BOUGHT
FOR REVENGE

Sarah Mallory

MILLS & BOON

First published in Great Britain 2013
by Mills & Boon, an imprint of Harlequin (UK) Limited.
Harlequin (UK) Limited, Eton House, 18-24 Paradise Road,
Richmond, Surrey TW9 1SR

© Sarah Mallory 2013

ISBN: 978 0 263 89843 9

Harlequin (UK) policy is to use papers that are natural, renewable and recyclable products and made from wood grown in sustainable forests. The logging and manufacturing process conform to the legal environmental regulations of the country of origin.

Printed and bound in Spain
by Blackprint CPI, Barcelona

Sarah Mallory was born in Bristol, and now lives in an old farmhouse on the edge of the Pennines with her husband and family. She left grammar school at sixteen to work in companies as varied as stockbrokers, marine engineers, insurance brokers, biscuit manufacturers and even a quarrying company. Her first book was published shortly after the birth of her daughter. She has published more than a dozen books under the pen-name of Melinda Hammond, winning the Reviewers' Choice Award from singletitles.com for *Dance for a Diamond* and the Historical Novel Society's Editors' Choice for *Gentlemen in Question*. Sarah Mallory has also twice won the Romantic Novelists' Association RONA Rose Award for *The Dangerous Lord Darrington* and *Beneath the Major's Scars*.

Previous novels by the same author:

THE WICKED BARON
MORE THAN A GOVERNESS
  (part of *On Mothering Sunday*)
WICKED CAPTAIN, WAYWARD WIFE
THE EARL'S RUNAWAY BRIDE
DISGRACE AND DESIRE
TO CATCH A HUSBAND…
SNOWBOUND WITH THE NOTORIOUS RAKE
  (part of *An Improper Regency Christmas*)
THE DANGEROUS LORD DARRINGTON
BENEATH THE MAJOR'S SCARS*
BEHIND THE RAKE'S WICKED WAGER*

**The Notorious Coale Brothers*

And in M&B:

THE ILLEGITIMATE MONTAGUE
  (part of *Castonbury Park* Regency mini-series)

To TGH

Chapter One

'The terms are very favourable, Mr Havenham. Messrs Powell & Son say their client is willing to pay the full asking price for Morwood and is ready to settle immediately.'

Annabelle looked hopefully towards her father to see how he would take this news.

'And what is this client's name, Mr Telford?' she asked. 'Do we know him?'

The lawyer adjusted his spectacles and studied the paper in his hand. 'A Mr Monserrat. Not a local man, I think.'

Mr Havenham sighed, the gold tassel on his cap dancing merrily as he shook his head.

'No one in Stanton has any money to spare. What with the war, and then last year's poor crops, it is a bad time for everyone.'

'Waterloo was more than a year ago, Papa,'

said Annabelle. 'And I know last summer was particularly bad, but the worst of the winter weather is over now and that always makes me feel hopeful. With a little economy, and the new mortgage Mr Telford raised for us on Oakenroyd, we shall come about.'

'Exactly,' agreed the lawyer. 'And the money from the sale of Morwood will pay off most of your creditors.'

'But not the gambling debts,' said Samuel. 'I should never have gone to Harrogate.' The regret in her father's voice made her heart ache, but Annabelle said nothing. Her father had gone to the spa town to take the waters, leaving her to run Oakenroyd, and he had returned with his health no better and his purse several thousand pounds lighter after being persuaded to enter the card room of the Dragon Hotel for several nights running.

Mr Telford shifted uncomfortably and sifted through the papers in his hand.

'No, not those. But I have had some correspondence with your, er, creditor at Harrogate. He is willing for you to pay off that loan in instalments.'

'But that is very good,' declared Annabelle. 'Once Burnt Acres—I mean Morwood—is sold and we have settled the other debts then we shall be able to pay him off, too. It will mean careful management for a few years, but nothing we cannot cope with.'

'I agree, Miss Havenham.' The lawyer nodded. 'That is the reason I think you should consider this offer very seriously, sir. If we act now then the sale of Morwood can go through before Lady Day.'

'But to sell Burnt Acres,' sighed Samuel. 'After all this time.'

Annabelle turned to him, taking his hands.

'Papa,' she said gently, 'We both love Morwood, with its trees and the ruins of the old Manor, but you know we have never made use of it as we should. Indeed, it is because it is so wild and neglected that I love it, but Morwood is the least profitable of your lands, and we must sell *something*.'

'We were very fortunate to find a buyer so quickly,' added the lawyer. 'And one who is willing to pay the full price.'

'Then I suppose it must be.'

'Indeed it must, Papa,' said Annabelle. 'We have no choice if we are to continue living here at Oakenroyd in the style we have come to enjoy.'

Mr Havenham straightened his shoulders.

'Very well, Mr Telford. Draw up the contracts. We will sell Morwood.'

The tree began to fall and Lucas stepped back, listening to the satisfying crack as the remaining section of trunk broke away. There was the swish of the branches sweeping down to the ground, the flutter of startled birds, then silence as everything settled once more. He lowered his long-handled axe and was contemplating his handiwork when the thud of hooves made him look round.

A rider was cantering towards him through the trees, a woman in a nut-brown riding habit mounted on a powerful grey horse that sidled and snorted as she drew rein. He guessed who she was, of course. No one else would be riding in this place save the daughter of its owner. The man he had vowed to ruin. Lucas had removed his jacket and waistcoat while he worked and he glanced at them now, knowing it was impolite for any gentleman to greet a lady in just his shirt. But she was the daughter of his enemy and he would not show her any courtesy. He watched her approach, acknowledging with reluctant appreciation the expert way she brought the powerful animal to a stand just feet from him.

'What are you doing?'

Her voice was low and musical, the tone not unfriendly, but Lucas was not minded to reply in kind.

'I should have thought that was obvious.'

Her brows went up. She said with a touch of

hauteur, 'Have you asked permission to cut down trees on this land?'

He regarded her in silence, knowing his cool stare was an insult. She frowned and it was with no little satisfaction he noted the spark of anger in her grey eyes. 'Well?'

He rested the axe against the newly felled tree trunk. 'As a matter of fact I haven't spoken to anyone about it.'

'Then I think you should cease work here until you have done so.'

He allowed himself a smile and took a step closer. 'Oh? And are you going to make me stop?'

'I shall report you to the steward.'

'I don't think so.' He reached out and caught the reins. The grey's ears came forwards and the animal snorted nervously.

'How dare you. Let go immediately.'

She kicked her heel against the grey's flank, but Lucas kept a tight grip on the reins and the animal merely sidled.

'You will learn I don't take orders from anyone,' he growled.

'Release my horse. You cannot keep me here.'

'I think you will find I can do whatever I want.'

Alarm flashed across her face, but it was

quickly masked. She said haughtily, 'Release the reins. I will not ask you again.'

He bared his teeth, his next words a deliberate, taunting challenge. 'Perhaps you should try *begging* me.'

Those grey eyes positively flamed now and she raised her riding crop. She brought her arm swinging down, but he was ready for her. He reached up with his free hand and caught her wrist. The horse, unsettled, reared and plunged, unseating the rider. Instantly Lucas released the reins and caught the lady as she fell.

He had braced himself for her weight and was surprised at how light she was in his arms. Her face was only inches from his own and he could see the tiny flecks of green in her eyes. For a few moments she was still, shocked, then she began to struggle, pushing against him.

'Let me go, you brute.'

'Brute, is it?' With a laugh he put her down, but kept hold of her arms, for although she no longer had her riding crop she tried to beat him with her fists. His hands slid to her wrists and he forced them behind her, pinning her to him. 'Now, madam, do you still call me a brute?'

He could feel her pressing against him as her breast heaved with indignation. The top of her head only came up to his chin. She was so delicate he thought he might crush her with one hand. She threw back her head and glared at him with an angry, fearless gaze.

'Monster,' she threw at him. 'Beast.... Certainly not a gentleman!'

He hardly heard her. His eyes were fixed upon her lips. They were red and full and without thinking he lowered his head and kissed her. She froze. Then, surprisingly, she yielded, becoming soft and pliant in his arms. But only for a moment. The next she was struggling to free herself. He raised his head, shaken by his actions. He had intended to antagonise her, but had been unable to resist the invitation of that extremely kissable mouth. Desire had leapt up immediately, fuelled by that one brief instant when she had leaned into him. He had sensed then a kindred spirit, a passionate nature to match his own. But even as his body hardened and the heated blood pounded through his veins he had known an overwhelming impulse to protect, to cherish the delicate creature imprisoned in his arms.

It would not do, he had no use for sentiment and must remember that she might well be a weapon he could use against his enemy. Better to befriend her, if he could.

'Ooh, that is, is *infamous,*' she declared, struggling to free herself. 'To steal a kiss when I am quite helpless to resist you. I shall add *thief* to the epithets I heap upon your head. Let me go this instant!'

He laughed, but self-preservation made him hold on to her.

'Very well. Only stop spitting like a wildcat and I will release you. Stop it, I say.'

She ceased her struggles and stared up at him, her eyes wary. He released her and stepped back.

'There. You are free to go, Miss Havenham.'

'You know my name?'

'Of course. Perhaps I should introduce myself.'

She tossed her head and turned away from him, saying over her shoulder, 'Pray do not. I have no wish to know you.'

She began to walk to where the big grey was quietly cropping the grass.

'Oh, but I think you should, since we are to be neighbours.'

That stopped her in her tracks. He felt a grim sense of satisfaction as she turned slowly back to face him.

'You are the new owner? Mr Monser…'

'Monserrat. Yes.'

'I did not think the contract was agreed yet.'

'I signed the papers yesterday. I have builders coming here next week, but in the meantime I thought I might remove a few of the trees that have sprung up on the drive.'

She went to collect her horse. Once she had picked up the reins she looked past him to the blackened shell of the old house.

'The house burned down over twenty years ago. No one has been here since then.'

'Save you.'

'Save me.'

'I do not know why your father bought it, if he did not plan to do anything with it.'

'I think at one time he was going to rebuild the house. Now he says it would cost a small fortune to put it right.' She scooped up her crop and as she straightened she looked across at him. 'Is that what you plan to do?'

'Yes. I plan to put things right.'

He stared at the old house. It was a stone-built building, two storeys high with a central porch and a wide, gabled wing jutting from each end. The sturdy walls were mostly intact, but the roof was missing and greenery had forced its way between the remaining blackened timbers. Ivy curled around the chimneys. The stone-mullioned windows had lost all their glass and stared like blind eyes across what had been the south lawn. It was now dotted with small trees, like the drive. It had been a fine property once, and he would rebuild it. But whether he could bring himself to live there again…

A slight sound brought his attention back to Miss Havenham. She was leading the horse away.

'Are you not going to ride him?'

The look she gave him was positively arctic. 'I cannot mount without a block. I shall walk home.'

'Let me throw you up.' He could see the indecision in her face and added, 'Come, Miss Havenham. Let me atone for my previous bad manners.'

'I don't think anything can do that.'

He grinned. 'At least let me try.'

She did not walk away and he took that for an assent. He approached and she waited warily, murmuring to the grey as she gathered up the reins.

'Steady, Apollo. Easy, boy.'

The horse seemed to know what was expected of him and stood patiently. Lucas ran a hand down the animal's muzzle.

'Apollo. A good name for him. He is a handsome creature.'

She did not reply, but placed the toe of her riding boot in his cupped hands. He threw her easily up into the saddle and she made herself comfortable, at the same time controlling Apollo with no more than a quiet word. Lucas made no attempt to help her, merely watching as she slipped her boot into the stirrup and arranged her skirts to cover an extremely dainty ankle. He stepped back.

'I shall be calling upon your father very soon, Miss Havenham. I hope to have the pleasure of seeing you again.'

'I shall tell Papa to expect you. I will also make it clear to our people that the manor is sold and is now out of bounds.'

'Please, feel free to ride here whenever you wish.'

She shook her head. 'I do not intend ever to come here again.' She looked around, as if committing the place to memory, then turned her horse and cantered away.

Lucas watched her go, a slight smile playing around his mouth. Perhaps he should have treated her more gently, but she had spirit, and he had enjoyed rousing her temper. He had enjoyed kissing her, too, although that had never been part of his plan, but she had looked so damned alluring there in his arms, how could he help himself? She was no beauty, the curls that peeped beneath her riding hat were a nondescript brown, but her features were regular and he had already discovered that her generous mouth was perfectly formed for kissing. She had a good figure, too—he recalled how well it felt, pressed against his. Smiling, he picked up his axe. How much greater would be Havenham's ruin if he lost his daughter as well as his fortune?

Nerves jangling, Annabelle struggled to keep Apollo at a steady canter. She did not intend to slow down until the chimneys of Oakenroyd were in sight. She was shaken by her encounter with the new owner of Morwood, but not overly frightened and that surprised her. To be accosted by a strange man, one so dark and foreign-looking, too, to be pulled from her horse—here she stopped herself. She must be honest. She had fallen from her horse and could have been badly injured if he had not caught her. And he had held her so easily, as if she had weighed nothing. The experience had been quite…exhilarating.

That did not excuse his behaviour afterwards, of course, when he had kissed her. She let herself go over that moment again. She could still recall the feel of his mouth on hers, and the moment when she had felt something in her leap to respond.

Outrageous!

From all she had been told, all she had read, she knew she should have been terrified at being imprisoned in those strong arms. She should have fainted quite away. Annabelle gave a little huff of impatience. She had never thought much of those heroines who burst into tears at the slightest thing and swooned as soon as a man touched them. Why, that would leave the man free to behave in whatever way he wished. Surely it was better to fight and struggle, as she had done?

And in the end he had let her go. Well, there was little else he could do. A poor start to his ownership if he was to ravish his neighbour's daughter at the outset. She wondered if he planned to settle at Morwood Manor. As its name suggested, it had once been the major property in the area. Her father had a watercolour of the house as it had been before the fire, a substantial stone building dating back to the time of the Tudors. The wealth of its owners had declined since then, and the last owner, Jonas Blackstone, was said to have been a poor landlord. That was well before Annabelle had been born, however. Her father had bought the manor lands soon after the fire, but although he had looked after the tenant farmers, he had never done anything with the house and grounds. Morwood had remained unused and untended, and Annabelle had grown up roaming freely through the woods and the ruins. They had been her playground, but that of course was ended now. She would avoid the manor and its odious owner in future.

Annabelle stabled her horse and went indoors. She decided not to tell her father of her meeting with their new neighbour. Papa was not yet sixty, but a serious illness a few years ago had aged him considerably and she felt very protective towards him. He had always been so much more than just a father to her. Annabelle had never known Mama, who had died giving birth to her, and the loss of her only brother ten years ago had brought her much closer to her one remaining relative. Papa was the very kindest of men and had always been both her mentor and confidant. She could not lie to him and details of her encounter with Mr Monserrat would grieve him deeply, so it was best not to speak of it at all. Besides, the man had acknowledged that he had acted improperly, had he not? So she would not dwell upon it, although she would make sure he never had the opportunity to repeat his outlandish behaviour.

Annabelle found her father in the morning room, reading beside the crackling fire.

'Ah, Belle, my love.' He put down his book. 'You have been a long time, I was beginning to worry.'

She glanced at the clock as she crossed the room, stripping off her gloves.

'I beg your pardon, Papa. But it has not been so very long, certainly no longer than usual.'

'I wish you would take Clegg with you, my

dear. I am always afraid you might meet with some accident.'

Annabelle's thoughts flew back to her encounter with Mr Monserrat. Could her groom have prevented that outrageous kiss?

'Mayhap I will then, in future.' Her eyes fell upon the little table beside his chair. 'I see you have been playing chess. Have you had a visitor?'

'Yes, Mr Keighley called and stayed to play a game.' He chuckled. 'I think his real purpose was to see you, but he bore your absence very well.'

'And so he might, since it gave him the opportunity to play with one of the finest chess players in the county,' she returned, smiling.

James Keighley was a widower and good friend to her father. Lately he had shown more of an interest in Annabelle and she suspected that he might be thinking of making her an offer. She was not sure how she felt about this, since he was on the shady side of forty and she had not yet reached one-and-twenty.

However, she knew the match would make her father happy. Mr Keighley's fortune was not inconsiderable and he owned a substantial property some five miles away from Oakenroyd. As his wife she would have every comfort. Except one.

Annabelle might despise the lachrymose heroines of romantic novels, but she had not set herself against the idea of marrying for love. She knew it was unlikely that a strong, handsome hero would appear to sweep her off her feet or save her from some hideous fate, but she still cherished the hope that she would meet a man for whom she could feel more than a tepid affection.

Unbidden, the image of their new neighbour rose up in her mind. There was no doubt of his strength. She recalled quite clearly the powerful thighs encased in buckskins, and the wide shoulders made even broader by the billowing shirt-sleeves, but in no way could she think of him as handsome. His rugged features, raven hair and coal-black eyes belonged more to a villain.

'…my dear, you are not listening to me.'

She gave a start at her father's gentle admonition. 'I beg your pardon, Papa, I was daydreaming.'

'I said Keighley has offered to take us up in his carriage when we go to dine with the Rishworths next week.'

'How kind of him. I confess I had hoped he would offer to bring us home, even if we had to walk to Rishworth Lodge.'

Her father tutted. 'But it should not be necessary to call upon anyone to drive us.'

'Now, Papa, you know we agreed it is an expense we can well do without.' She sank down beside him. 'The cost of the coachman, plus the horses eating their heads off in the stable, was far too much, especially when we rarely go farther than Stanton these days.'

'But to have no carriage—'

'We have the gig, Papa, and that is more than sufficient. Now,' she said brightly, determined to turn his thoughts, 'I will put off my riding habit and then perhaps you will give me your arm for a stroll around the gardens. We need to be thinking about the summer planting.'

She hurried away to change her gown. There was no doubt that her father was finding it difficult to come to terms with the economies they were forced to make, but she had every confidence that in a year or two they would be able to resume their previous mode of living, and possibly even use their own carriage again. Of course, if she married James Keighley their fortunes would alter overnight. But was that sufficient incentive to marry a man for whom she felt only a mild liking? It was a vexing question.

'But not one you need to answer yet,' she said, frowning at her reflection as she tidied her hair. 'Time to make a decision if and when he asks you, my girl.'

Chapter Two

'So, Mr Monserrat has arrived,' said Mr Havenham.

They were at breakfast. Annabelle was buttering a freshly baked muffin and did not look up.

'Has he, Papa?' She kept her tone decidedly cool.

'Yes, Telford mentioned he was the new owner of Burnt Acres, did he not? Although I suppose we shall have to call it Morwood Manor again now. He has written me a very civil letter and I have invited him to call today.'

'Oh, that is unfortunate. I have arranged to visit old Mrs Hall in Stanton and shall not be able to meet him.'

'But I have not yet told you the time, my dear.'

'I know, dear Papa, but I am engaged to go on to Mrs Ford's for a fitting for my new gown.'

She gave him her sweetest smile. 'If I'd had more notice I should of course cry off from both these appointments, but as it is…'

'No, no, you must go, especially to visit Mrs Hall, I would not have you backward in your attentions to such an old friend. Very well, my dear, off you go. I will give our new neighbour your apologies.'

'Mr Monserrat, sir.'

A very correct butler showed Lucas into the sunny drawing room at Oakenroyd, and as the door closed quietly behind him Lucas took the opportunity to study the man waiting for him.

He suffered something of a shock. In his mind he saw a tall, upright man with brown hair and grey eyes, very like his daughter, but his host was an elderly gentleman, his shoulders slightly stooped and his hair silver white. He came forwards now to greet his guest. His grey eyes were smiling, but Lucas had the impression of a pervading air of gentle sadness about the man.

No sympathy, Lucas reminded himself. *Havenham is your enemy. Smile, play his game of friendliness, but keep your distance.*

Lucas listened to his words of welcome. They seemed sincere, uttered in a quiet voice that matched his mild demeanour. There was no hint that Miss Havenham had told him of their meeting. Surely if she had done so his welcome would have been less cordial?

Lucas took a seat, accepted a glass of wine. After all, that was the civilised thing to do. It did not imply that they must therefore be upon good terms. In the past he had shown equal courtesy to a captured French officer, knowing that if they met on the battlefield they would neither of them have the slightest hesitation in killing the other.

But this is underhand. Havenham doesn't know you are his enemy.

The thought was unwelcome, but Lucas pushed it aside. Havenham's conscience should tell him that retribution would come, one day. He dragged his attention back to what his host was saying.

'I regret my daughter is not here to greet you. She is gone on a visit of duty that could not be put off.'

'That, sir, is my loss,' murmured Lucas. So she was avoiding him? Well, there was plenty of time to renew that particular acquaintance.

'No, no, she is eager to meet you.' The old man smiled. 'She will want to see the new owner of Morwood. The house has been empty since before she was born and she has grown up running free in the grounds.'

'Really? I am surprised you allowed her to wander so far from home.'

'It is safe enough. She was always accompanied by a servant, or her brother, when he was alive.' A hesitation, a flicker of pain, quickly brushed aside and Havenham continued. 'Now she is grown, of course, she does ride unaccompanied, but I do not worry about her going there. The locals never venture on to the estate. They believe it is haunted.' The old man fell silent, looking dreamily into the fire.

'And is that what you believe too, sir?' Lucas prompted him. 'Is that why you have never done anything with it?'

'No, but it holds painful memories for me.' Lucas saw another shadow of pure anguish cross the lined face, then Samuel seemed to shake himself out of his reverie and said brightly, 'But that is all in the past now. You are about to bring Morwood alive again and I am very glad of it.'

Lucas stayed for no more than the required half hour, fending off questions he did not wish to answer and making enquiries of his own about Morwood. All the time part of him was marvelling that he could sit so calmly exchanging pleasantries with a man whom he had hated for so many years. A man he planned to destroy.

Annabelle had been thankful to escape from the house and from a meeting with Mr Monserrat. She would have to meet him sometime and part of her was a little ashamed that she was putting it off, but she stifled the quiet voice that was her conscience and went in sunny spirits to call upon the elderly Mrs Hall. However, when she sat down to dinner that night she could not forbear asking her father about his visitor.

'I am sorry you missed him,' said Samuel as he took his seat opposite her. 'He has great plans for the manor, and I am glad of it. I should have done more with the house...'

'And is this Mr Monserrat a gentleman, sir?' Annabelle prompted him in an attempt to dispel his wistfulness.

'Oh, I think so, my dear, although he is very dark. He was a soldier, you know, at Waterloo and before that in the Peninsula. I have no doubt the hot sun is responsible for his complexion, he is almost swarthy.'

She was about to say that could not account for his black eyes and hair, but she remembered, just in time, that her father did not know she had met their neighbour.

'In fact, he reminds me of someone.' Her father leaned forwards, a slight crease in his brow as if he were trying to catch some fleeting thought. He smiled and shook his head. 'No, it will not come and is probably a nonsense. But you shall see for yourself when you meet him.'

'I will indeed.' Annabelle turned her attention to her food, hoping that it would be some time before she was obliged to see Mr Monserrat.

Samuel had been looking forward to dinner with the Rishworths, but when Annabelle had helped him into Mr Keighley's carriage, she knew he would be comparing it unfavourably with their own well-padded barouche, which was now stored away at the back of the coach house.

'Mr Havenham, welcome, sir, and Miss Havenham.' Lady Rishworth greeted them with her usual jolly smile before turning to welcome Mr Keighley, who followed them into the drawing room. A number of guests had already arrived, all of them known to Annabelle. She considered it a misfortune that the closest was Mrs Kensley, a widow as colourless as her grey garb but with a waspish tongue. She gave Annabelle a false smile as she expressed her surprise at seeing them there so early.

'I had thought you would be walking here tonight, Mr Havenham, and did not expect you for a good half hour yet.'

'No, no, ma'am, Mr Keighley was good enough to call for us.'

Annabelle admired her father's calm and good-natured response.

'But it must be such a blow to lose your own

horses,' the widow continued. 'Times are very hard indeed when Oakenroyd must close its stables.'

'They are not closed, ma'am,' Annabelle corrected her. 'It is only the carriage horses that have been sold. Old Simmons the coachman gave notice that he wanted to retire and we decided that we would not replace him for a while.'

'My dear, you do not need to explain to me.' The widow patted her arm and it was all Annabelle could do not to pull away from the condescending gesture. 'So many Stanton families are struggling at present. No doubt you are regretting spending all that money on your presentation...'

Annabelle's ill humour disappeared and she laughed at the absurdity of the remark.

'My dear ma'am, that was two years past. But since you mention it, I do not regret a groat spent on a London Season.' She continued, knowing what the widow's next comment would be, 'Neither do I regret returning unmarried. It means I can look after my father and be mistress of Oakenroyd. What more could I ask for?'

Annabelle watched with no small measure of satisfaction as Mrs Kensley blinked and opened her mouth to respond, then closed it again. She was well aware that the widow had prepared any number of sympathetic and patronising comments, but none would be appropriate now. Her father touched her arm.

'My dear, let me present our new neighbour to you.' Annabelle's head came up. 'Mr Monserrat, my daughter, sir.'

So he was here and looking very different from their previous meeting. In the confines of the Rishworths' commodious drawing room he looked even larger than she remembered. The superb cut of his black evening coat did nothing to lessen the width of his shoulders, and the snowy whiteness of his cravat and shirt-points accentuated the deep tan of his skin. His hair, black as jet, was brushed back from a face that was more rugged than handsome with heavy brows that gave his aquiline features a rather hawkish look. She could more readily believe him a soldier than a courtier, yet when he made his bow to her she could not fault it.

'We have met,' he said, not taking his eyes from her. 'I am glad to see you are none the worse for your little tumble, Miss Havenham.'

'Tumble?' Samuel was immediately on the alert. 'When was this?'

She glared at the man, but he met her furious gaze with a bland smile as he replied.

'On Monday last, sir. Miss Havenham had the misfortune to come off her horse and I was able to assist her.'

Mrs Kensley tittered. 'Have I not always said that big horse is no mount for a lady?'

Her remark was ignored. Mr Havenham turned a frowning look upon Annabelle.

'My dear child, you said nothing of this to me.'

'Because it was of so little importance, Papa.'

'But you did not tell me you had met Mr Monserrat.'

'We were not introduced,' she explained, keeping her voice cool. 'And he merely helped me back into the saddle.'

'Oh, my love, have I not said you should take your groom when you are out riding?'

Her tormentor nodded. 'Let me add my entreaties to your father's, Miss Havenham. You can never be sure what dangers you might meet in the woods.'

She almost gasped at his impertinence, but contented herself with a swift, angry glance as she addressed her father. 'You have, sir, and in future I shall make sure I am always accompanied.'

Mrs Kensley was watching the interchange closely. She gave a little cough to remind everyone of her presence.

'Perhaps you should consider selling such a dangerous brute, Mr Havenham,' she suggested. 'That would save you a deal of worry.'

Annabelle felt her temper rising, but support came from a surprising quarter.

'Oh, I doubt that,' remarked Mr Monserrat. 'I suspect the lady would be a most uncomfortable companion if she was obliged to give up her riding.'

'You are very right, sir. My poor father would soon be at his wits' end with me. No, Mrs Kensley, it will be a sad day indeed when I am forced to part with Apollo.'

With a tight little smile she led her father away, muttering under her breath, 'Insufferable woman! She delights in our troubles.'

Her father patted her arm. 'Hush now, Belle. People are bound to talk about our economies. We must bear it as best we can. It will soon pass, when there is more fruitful gossip to be had.'

'You are right, Father, and I beg your pardon. I am not as forbearing as you.'

'You are young, my love, and impatient of adversity. These little setbacks happen and there are always those who will revel in others' misfortune. We will smile and show them it is a small matter.'

'Always so kind, Papa, always so gentle. I will try to learn from your example.'

'You are a good girl, Belle.' He patted her cheek. 'Now, let me sit by the fire with my old friends while you go and enjoy yourself with the younger set!'

* * *

The Rishworths were well known for their
lively dinners, and when they sat down at the
table Annabelle found herself with a group that
included Celia Rishworth and Lizzie Scanlon,
two young ladies who were determined to enjoy
themselves. She was some distance from her father, but since he was seated comfortably between his hostess and Mrs Hall she knew he
would be happily entertained during the meal.
Mr Monserrat was also at that end of the table.
He appeared to be at ease with his company, but
throughout the meal she was aware of his dark
and enigmatic presence, watching and listening.

The dinner was excellent and the company
determined to be pleased. Lucas set himself to
entertain the ladies on either side of him, expertly drawing them out to talk about themselves
and deftly turning aside all questions about his
own background. On one side was Mrs Kensley,
the widow whose caustic remarks had inflamed
Miss Havenham. While cleverly eluding all her
attempts to learn more about him, he encouraged
her to talk. Lucas had her measure and took none
of her comments or opinions at face value, but
from her artless chatter he gained a great deal of
valuable information about the neighbourhood.
As the meal progressed he studied Samuel

Havenham, seated across the table from him. He had learned that Havenham's health was not good, but this merely confirmed his own impression. The old man ate sparingly, just enough to avoid offending his hostess, and his wine glass rarely required topping up. However, it was easy to see that Samuel Havenham was a well-respected figure in the area, and despite being obliged to give up his carriage he was still regarded as a man of some standing. Lucas let the conversation flow around him as he continued to watch Samuel. He noticed how often his eyes strayed to his daughter, sitting at the far end of the table.

'Miss Havenham is the belle of our local circle,' offered Mrs Kensley, following his glance.

'Is she?'

The widow tittered at his cool response. 'Oh, she is not as pretty as Miss Rishworth, nor Miss Scanlon, but she *is* Miss Havenham of Oakenroyd.'

'You mean it is only her fortune that makes her so appealing.'

Mrs Kensley gave an arch laugh. 'Oh, Mr Monserrat, that is very wicked of you, of course I do not mean any such thing! Miss Havenham is a very good sort of girl. She has been a little spoiled perhaps, but then her papa quite dotes on her. Although that is no wonder, Miss Havenham being his only surviving child. However, for my part, I find her manners a little too forward for one so young.'

'And how old is she?' he enquired, helping the widow to another slice of lemon tart.

'Not yet one-and-twenty, although she rides around on that big horse of hers as if she were lady of the manor.' Mrs Kensley stopped, her knife and fork poised in mid-air. 'But of course *that* will have to end now, won't it, sir, since *you* are now the owner of Morwood Manor.' She gave another of her irritating titters. 'Unless, that is, you are tempted to offer for her? I warn you, Mr Keighley is there before you.'

Lucas smiled vaguely and sipped at his wine. The young people at the other end of the table were enjoying a lively conversation, with Annabelle Havenham at their centre. Mrs Kensley was right, the two other young ladies would be considered more beautiful than Annabelle Havenham. Her figure was good, but no better than others he had seen, her features were regular and her soft brown hair was simply dressed. Celia Rishworth's vivacity made her dark curls dance about her head and Miss Scanlon's fair prettiness was set off by an over-decorated gown that must have cost her father a pretty penny, but there was something about Miss Havenham's quiet elegance that caught the attention. He remembered she had looked magnificent when riding and it was hard to forget the disconcertingly direct gaze of her grey eyes.

His own gaze moved on around the table until it reached James Keighley. A widower, he had been informed. They had been introduced earlier and Lucas had summed up Keighley as a country gentleman of comfortable means, some years older than himself. Was there an understanding between the man and Miss Havenham? Keighley had brought the Oakenroyd party in his own carriage, but Lucas had noticed no special attention between the pair since then. If he had been enamoured of the lady, or if he had been a hot-headed young suitor then he might have been a nuisance, but Lucas did not think Keighley's interest in Miss Havenham was likely to affect his own plans.

When the ladies withdrew, their host gave a signal to the butler.

'Now we can be comfortable.' He leaned forwards to address Lucas. 'I know you were a military man, Monserrat, but I hope you won't think us unpatriotic to bring French brandy to the table now that the emperor has finally been defeated.'

'Not at all,' returned Lucas, pushing his glass out to be filled. 'I am pleased to see you are supporting the new regime.'

'We are, sir,' declared Mr Scanlon, 'and since Sir John is magistrate for these parts you can be sure that the duty has been paid on the brandy, too!'

There was general laughter at this.

'So you were in the army, Mr Monserrat,' remarked Mr Keighley. 'What is it brings you to Stanton, sir?'

'Have you not heard?' said Scanlon. 'He has purchased Morwood Manor and means to restore it. Ain't that right, sir?'

'It is,' averred Lucas.

'Well, now you are here,' said Rishworth, 'perhaps you would be interested in investing locally.'

'That depends upon the investment.'

Sir John Rishworth sat back in his chair, preparing to expound upon what was clearly a favourite theme.

'Our new toll road, for example. A number of us subscribed to the venture two years ago, to build a new road running around Dyke's Ridge. The old road, you see, dips down very steeply past Oldroyd Farm to cross the ford, but the valley bottom is almost a bog. In winter the road is well nigh impassable. We hope the new road will improve trade to the town.'

'Unfortunately it has not done so yet,' observed Mr Keighley.

'No,' agreed Sir John. 'Last year's bad harvest means trade in Stanton has been very poor and we have not yet recovered our costs.'

Samuel Havenham sighed. 'I had hoped we would have turned a profit by now.'

'You could always sell your share in the venture,' suggested Lucas.

Havenham shook his head. 'No, no, we shall come about. Besides, the subscription was not so much an investment for me as for my daughter. A little something for her when I am gone.'

His neighbours cried out at that and declared they hoped Mr Havenham would be with them for many years to come.

'If you are interested, Monserrat, there are several of us who might wish to sell on our shares to you,' called a bewhiskered gentleman from the far end of the table.

'Aye,' cried Scanlon. 'You may have mine with pleasure. I haven't seen any improvement to business in Stanton or recovered my costs yet.'

Sir John waved one hand in a placating gesture. 'Be calm, gentlemen. Once the mail coach begins to use the new road next summer our fortunes will improve, trust me.'

'Perhaps Mr Monserrat has more patience than I,' retorted Scanlon. 'What do you say, Monserrat, would you like to take my shares off me?'

'I will consider it.'

'I think he is better keeping his funds to restore Burnt Acres,' laughed the bewhiskered gentleman.

Lucas raised one black brow in enquiry. 'Burnt Acres?'

'Morwood Manor. Burnt Acres is what we've called that land for more years than I care to remember.'

'Oh?' Lucas kept his face impassive. 'Why is that?'

'Goes back to when the house burned down five-and-twenty years ago,' explained Sir John. 'Owner and his wife lost their lives in the fire.'

'Aye, sad business.' Mr Scanlon shook his head. 'It followed a particularly dry spring. Burning debris from the house was caught up by the wind. It set fire to the surrounding trees and the gorse. By morning the house was a ruin and everything around it was scorched and blackened.'

A chill was spreading through Lucas, but he forced himself to ignore it. He asked his next question with studied indifference. 'What caused the fire?'

Rishworth shrugged. 'Angus Dutton was the magistrate then, so I am not familiar with the details, but no one knows for sure. It is thought it started in a bedchamber—the mistress of the house was a foreign lady from warmer climes and didn't like this northern cold. She insisted on a fire in her room, day and night, at all seasons.'

Lucas, my love, come and read with me by the fire.

Samuel Havenham shifted in his chair. 'Let us hope Mr Monserrat will bring some happier memories to the place.'

Their host signalled to the butler to fill the glasses again. 'You've taken on a deal of work there, sir,' he remarked.

'Aye, but it's brought some much-needed employment to the town,' remarked Mr Scanlon. 'Isn't that so, Mr Monserrat?'

'Yes, I use local labour where I can.'

'Good for you, sir. And where are you staying while all this work is going on at Morwood?' asked the bewhiskered gentleman. 'I haven't been there for years, but I understand the house is merely a shell.'

'It is. I am staying at the Red Lion.'

Rishworth chuckled. 'Ah, then let me warn you to watch out for the ladies, sir. The Red Lion holds the monthly assembly, and with you living there, they will expect you to attend.'

'Aye,' laughed another who had reached the roistering stage and was banging the table. 'They'll have you marked down as a dance partner and maybe more, if they have daughters to marry, eh, Sir John?'

Their host laughed. 'I ain't looking for a husband for Celia yet, but her mother is no different from the rest, looks upon every single man as a possible catch. Sorry to put it so bluntly, Monserrat, but there it is…'

Lucas smiled and shrugged and the conversation moved on, growing louder and more boisterous as the brandy and port flowed freely. By the time Sir John led them back to the drawing room to join the ladies, many of the gentlemen were decidedly rosy-cheeked. Lucas had drunk comparatively little and as the gentlemen ambled their way out of the dining room he hung back to wait for Samuel Havenham. Slowly they crossed the hall together.

'I hope my neighbours' little jests did not offend you,' said Havenham in his mild way. 'They are as good a set of gentlemen as one could hope to find, but the wine and the brandy, you know…'

'I understand,' said Lucas. 'I am pleased at the warm welcome I have received since I came here.'

They were entering the drawing room and Lucas observed that Annabelle was watching him from across the room. A wry smile tugged at his mouth. There was one person whose welcome had been anything but warm. Havenham was still talking and making his way slowly but surely towards his daughter. Lucas wondered if he should excuse himself and move off, but an inner demon kept him beside the older man.

'We have not done much entertaining of late at Oakenroyd,' said Samuel. 'My health, you know. I keep very much to the house during the winter months, but your coming puts me in mind of my obligations. Annabelle, my love, I was just saying to Mr Monserrat that we should hold a dinner. What do you say?'

'Of course, Papa. Perhaps at the end of May. The weather will be more settled then and that will give me time to arrange everything. I do hope you will be able to join us, Mr Monserrat.'

She was clearly accustomed to playing hostess for her father. Her response was cool and collected, although Lucas noted how she avoided his eyes.

'May? We cannot wait nearly two months to invite our new neighbour to dinner,' objected Havenham.

'Papa, I cannot possibly organise something in any less time. Invitations will need to go out and guests must have time to reply, then Mrs Wicklow must open up the guest rooms, and Cook, you know, will need notice to prepare.'

'Yes, yes, I quite see that is the case if we are going to have a *grand* dinner, but in the meantime Mr Monserrat must take pot luck with us. Next week. A man cannot dine every night at the Red Lion!' He touched Lucas's arm. 'Come as soon as you wish, sir. Name your day. You will find Belle keeps a very good table, you will not go hungry. And if truth be told her efforts deserve more appreciation than I can give them.'

'You are very good, sir, and I will take you up on your invitation, gladly.' He felt rather than saw the lady's grey eyes upon him and turned to meet her frosty look with a blank one of his own. 'Thursday next week would suit me very well, sir, but I would not want to inconvenience Miss Havenham.'

He could almost see the thoughts whirling through her head. She wanted to refuse, to make some excuse to put him off, but in view of her father's invitation that was not possible. The devilish imp prompted him to say with false deference, 'Perhaps Thursday is not her best day for cooking...'

'Heavens, Mr Monserrat, I would not cook for you *myself*.' The honeyed tone was as insincere as his own. 'However, I can assure you that our cook is equal to feeding guests on any day of the week.'

'Thursday it is, then,' cried Mr Havenham, oblivious of the tension around him. 'Splendid, splendid.'

He wandered off, but Lucas remained with Annabelle. 'I look forward to improving our acquaintance, Miss Havenham.' Silently she turned to walk away, but he kept beside her. 'Ah,' he murmured. 'You are speechless with anticipation.'

'I am speechless at your effrontery, first at Morwood—'

'And now I only want to make amends.'

He could smell her perfume, not too sweet, and with a hint of citrus. He found himself leaning closer to breathe it in.

'Let it be enough that I do not cut your acquaintance,' she hissed.

'But then everyone would want to know why.'

'And you would delight in telling them, I suppose.'

'No, no, I would not *delight* in it, Miss Havenham.'

She bit her lip and glared at him. He thought that if they had not been in Lady Rishworth's drawing room she would have stamped her foot. He laughed suddenly and held out his hand to her. 'Come, madam, your father likes me. For his sake, cry friends.'

She hesitated. Slowly, her hand crept up and into his. 'Not friends, sir,' she said quietly, 'but for my father's sake, not enemies.'

They did not speak again and later, when he lay down on his bed at the Red Lion, Lucas went over the events of the evening. He had enjoyed himself. Moreover, he had enjoyed the verbal sparring with Annabelle Havenham, so much so that when she had at last given him her hand he had felt a surge of pleasure.

He shifted uneasily. Havenham was a gentle, scholarly soul. In other circumstances he would have liked him, but it was not part of his plan to grow too fond of Samuel Havenham. Or his daughter. Lucas turned over and prepared for sleep, seeing again in his mind's eye Annabelle's clear eyes, the slight blush tinting her cheek during their last encounter.

On the other hand, it would do no harm at all if Annabelle Havenham grew too fond of *him*. Perhaps he should revise his plans. To force her to marry him to save her father would, of course, have its merit, but how much sweeter would his revenge be upon Samuel Havenham if Annabelle was to fall in love with him?

Chapter Three

Mr Havenham was sanguine about the invitation he had issued to Mr Monserrat to dine at Oakenroyd, but Annabelle could not rest. She knew her father would enjoy the evening, so she stifled her own misgivings and set about preparing a sumptuous dinner to show their new neighbour that Oakenroyd was a household of some standing in the neighbourhood. She made several journeys to the housekeeper's room to change her mind about the dishes they should offer their guest, until at last the housekeeper, Mrs Wicklow, gently but firmly refused to discuss it any further.

'Cook has been in charge of the kitchens for the past twenty years, Miss Belle, as you very well know, and if I tell him that you have changed your mind *again* he is likely to pack his bags and go off in high dudgeon, and then where should we be?' She ushered Annabelle to the door. 'Now, miss, I suggest you take yourself for a nice walk around the gardens while the sun is shining. The roast beef and cod loin will do very well, then we have a fine ham and apple dumplings, and I am sure we will find a few dainty sweets for when the covers are removed. Don't you worry, my dear, your guest will not be disappointed.'

A similar indecisiveness struck Annabelle over what to wear.

'I am mistress of this house,' she muttered to herself as she pulled out and discarded various gowns. In the end she chose a high-waisted robe of pale-green silk, cut low across the bosom and with tight-fitting sleeves to offset the chill of a March evening. One of her many cream-muslin gowns would have been more suited to a young unmarried lady who had not yet attained her majority, but following their previous meetings she wanted Lucas Monserrat to see her as mistress of her father's house, composed and in command.

Their guest arrived promptly and was shown into the drawing room by the butler. He was again dressed in the regulation dark coat and tight-fitting breeches, and his manner of greeting was just as it should be. She met him coolly, alert for any sign of insolence in his manner, but he was perfectly polite. Relieved, but not yet wholly convinced, she took her embroidery to a chair by the window and left her father to entertain him.

The winter weather took its toll on her father's health and he was not able to enjoy the local society as much as he would wish, so by the spring he was always ready for company. Despite their distance from London, her father was well informed and the two men conversed easily together on a wide range of subjects, leaving Annabelle free to set her stitches and listen to their conversation with growing interest. Perhaps the evening would not be too much of a trial after all.

The good mood continued throughout dinner. Mr Monserrat directed his attention towards his host. Their discussions ranged from politics and the price of corn to the recent war. As the meal progressed Annabelle found herself relaxing. She forgot her previous animosity and even interjected her own comments into the conversation upon occasion—it was hard to remain coldly aloof with a guest who entertained her father so well.

At the correct time she excused herself and left them to their port, but it was not long before they joined her in the drawing room. Darkness had fallen and the shutters were closed. She had ordered the log fire to be built up and a quantity of candles burned steadily about the room. Annabelle glanced around her with satisfaction. No hostess could be displeased with such comfortable and elegant surroundings.

'Mr Monserrat has great plans for the manor, my dear,' remarked her father as she helped him to his favourite chair beside the fire. 'He intends to restore it, very much as it was.'

'That is admirable, sir.' She favoured their guest with a faint smile. 'I hope you succeed.'

'I intend to.' His dark eyes rested on her, cool and considering. 'I succeed in everything I undertake.'

A *frisson* of disquiet ran through her, but she tried to ignore it.

'How fortunate for you.'

'Fortune has little to do with it.' He waited until Annabelle was seated, then lowered his long frame into a chair. 'I make my plans and stick to them.'

Her father chuckled. 'But you are a young man still, if you do not mind me saying so. Life has a way of upsetting the best-laid plans.'

'Not yours, sir, surely.' Those dark eyes flickered about the room. 'You look to be very comfortable here. Everything you need to make you happy.'

'Not quite everything.'

Annabelle was immediately aware of her father's sadness. It was in the slight droop of his shoulders and the faint change to his expression, imperceptible to a stranger.

'Papa.' She flew out of her chair and dropped down at his side. 'Do not talk of it if it makes you unhappy.'

He placed one gnarled hand upon her head while he addressed his visitor.

'I lost my wife when Belle was born, and my son died of a fever some years ago.' He raised his eyes. 'So you see, young man, I too have had my share of sadness. Belle is now my only joy.'

The silence following his words was broken only by the faint tick of the clock and the logs crackling in the fireplace. Belle expected their guest to say something, to murmur a word or two, of comfort, perhaps, or at least sympathy, but he said nothing. His face was impassive, the dark eyes thoughtful. She sought for something to break the silence, but within moments her father had roused himself and was smiling again.

'We have a painting of Morwood Manor, Mr Monserrat. A watercolour. Perhaps you would like to see it.'

'I would indeed, sir.'

'It hangs on the landing. Annabelle, my love, perhaps you would accompany our guest? It is at the top of the stairs, you see, sir, and my legs are not what they were.'

'I quite understand and would be obliged if Miss Havenham will show me the way.'

Annabelle wavered, wondering whether to suggest viewing it another time, in daylight, but that would require a further invitation. No, better to get it over with. She rose.

'Of course, sir. Let us go now.'

She picked up a branched candlestick as they crossed the hall, explaining that they would need the extra light to see the painting properly. Her spine tingled as she led the way up the stairs, aware of his presence, the faint whisper of his footstep behind her, his warm breath on her neck—or was that her imagination? Surely he was not that close. She forced herself not to look around.

When they reached the landing she stopped by a small painting in a plain wooden frame.

'Here it is.' She lifted the candles higher. She had seen the painting many times before. It showed a long stone-built manor house with a slate roof and a gabled wing at each end. It had been painted in high summer. The creamy stone glowed against the backdrop of dark trees, and where there was now only rough grass and young saplings the artist had lovingly painted a sweeping drive curling between manicured lawns. 'We keep it here on the upper landing so that it is out of direct sunlight and will not fade so quickly.'

He stepped closer to study the picture and Annabelle found herself looking at his profile, the hawkish nose and strong jawline, the lines of his face, so harsh they might have been carved from stone. In the dim light his hair was black as ink, his colouring so dark that even though his cheek was freshly shaved it bore a faint shadow. A man of dark thoughts, not one given to smiling. Strength emanated from his powerful frame. For all his fine clothes and good manners, he was not a man to be crossed.

Suddenly she was uncomfortable being here alone with him. The gloom and stillness were unnerving. She shivered and a few droplets of hot wax dripped on to her hand, making her gasp.

'Here, let me hold that.' He took the candlestick from her, his fingers brushing her skin and causing her to suppress another shiver, this time at the shock of his touch. She began to chatter to cover her nervousness.

'This was painted just before the manor burned down. It is one of my father's most prized possessions.'

To her relief he turned his attention again to the painting.

'It is a good likeness.'

'Is it? I have never seen another painting of the manor, so I cannot tell you.'

'Who is the artist?'

'I do not know…'

'There is a signature.' He held the candles closer and she peered at the faint scrawl.

'I have never thought to look before… M.M.B…'

'Maria Blackstone.'

She blinked. 'Blackstone was the name of the family who lived there. Look—' she pointed '—there is a small figure on the lawn.'

'Yes, I see it. A tiny detail, easily missed.'

She leaned closer. The painting had been on the wall for as long as she could remember and she had not studied it for years.

'It is a little boy, I think. I wonder who—'

'Shall we go?'

His tone indicated that his interest was at an end. At the top of the stairs he put a hand beneath her elbow. Startled, she looked up and their eyes locked. His were black, unfathomable, yet she sensed danger and her breath caught in her throat. Panic gripped her, setting her heart thudding wildly, and the blood pounded so loudly in her ears that she was sure he would hear it in the gloomy stillness.

Annabelle swallowed nervously. She was being fanciful and foolish beyond permission. Straightening her shoulders, she moved away from him and began the descent, although she kept one hand lightly on the banister in case her shaking legs failed to support her.

Back in the drawing room, the tea tray had arrived.

'It is a few miles to the Red Lion,' explained Samuel as they came in. 'I know you will want to get back while the moon is still high.'

'I will indeed, sir.' Lucas replied. He noted Annabelle's tense countenance and could not resist teasing her, saying quietly, 'Patience, Miss Havenham. Your ordeal will soon be over.'

Her brows rose and she muttered with icy politeness, 'It is no ordeal, sir, I assure you.'

'What thought you of the picture?' Samuel enquired, unaware of the interchange.

'Very interesting, sir.'

Samuel nodded. 'It is an accurate representation of the way the manor used to be. Feel free to call again and look at it whenever you wish. Bring your architect, he may want to copy the detail.'

Lucas felt a smile tugging at his mouth when he saw the flicker of alarm in Annabelle's eyes.

'I am not employing an architect, Mr Havenham,' he said. 'I have drawn up my own plans for the builder.'

'Such a lot of work,' sighed Samuel. 'The

place has been sadly neglected. I always intended
to do something about it, but…'

He trailed off and Lucas said cheerfully, 'I do
not despair of returning it to its former glory.
The house is already under way and I have made
a start on taming the wilderness that was once
the park.'

'I wish you good fortune, then, Mr Monserrat.
If we can help in any way, you only have to ask.
In fact…' Samuel straightened in his chair '…if
anyone knows the lie of the land it is Belle. She
grew up playing in those woods and grounds.'

'Oh, no, Papa. I am sure Mr Monserrat would
be better advised to study a map.'

'Nonsense, my love, you know every dell,
every spring and stream at Morwood.'

'But surely you could be more helpful to him,
Papa,' she persisted. 'After all, you remember the
house and grounds as they were before the fire.
You have not yet given up your horses, a gentle
ride would be good for you.'

A strange look came over Samuel's face. Fear?
Revulsion? Lucas could not decide, but a defi-
nite tremor ran through the old man as he shook
his head.

'No, my dear,' he said quietly. 'I do not care
to ride there any more.'

'I would be honoured if Miss Havenham
would give me the benefit of her knowledge,'

said Lucas. 'Perhaps, ma'am, you would ride out with me one day and show me these, er, streams and dells.'

'An excellent idea,' put in his host, rousing himself once more. 'And you should do it soon, while the weather holds. What about tomorrow, sir?'

'Papa, I do not think—'

Samuel was so caught up in his own thoughts that he did not hear her.

'Yes, if you are free, Monserrat, I think tomorrow would be most convenient. I know Belle intended to spend the day at home, but Dr Bennett is coming over to play chess with me in the afternoon, and it is very dull work for a young lady to be sitting with two such elderly gentlemen when she would much rather be roaming free over the fields, what?'

Annabelle opened her mouth and closed it again. Her father had anticipated every objection. Lucas rose.

'Then it is settled.'

Lucas came towards her, smiling with unholy amusement at her consternation.

'I must be going. I shall call for you tomorrow, Miss Havenham.' His back was to his host and he added quietly, 'It seems you are not rid of me quite so easily.'

She bit her lip before replying with much feeling, 'Nothing about you is *easy*, Mr Monserrat.'

Apollo was fresh. The big grey sidled and sidestepped playfully when Annabelle rode away from Oakenroyd, and she was glad that she could give her attention to controlling her mount and did not have to make conversation with the man who rode beside her, mounted on a hunter of equal size and strength to Apollo.

'I am somewhat surprised you agreed to ride out with me, Miss Havenham.'

'I did not choose to do so.'

'If you really did not wish to come, you could have told your father the truth about our first meeting.'

Apollo took exception to a wood pigeon flying out of the hedgerow and she quietened him before making her reply.

'That would upset him and he would be obliged to cut your acquaintance. I would not have him on bad terms with a neighbour.' She glanced behind her. 'And as you see, I have Clegg with me today.'

'You would be quite safe, even if you had not brought your groom.'

His tone was perfectly sincere, but Annabelle had not forgotten his insolent manner, nor the hard looks he had given her when she had come upon him at Morwood.

'Perhaps,' she said coldly. 'I would rather not put it to the test.'

'I can see I have some work to do to gain your good opinion, Miss Havenham.'

'A great deal,' she retorted.

'But you will allow me to try?'

'That implies good behaviour does not come naturally to you.'

'Of course not. I was in the army for fifteen years and they teach one discipline, but not society manners. Pray allow this boorish soldier a chance to redeem himself.'

He smiled, softening the harsh features. The dangerous look in his eyes disappeared, replaced by something warmer, an invitation to share his amusement. Annabelle was shaken by the transformation and had a great desire to smile back. Instead she looked away, not ready to capitulate. She pointed to a nearby lane.

'If we turn in here, we can go across the moors and gallop the fidgets out of these horses.'

The exertion, the sensation of flying over the ground, did much to ease the tension Annabelle was experiencing. They raced neck and neck along the track that cut through the rough moorland. The gorse was coming into bloom; in a few more weeks there would be huge splashes of brilliant yellow dotted over the moors, contrasting sharply with the black, almost lifeless heather that would turn first dark green, then purple as the summer progressed. She felt at home here, free to roam, but the approaching woods reminded her that her freedom was now curtailed. That wall of trees was her boundary. The land surrounding Morwood Manor was no longer hers to ride over as she wished. She tried not to be downhearted. Her father still owned sufficient land for her to enjoy a daily gallop. She must not be greedy.

They pulled up in the shadow of the trees and waited for Clegg to catch up before joining the track that wound its way down through the woods to Morwood. Annabelle saw immediately that changes were in progress. The encroaching undergrowth had been cut back to make the path through the woods once again wide enough for a carriage.

A laugh escaped her. 'It is like "Sleeping Beauty."'

'I beg your pardon?'

She had been so engrossed in her thoughts she had forgotten her companion. A self-conscious flush touched her cheeks.

'When the prince arrives and wakes the princess. The forest has been growing around the castle for a hundred years and he has to hack his way through the brambles.'

He looked around. 'Just five-and-twenty years has been enough to change the woods out of all recognition.'

They continued towards the house. Even before it was in sight, the sound of hammering could be heard ringing on the breeze, along with snatches of song from the workmen.

'Your coming is timely, Mr Monserrat,' she conceded. 'You have brought a great deal of work to Stanton at a time when it is much needed.'

'I have heard the harvests were bad last year.'

'Dreadful. They called it the year without a summer, the crops rotted in the fields. The farmers had nothing to harvest, so the labourers had no work and no money was spent, thus the tradesmen suffered too.' She shook her head, remembering the sad, strained faces in the town. 'My father did what he could, set men on to renew the road from Oakenroyd to Stanton and rebuild the stone walls.'

'And he borrowed money to do it.'

'Yes.' She looked across, frowning slightly. 'How did you know that?'

'A guess, merely. Ah, here we are.'

They emerged from the trees and the house now stood before them. It was just over two

weeks since Annabelle had ridden here last—
and been so rudely accosted, but she must try
to forget that. She was astonished by the transformation. A forest of scaffolding was growing
up around the old walls, the sweeping drive was
covered with wagons and much of the ground between the house and the woods had been cleared
of weeds and saplings.

'I shall lay new lawns, of course, but not until
the builders and stonemasons have finished their
work.' He pointed to one side of the house. 'I
propose to plant a rose garden there, on the west
front.'

'In the painting the roses are on the other side
of the house.'

'Yes, but they never prospered there.'

'You were fortunate to find anyone to remember such a detail.' She gazed at the busy scene
with mixed feelings. Of course it was a good
thing for the manor to be restored, but the abandoned ruin of the old house had been so peaceful, a tranquil haven that she had come to look
upon as hers alone. That was all gone now.

Lucas watched the play of emotion on her
face. She had grown up here, she considered it
hers. He quickly stamped down the tiny flicker
of sympathy. Annabelle Havenham was merely
losing her playground: twenty-five years ago he
had lost his home and his parents, everything

he held dear destroyed in one terrible night. He was obliged to push the memories aside so that he could continue.

'I have a stonemason inspecting the old walls of the house,' he said. 'To see which of them can be made sound. Much of the house will have to be rebuilt. Strange thing is that where the walls have collapsed much of the stone has gone. Robbed for other buildings, perhaps.'

'There is an abundance of stone on the far side of the rise.' She pointed with her crop to a tree-covered hill behind the house.

'Will you show me?' Lucas turned his horse. 'We could go there now.'

She led the way. The old path around the base of the small hill was just passable, but although the trees were still bare of leaves she had to push the grey through the undergrowth, where the brambles were so high they snagged at her skirts. Eventually they reached a very uneven area of ground. The trees were much thinner here, growing between haphazard grassy mounds. Annabelle walked Apollo beside one particularly large mound and reached down to push aside some of the vegetation with the end of her crop.

'This whole area is made up of piles of cut stone. It is very overgrown and the stones themselves are covered in lichen, but you will see that they are all dressed, ready to use.'

'And use them we will. Thank you, Miss Havenham. I wonder why it was brought here?'

'I think my father had some idea of building a house on this spot.'

'Surely it would have been better to rebuild the old manor? The views are much better from that side of the hill.'

'I am sure he had his reasons.'

He did not press her to explain, saying instead, 'Tomorrow I will set men on to clear a path for the wagons. There is sufficient material here to rebuild the west wall and it should keep the builders supplied with stone until I can open up the delph again.'

'You know about the old quarry? I suppose someone in the town told you, I did not think any of them would remember it.'

'Clearly you were wrong.'

The frank grey eyes met his for a moment, a faint twinkle in their depths. 'Then they have stolen my thunder, sir. I meant to amaze you with my local knowledge.'

It was the first crack in the wall of ice she had put around herself.

Lucas was heartened.

'I am sure there is plenty more for you to show me.'

He smiled at her, but the defences were up

again. She replied coldly, as if to make up for her momentary lapse in hostilities.

'My father instructed me to show you everything that might be of interest, Mr Monserrat.'

She turned the big grey and rode on. He followed her to the valley where the natural springs welled up from the ground and she pointed out the damaged and dry culvert that had once carried water to the house. Moving into the surrounding woods, she showed him the heavily overgrown tracks that cut across the Morwood land.

'Odd that they should have been allowed to fall into disuse.'

'Not really. They lead only to the old house. Once that was abandoned there was no need for them.'

'But all this woodland, untended. Do the local people not come here to gather firewood, or snare rabbits?'

'I have never seen any sign of that. Perhaps they are afraid of the ghosts.'

Lucas looked around. In every direction the trees grew tall and thick, cutting out all sound from the rest of the world. At night it would be a very different place, dark and sinister, a place for hiding secrets.

Lucas, your father, he has the black temper

*this morning. You had best go away and play,
my love. Keep out of his sight.*

He shivered and his horse sidled as his hands
clenched on the rein. Annabelle glanced at him,
brows raised.

'Have I unnerved you, with the talk of ghosts?'

'There are no ghosts,' he said shortly. 'Only
memories. Let us move on.'

They made their way to a sunlit valley where
the warmth of the spring sunshine dispelled his
melancholy and he was able to concentrate on
winning over his companion.

He went carefully, showing an interest in the
land, asking questions, drawing her out to tell
him what she knew of the estate's history, encouraging her to share her memories. He might
tease her gently, but he maintained a rigid pro-
priety and gradually, as the day went on, the ice
maiden thawed a little.

The tour took much longer than Annabelle
had anticipated, partly because the overgrown
paths meant their progress was slow. They had
to take long detours to reach the points of interest she wanted to show the new owner of
Morwood. He was eager to see everything and
she was surprised at how much she enjoyed ac-
quainting him with the land where she had spent
so many happy hours. It was impossible to stay
aloof, although she caught herself up at times,

refusing to respond with more than a tight smile to his pleasantries. She was still unsure of Mr Lucas Monserrat.

Clegg reminded her of the time and Annabelle was surprised by a tiny stab of regret as they left the old house and its neglected grounds behind them. They rode in silence until they reached the highest point of the moor. A sudden tinkle of bells was carried on the wind and she slowed, looking up to see a packhorse train trotting across the distant hills, while in the valley below Oakenroyd and its gardens basked in the weak sunshine. How she loved this place!

'Your knowledge of Morwood is invaluable, Miss Havenham,' said Lucas.

'Thank you.' Her response was cool. Not for the world would she let him know that she appreciated his praise, nor how much she had enjoyed herself. 'You could gain as much from a map, I am sure.'

'All the maps in the world are not as useful as someone who knows and loves the land. Perhaps you will come again? We have not yet seen everything.'

'No, but there is only the Home Wood to explore. The rest is mainly farmland, and that has been well tended and needs no explanation from me.'

'But I thought you might show me the lake.'

She looked at him, surprised. 'You are particularly well informed, sir.'

'You would not expect me to purchase an estate without making some push to find out what I was buying.'

'No, I suppose not.'

'And you will come again and be my guide?'

She bit her lip. It was tempting, but she must not succumb. 'You do not need me.'

'Oh, I think I do, Miss Havenham. Having seen how treacherously overgrown the paths have become, I might well lose myself in the wilderness that is now the Home Wood. Remember "Sleeping Beauty." It could be a hundred years before anyone comes to my rescue.'

His reference to her earlier comment surprised a laugh from Annabelle. He grinned back at her.

'So you will come. Tomorrow?'

She shook her head. 'I have an engagement.'

'Monday, then, if the weather is good.' Still she hesitated and he continued, 'I intend to be at the manor all day, so come if you can.'

It had been such a pleasurable day, why not repeat it? She was sorely tempted.

'We have reached the edge of the Oakenroyd Park,' he said, bringing his horse to a stand. 'I shall leave you here and hope to see you on Monday.'

'I— Do not look for me.' She was suddenly unsure.

The brim of his hat shaded his face and she could read nothing from his look, although she knew those black eyes were fixed on her. Unsettled, she touched her crop to Apollo's flank and set off at a gallop across the park. She did not look back, but it was an effort. She wondered if he was still watching her, or had he ridden away, putting all thoughts of her from his mind?

Annabelle entered the house by a side door and went to find her father. He was in his study, but he put down his book when she entered.

'So you are back at last, my love. Did you enjoy yourself at Morwood?'

'The time went very quickly,' she answered him evasively. 'We covered everything to the south and east of the house. Mr Monserrat has a lot of work to do to make Morwood habitable again.'

'But it is time. I should have done more with it.'

'You once had plans to build another house there, did you not, Papa?'

'Yes. I thought I might do so.' He sighed. 'I was going to demolish the old manor, but when it came to it…' He sighed again. 'Perhaps I should have sold Morwood then. Perhaps I should never have bought it.'

'Too late to fret over that, sir,' was Annabelle's bracing response. 'Instead let us be thankful that it is now being restored.'

'Yes. Do you know, my love, I think Mr Monserrat's coming will prove beneficial to the whole area. I am glad you have shown him over the grounds, Belle. I would not want him to think us anything less than good neighbours.'

She walked to the window, gazing out at the tranquil gardens, everything so neat and orderly.

'He has asked me to ride out with him again, Papa. On Monday.'

'And will you go, Belle?'

She raised her eyes, looking past the well-kept domesticity of Oakenroyd to the rugged moors beyond. Even in the sunshine they had a barren look to them, a wildness that attracted her. And beyond the moor lay the neglected groves of Morwood and their enigmatic owner.

'Belle?' Her father spoke again. 'Will you ride out with Mr Monserrat?'

She smiled.

'Yes, Papa. I think I shall.'

Chapter Four

It was gone noon and Lucas was helping the men to winch a particularly heavy section of the pediment into place over the main door when the sound of hooves made him look around. Annabelle was approaching, cantering out of the trees.

The rush of pleasure he felt at the sight of her surprised him. Quickly he turned his attention back to the job in hand. The stone was inching upwards amongst a complicated web of ropes, the stonemason on the scaffolding above them shouting instructions. At last the block was in place and he could release his hold and leave the others to finish the work.

Annabelle had brought Apollo to a stand well back from the bustle and disorder in front of the house. Lucas picked up his discarded jacket as he walked over to meet her. He was aware of her watching him as he shrugged himself into his coat. How must he look to her in his workaday buckskins and simply knotted neckcloth? Did she think him beneath her?

No. That was not her way. Everyone he met told him that Miss Havenham was an angel, not at all proud or disdainful. Unless one treated her with insolence, as he had done. Then she was justly indignant, her grey eyes darkening with anger and she became a force to be reckoned with. He smiled to himself. There was steel beneath that soft exterior. It would be interesting to discover just how much.

Lucas approached her, reaching up to rub Apollo's great head.

'You came.'

'Yes.' She looked a little uncertain. 'If you are too busy it does not matter—'

He smiled. 'No, not too busy at all. Wait there while I collect Sultan.'

The Home Wood lay at the western edge of the Morwood estate. The road to it lay through what had once been the park, but the smooth grass had been left to grow uncropped and the elegant trees now rose up amongst a mass of weeds and brambles. Lucas looked about him, frowning.

'Did your father tell you why he bought Morwood?' When she shook her head he continued, 'Much of it shares a boundary with Oakenroyd. Perhaps he thought it a good opportunity to increase his property.'

'Perhaps, although Papa has never been ambitious in that way.'

'So he just shut the gates and left it to rot.'

She flushed. 'He intended to build a new house and give it to my brother—' She broke off, biting her lip. 'I think, when Edwin died, he lost heart.'

'He should at least have maintained the woods and the grounds.'

He heard the defensive note in her voice when she responded. 'My father must have had his reasons for leaving Morwood as it was.'

'Oh, I am sure he did.' Annabelle was looking at him, a faint crease in her brows. It was not part of his plan to antagonise her, so he threw off his black mood and smiled. 'Let us not waste time upon conjecture, Miss Havenham. You are here to show me the Home Wood and I am eager to see it.'

They picked their way across the neglected park and Annabelle led him unerringly to the remains of a path meandering through the trees.

'My father told me this was once a carriage-way here, used by the family for pleasure trips around the grounds.'

'It leads to the lake.'

'Yes, you are right. How…?'

'One of the locals told me.'

'What good memories they have, when no one ever comes here now. It is still possible to reach the water, although I haven't ridden this way for a while and the weeds will already be invading the path. Would you like to see it?'

Annabelle turned Apollo on to the little-used track. Lucas followed, enjoying the view of her elegant figure twisting and bending to avoid the overhanging branches. The encroaching brambles snared her skirts, but she kept the big horse moving forwards. Gradually the sounds of the building work disappeared and only creaking leather and the jingle of the harness could be heard, along with the occasional trill of birdsong high up in the trees. Sunlight filtered through the young leaves and painted a fine tracery over everything, and as the hooves disturbed the soft loamy soil the pungent scent of damp earth rose up to meet them. As he followed Annabelle through this strange, unfamiliar world, an unaccustomed peace settled over Lucas. It was the most relaxed he had felt for a long time.

The path began a gentle slope downwards and they picked their way, avoiding the tree roots and the occasional stone protruding through the earth. Finally, through the trees ahead there was the glint of sunlight on the water.

'We are nearly there.'

Even as she called over her shoulder the trees gave way to a grassy bank that ran down to the water's edge. Before them stretched the lake, a large, serpentine expanse of water enclosed by trees that grew thickly over the slopes of the surrounding hills. It was a sheltered spot and the spring sunshine was surprisingly hot.

Belle stopped and waited for her companion to bring his horse up beside her. 'There. Was that not worth pushing through the undergrowth?'

'It is every bit as beautiful as I...as I was led to believe.'

'You can still see the line of the old path around the lake.'

'Shall we follow it?'

She shook her head. 'Clegg took me around the lake once, a few years ago, but even then the path was barely passable in some places and we were in danger of being tumbled into the water.' She threw her groom an affectionate look. 'He refused to ride that way with me again and made me promise never to do so alone.' She pointed along the bank. 'There is a boathouse over there, but to get to it you must cross the old wooden bridge across the inlet. It has not been maintained and I have no doubt the timbers are rotted away by now.'

He jumped down and handed his reins to Clegg. 'I shall go and find out.'

She watched him stride off, torn between wanting to remain aloof and curiosity. Curiosity won. Kicking her foot free from the stirrup, she slid to the ground.

'Wait for me!'

'Now, Miss Belle—' The groom's remonstrance had little effect, save to make her smile at him as she had done so many times in the past when she wanted her own way.

'Pray, look after the horses, Clegg. We will not be long and I *will* be careful.'

Lucas waited for her to catch up with him.

'Are you sure you will be safe?'

'We are only going to the bridge. Clegg will always be in sight.'

'But he will not be in earshot. I might insult you verbally.'

'You might, of course.'

'You do not think I will?'

'You have shown no inclination to be so ill-mannered since that first meeting.' She slanted a glance at him, a slight frown in those clear grey eyes. 'Why *were* you so rude to me then? We had never met, I had done nothing to deserve such treatment.'

Nothing, save be the daughter of a man I am sworn to destroy.

Lucas could not tell her as much, especially now he had decided her affection would prove a better weapon than her disgust.

'Perhaps you were fatigued,' she offered helpfully. 'That can make one irritable.'

By heaven, she was even giving him his excuses! Looking into her eyes, he saw a faint, shy smile lurking there and he was obliged to squash a slight prickle of unease at making use of her in this way.

'Yes, that was it.'

They were approaching the wooden bridge. Lucas could now see just how poor a state of repair it was in. The side rails had broken away and the boards looked grey and rotten. He stepped on to the bridge and tested one of the boards with his foot. It crumbled beneath his weight. He exhaled impatiently.

'Sheer foolishness to leave it in this state. If it is so dangerous, it should have been rebuilt or removed.'

'It should, of course, but no one ever came here to use it.'

'*You* came.'

'Not for years. Not since…' She looked about her, and Lucas had the impression she had withdrawn from him. It lasted only a moment, then she shook off her reverie and said in a robust tone, 'If you are going to reinstate the lakeside drive, then a stone bridge would look very well here.'

He replied absently, 'Yes, I have always thought so.'

She laughed. 'Now I *know* you are teasing me, Mr Monserrat. You have but this minute seen this place.'

He recovered quickly. 'But I have studied the plans, and this point faces due west, into the sunset.'

Come, Lucas, let us go down to the lake and watch the sunset from the bridge.

'Are you mentally landscaping the lake, sir? Perhaps you want to return it to its former glory. I am afraid that is not something I can help you with, since I have only seen it as a wilderness.'

It took Lucas some time to realise she was talking to him. 'I beg your pardon, I was… dreaming.'

She waved aside his apology. 'It is your home now, sir. Of course you want to take it all in.'

He looked across to the boathouse. 'I wonder if the boats are still there.'

'No. My brother and I looked in once. Papa said he had them broken up because they were unsafe. But the oars were on the walls then and there were some old fishing rods upstairs…'

'There were?' His eager response caught her attention and he was quick to explain. 'I mean, I am surprised that they should have been left there, that no one would have taken them away.'

'From what I understand Mr Blackstone was very severe with trespassers and the local people learned to stay away from his land. After he died they said he had left a curse over it.'

'More ghosts, Miss Havenham?'

She gave a little shrug and a smile. He tested the bridge again.

'What are you doing?'

'The thick timbers spanning the inlet appear to be strong enough. I am going to have a look in the boathouse.' He looked back to find her watching him, a wistful look in her eyes. 'Will you come with me?'

'The water is not deep here. I suppose the worst that can happen is we would get a ducking.'

'Come along, then.' He held out his hand. 'Keep your weight over the main beams…that's it.'

Her fingers clung to his as she carefully followed him across the bridge. He wanted to tease her, to say something about having to trust him, but he did not want her to withdraw again. She was clearly aware of their situation, for she kept her eyes lowered and a delicate flush painted her cheeks. As soon as they reached the far bank she disengaged her hand and began to stride ahead of him.

The boathouse was built out over the lake on the southern side of the bridge. The waterside opening yawned black as they approached, but when they drew closer they could see the water lapping gently against the stone walkways inside. The sturdy walls of the building were intact and a set of stone steps ran up the outside to the upper floor.

The wooden door to the lower part of the building had long since parted from its hinges and lay almost hidden in the long grass. The double glass doors in the gable end over the boathouse entrance had fared better and were still in place.

'I suppose that is where they would have fished from,' remarked Belle, gazing up. 'The iron railings across the opening would have prevented anyone from falling into the lake.'

She put her foot on the first of the stone steps, but Lucas caught her arm.

'No, let me go first. It may be dangerous.'

She followed him. There was no handrail, but the steps were wide and caused her no problem. The old wooden door at the top of the steps was swollen and Lucas had to put his shoulder to it to push it open. He moved inside, carefully testing the boards as he went.

'The floor here is in better condition than the bridge,' he remarked.

'The roof is still intact. That has protected it.' Belle followed him into the room. 'I haven't been here since Edwin was alive. It must be ten years and it is just as we left it.'

Belle looked around, remembering her excitement when they had found this miniature house with its little table and chairs, the wall sconces on the wall still bearing half-burned candles although their brass reflectors were pitted and dull with age. Now she could imagine the gentlemen—and perhaps ladies too—sitting at their ease on the chairs by the open doors, fishing rods draped out over the railings.

'You discovered this place all those years ago, but never came back?'

'I gave Papa my word,' she said simply.

'I do not think that would have prevented me.'

'Then you have a more rebellious spirit than I,' she replied, smiling. 'Papa is a loving parent who rarely demands my obedience. When he does I am happy to give it.'

'My parents died when I was ten years old.'

'I am so sorry.'

Impulsively she put her hand on his arm and squeezed it. It was a friendly gesture, but too intimate for their fragile acquaintance. Blushing, she drew back. Looking for distraction, she turned to the fishing rods fixed to the wall. They rested on their hooks as if they had been placed ready for another day's fishing, which had never come. Now they were grey with age and dust. One rod was much smaller than the rest and she pointed to it.

'That must be for a child.'

'Yes.' He took it down and weighed it between his hands. He looked towards the glass doors. 'Father and son, enjoying a rare moment of peace together, fishing.'

Belle smiled at the image. 'Is that how you see it, sir?'

'Oh, yes. They would sit here in companionable silence…'

You and your father should spend more time together, Lucas, so I will not come with you. But be sure to bring me back a fish for my dinner!

'I do not think my father ever enjoyed the sport. He certainly never took my brother fishing. Edwin liked that little rod. He was going to take it home and put a new line on it.'

Lucas pushed aside the memories that were crowding him and carefully put the rod back in its place on the wall.

'So why didn't he take it?'

'I said we should ask Papa before we disturbed

anything here.' Belle shivered and went back to the door. 'We should go. Clegg will be growing anxious.'

'And did your father object to your brother taking the rod?' he asked the question as he followed her down the steps.

'No.'

'Then why is it still there? Belle?' She began to hurry away from him, but he ran to catch up with her. He saw the tear on her cheek before she dashed it away. He said gently, 'What happened?'

She stopped. 'We were caught in a heavy shower of rain that day, on the way home. Edwin became ill. Inflammation of the lungs. He never recovered.'

'I see. How old was he?'

'Just eleven years old.'

He watched as she looked into the past, such desolation about her that he wanted to reach out and pull her into his arms, but that was impossible. He of all people could not give her sympathy.

'I am very sorry,' he said at last.

'It was such a time ago, but I still feel his loss, greatly.'

'I know. The pain never goes away.'

'I am sorry,' she said. 'About your parents.' She stood for a moment, looking out over the water. Then with a sigh she tucked her arm in his. 'We have become very maudlin, Mr Monserrat. Let us move on now. There is still a great deal to see, including the hermitage.'

He recognised her attempt to distract him and responded in kind. 'A hermitage? That is something I did not know about. That will put me in the very kick of fashion!'

She chuckled. 'Unfortunately, it is not a grotto but a natural formation of the rocks, but Edwin and I thought it would be the perfect habitat for a hermit.'

'Then take me to it, Miss Havenham!'

He helped her back across the bridge and this time she did not pull her hand away, but allowed him to draw it onto his arm as they strolled back to where Clegg was waiting with the horses.

'Let me help you to mount.'

Belle met his eyes for a fleeting moment, remembering the first time he had thrown her into the saddle. Did he recall it, too? How differently she had felt then. It would not be wise to mention it in front of Clegg, however. He was already looking disapproving about her being alone and out of sight with Lucas for so long, and if he knew of that first encounter he would most likely deliver a long homily upon the consequences of a young lady's venturing forth without her groom. So she allowed Lucas to assist her and tried to look unconcerned while a storm of conflicting thoughts and feelings raged inside her. His touch, his nearness, both frightened and excited her. Instinct told her to beware this man, yet some power beyond her control drew her to him. He seemed to understand her love for this place and she wanted to share with him her memories, the happy days she had enjoyed running free in the woods and glades. She tried to explain it as they rode away from the lake.

'Even after Edwin was gone I still liked to come here. Often I would ride my pony through the woods, exploring.' She chuckled. 'It was a chance to escape from my governess for a while. I liked being alone here, especially if I was unhappy, or there was some little problem I wanted to think about.'

'I hope you still feel you can do that, Miss Havenham.'

She shook her head. 'No. It is your land now, sir.' She urged Apollo on. 'We need to press on, if we are to see much more today.'

The Home Wood was extensive and they had not covered the half of it when Clegg drew her attention to the sun, which was sinking low towards the horizon. Belle looked about her, surprised. Had they really been riding for so long?

'We should be turning back,' she said. 'Papa will worry if I am late.'

'I hope you have enjoyed your time with me, Miss Havenham.'

'I have, very much.' Heavens, he would think her far too friendly! 'But I would have enjoyed pointing out the hidden valleys and bubbling springs to anyone who showed such interest.' Now she was too casual and felt compelled to compliment him. 'You are a good student, Mr Monserrat, and you already know a great deal about Morwood.'

'I have made it my business to study the ground plan and talk to the locals,' he told her. 'Those who are not afraid of the ghosts.'

She knew he was teasing her and chuckled. 'If there are ghosts here they are friendly ones, for I have never felt in the least uneasy, even in the ruins of the house itself. But I have never seen anyone from Stanton here, which is why I am surprised they know so much about it.'

'Ah, but I pick up a great deal of information from the taproom of the Red Lion, so perhaps the people I have spoken with make more, er, nocturnal visits.'

'You mean poachers! That is much more likely. I hope you are not planning any dark nefarious deeds of your own, sir!'

Instead of the laugh she expected, his face darkened and there was a dangerous glitter in his eyes. It was gone in a moment and Annabelle wondered if she had imagined it. Mayhap it had been a cloud passing across the sun, because now he was smiling at her again.

'We have not seen the half of the Morwood estate yet, Miss Havenham. I would like to ride out with you again, if you will?'

'Why, yes, if you wish—and if the weather holds.'

She gave him a shy smile. Again Lucas felt that uncomfortable prickle of conscience. He shrugged it aside. He meant the chit no real harm, after all.

The afternoon was well advanced by the time they returned to the manor house.

'I would ask you to stop and take some refreshment with me,' said Lucas, 'but I fear there is only water or the builders' ale to be had.'

'Then I shall decline gracefully and go on my way.' A workman was approaching, mopping his brow with a red handkerchief. She recognised him as one of her tenant farmers and nodded. 'Good day to you, Elias. You have plenty of work here, I think.'

'Afternoon, Miss Havenham, Mr Monserrat.' The man tugged his forelock. 'Aye, there's work aplenty here for us, which is good, seeing as how the harvest failed last year. We've had to buy in seed for this year and this'll go some way to pay for it.'

'I have taken on Greenwood as my foreman,' explained Lucas. 'And he is a very good one, too.'

'Aye, well, it helps to be able to turn a hand to summat else when times is bad. Which reminds me, sir, if you've a minute, I need to ask you about the stone lintel for the new porch. It don't look quite right to me.'

'And I must be going home,' said Annabelle quickly. 'Pray do not think you have to escort me back to Oakenroyd, sir, you will be far more useful here, working on your house.'

Lucas hesitated. 'If you are sure.'

'Very. I have Clegg with me, after all.'

'Then I shall take you at your word and stay.' He leaned across and held out his hand to her. 'I only wish I could offer you hospitality.'

'All in good time, sir. Perhaps when the manor is finished—' Annabelle broke off, feeling the blush steal into her cheeks again. Was she being far too forward? After all, it was not long since she had vowed never to speak to this man. Now, with her fingers snugly clasped in his, she was inviting herself into his house.

'When it is finished I shall be delighted to welcome you here.'

His voice was quiet, but there was something

in his tone that made her blush even more. She tried to look up, but could only raise her eyes as far as his mouth. The lips were curved upwards into a smile and the lines at each side had deepened. How could she ever have thought him unattractive? Shaken, she disengaged her hand and busied herself with the reins.

'I must go.'

'Of course. And thank you for your company today.'

'Not at all. I hope it was of use.'

'It was,' he responded. 'I am very grateful.'

She could think of nothing else to say, but still she could not bring herself to go. They stayed thus, not speaking, with Elias Greenwood watching them, his eyes shifting from one to the other. Apollo grew restless. He threw up his head impatiently and Annabelle shook herself out of the unaccustomed inertia. With a final murmured goodbye she turned the grey and trotted away.

Chapter Five

Lucas watched her ride off, admiring the way she handled Apollo, the straight line of her back, the proud set of her head. Had he really thought her such a nonentity when they first met? He glanced down at his fingers. They still tingled from the shock he had felt when she clasped his hand, the excitement that had pulsed through him, the sheer exhilaration of touching her. He had not expected that.

He heard someone clearing his throat and realised that Greenwood was still there, watching him.

'Ah, yes. The porch lintel. We'll go and look now.' He jumped down and tethered Sultan to a post. He took a final look at the lane, but Annabelle was no longer in sight.

'No need to worry,' said Greenwood, grinning. 'Miss Belle's a cracking rider. She'll get home safe enough.'

'Miss Belle?'

'Aye, that's how we've always known her. Grand lass she is, too. Not a bit high in the instep, for all she's mistress of Oakenroyd.'

For some reason the information did not please Lucas.

'Is she not a little spoiled?' he asked casually. 'After all, she is Havenham's only child. He says himself he dotes on her.'

'Oh, he does, but she has the sweetest nature. Why, when my wife were lying in last year and having such a bad time of it, Miss Belle goes herself to fetch the midwife, then stays looking after the little ones so's I wouldn't miss market day, such as it was. She's a good 'un, sir, and no mistake. Thinks well of everyone, or tries to.' Elias paused, then added slyly, 'She'll make someone a good wife, I do reckon.'

Lucas affected not to hear this last comment. He began to stride away towards the house. 'Right,' he said curtly. 'Let us see what is wrong with that lintel!'

A period of dry sunny weather followed and Annabelle rode with Lucas almost every day. No arrangement was made, but as she rode across the park each morning Annabelle would look out for him on the moors above her, the black figure of a horse and rider outlined against the eastern sky. He would gallop down to meet her and they would ride over the Oakenroyd land, then across to Morwood, where she accompanied him to the outlying farms, explaining the histories of his tenant farmers and their families, details that the taciturn northern people would never tell him themselves, such as how young John Sutcliffe had struggled to rebuild the farm after his father was killed in a riding accident two years ago, and how Matthew Crabtree bred the best milch cows in the county and Jonah Oldfield the miller might appear surly at first, but he had a heart of gold, while his wife Hannah had a gift for healing. Lucas remembered Elias Greenwood's words: *Thinks well of everyone, or tries to.* What would she think of him, when she knew the truth? He pushed the thought away.

By the time April was sliding gently into May they had covered the whole estate and Belle declared that Lucas had no further need of her. They were within sight of Oakenroyd, the point where the path to her home parted from the road into Stanton.

'Are you tired of my company, then, Miss Havenham?'

'Not at all, but…'

She hesitated over her next words. She was aware that spending so much time in Lucas's company was giving rise to comment. Even Mr Keighley had mentioned it when he called at Oakenroyd recently. Her father had been quite sanguine.

'I fear it is my fault,' he had said in his gentle way. 'Belle is standing in for me by showing Mr Monserrat over his new lands and introducing him to his tenants. I do not ride so often now, you know, and never to Morwood.'

'Then the rumours of an alliance are unfounded?' asked Mr Keighley.

'Oh, completely,' Samuel had replied comfortably. 'I'm afraid I quite bullied Annabelle into going out. She is merely being neighbourly.'

'Then I shall make sure I dismiss any speculation I hear.'

'Aye, do, sir,' cried Annabelle, her cheeks burning, and not only with indignation. 'It is a poor thing if one cannot ride out with a neighbour!'

The exchange had left her feeling slightly uncomfortable. During their rides together Lucas never did or said anything untoward, but she was very much aware of his physical presence, of the warm note in his voice when he addressed her, and there was a curious lightness in her chest whenever she met his smiling eyes. It was nothing more than friendship, she told herself, but sometimes, in the dark reaches of the night, she hoped—dreamed—one day it might be more than that. Not that she could admit as much to Lucas, of course, so now she prevaricated a little.

'I fear I am taking you away from the building work.'

'You are not. I still make regular visits to the manor. To be truthful I think the builders are relieved that I am not on site all the time.'

'I know most of them,' said Annabelle. 'They are good men and do not require constant supervision.'

'I am aware, and it is not why I spend so much time there. I like to be involved, to get my hands dirty.'

Her eyes dropped to those hands, gloved in the finest leather and resting lightly on Sultan's glossy mane. Strong, capable hands. The memory of those same hands spanning her waist, lifting her down from Apollo, suddenly made her grow hot and she looked away.

'So will you be riding again tomorrow?' she spoke quickly, to defuse the sudden awkward tension she could feel around them.

'Not tomorrow. I would like to do something different.' He smiled at her enquiring look. 'I sent Rudd to fetch my curricle and he returned

yesterday. I would like to take you out in it, if
I may.'

She could feel the smile bursting out from inside her. There was no question of refusing such
a tempting invitation.

'Oh, yes, if you please! I should like that very
much. I have never been in a curricle and always
wanted to do so. Sir John has a phaeton and it is
very elegant, but a curricle—is it a racing one,
sleek and low?'

He laughed at her enthusiasm. 'Yes, it is and
tomorrow you shall have your wish and drive
out in a curricle, Miss Havenham!'

Belle was waiting at the door when Lucas
swept around Oakenroyd's curling drive the following morning. She did not come immediately
to the carriage, but instead her attention was all
on the matched bays pulling it.

'What magnificent creatures,' she declared
as Rudd jumped down from the rumble seat and
ran to their heads. 'May I?'

She would not approach until she had obtained
the groom's consent, but once he had nodded she
moved closer, murmuring endearments and rubbing each velvet nose in turn as she ran a practised eye over the bays.

'They are beautiful,' she said. 'Small heads,
deep chests—I imagine they are very fast?'

Lucas was thankful she addressed her question to Rudd, for he was incapable of speech. He was looking at her, a slight smile playing about his mouth. She was wearing her olive-green riding habit with its military-style gold frogging, the one she often wore for riding out with him but now, as she moved gracefully around the horses, discussing their finer points with Rudd, her countenance beneath the stylish beaver hat was quite animated and she took his breath away.

'They are indeed fast,' he said when at last he handed her into the curricle. 'They are good for sixteen miles an hour on a fast road.'

'You will find very few highways of that standard here,' she told him. 'Except the new toll road at Dyke's Ridge.'

'Then we shall go there first and I will put them through their paces for you.' He saw Samuel standing in the doorway and turned to him. 'That is, if you have no objection, sir?'

'By all means,' Samuel replied. 'I saw you drive in and I do not doubt your ability. You have an excellent turnout there, my boy. If I were twenty years younger, I should like to try them myself.'

'Then go in my stead,' said Belle immediately. 'I am sure Mr Monserrat would take me another day...'

'No, no, my love, my racing days are over. We

will enjoy a gentle ride together later, perhaps, but now off you go and enjoy yourself. Take care of my daughter, sir!'

'I will, sir, you may be sure of it.'

Driving off with Annabelle beside him, Lucas felt unusually exhilarated. It was easy to ignore the tiny pinprick of conscience he had felt when Samuel had adjured him to look after his daughter. He intended to do just that. He also wanted to impress her and he found himself reining in his own exuberance as well as keeping his horses in check. They skirted the town of Stanton, maintaining a steady pace through the rough lanes, but once they had climbed to the high road and left the old track to Oldroyd he dropped his hands. The bays leapt into their collars and sped away. The new road followed the curving ridge; to one side the moors stretched upwards, ending in a grey outcrop of rocks on the skyline, while on the other the land fell away, sharply at first, and the curricle swept around the first bend where the road came close to the edge of the ridge, with only a thin, grassy strip between the road and a steep valley. Once past the bend the land flattened out and a series of fields dipped gently to the old track which could be seen cutting through the valley, dropping down to the ford at Oldroyd Farm before snaking upwards again to meet the new road a mile or so past the toll house.

Instinctively Annabelle put her hand up to her bonnet. Lucas glanced at her.

'Frightened, Miss Havenham?'

'Not a bit of it,' she declared, laughing. 'I love racing along like this!'

They drew up for the toll, paid their fee and were off again. The bays flew over the ground, making short work of the last stretch of new road and all too soon they were dropping down to Holmeclough, from where they made their way back through the winding lanes towards Stanton. They passed few carriages, but there were several figures in the fields who straightened up to watch them race by and Mr Keighley's words came back to Annabelle.

'I fear we shall be the subject of some gossip, Mr Monserrat.'

He flicked a glance at her. 'Riding in an open carriage, with my groom perched up behind us? There is no impropriety in that.'

'No, of course not, but—'

'Are you not enjoying yourself, Miss Havenham?'

'Oh, yes, very much!'

'Would you like me to curtail our drive and take you home now?'

The very idea made her heart sink. 'No!' She

put up her chin. 'As you say, we are doing nothing improper, and we have my father's blessing for this trip.' Having persuaded herself that no one could object, she settled herself more comfortably beside him. 'Where do we go now?'

'I am going to take you to Morwood, if you are agreeable. We have ridden around the land and you have seen the building work, but there is one improvement you have not yet seen. What do you say?'

Belle had readily agreed and soon they were driving along the tree-lined drive to the house. Not only was the road much improved, but the trees on either side had been thinned out and the undergrowth cut back, allowing sunlight to dapple their path. Instead of turning towards the house, Lucas kept his team on the path around the edge of the park, making for the Home Wood. As they approached Belle gave a little gasp.

'You have opened up the drive to the lake!'

'I have indeed. I set a team of men on to it after our first visit there.'

Where she had known only an overgrown track there was now a wide carriageway. Fresh gravel scrunched beneath the wheels as they followed the meandering route down through the trees to the lake. The new drive ended in a turning circle close to the water's edge.

'Eventually I want to extend the carriageway all around the lake, to rebuild the bridge and refurbish the boathouse, as it used to be, but for now this is as far as we can go.' He drew the curricle to a halt, facing the calm waters of the lake.

'An amazing transformation,' she declared, looking about her. 'Your men have worked so hard, but why, when there is so much yet to do at the house?'

'I have more than enough men working there. These were hired specifically to clear this path.'

Lucas knew he should not have done it, for it was outside the budget he had allowed for the rebuilding work, but Annabelle's reaction made it worthwhile.

'Extravagant, Mr Monserrat.'

She was smiling and Lucas felt the breath catch in his throat. She exuded happiness, her beaming smile, the bright sparkle in her eyes and the delicate flush on her cheeks. He wanted to lean closer, to soak up her radiance.

He returned her smile, holding her eyes, enjoying her innocent friendliness until he became aware of a subtle change. She was still smiling at him, still trusting, but anticipation filled the air around them. She was expecting something—that he would kiss her, perhaps? He wanted to do so, he wanted it very badly, but even as his head began to dip towards her, Samuel's parting words echoed in his mind.

Take care of my daughter, sir!

A sudden, delicate cough from his groom settled the matter.

'You won't want to be keeping your horses standing too long, Major, there's a sly breeze coming off the moors.'

Lucas drew back, but when he looked at Annabelle she was not blushing, there was no conscious, awkward look. Instead her eyes were brimming with laughter and the desire to take her in his arms was greater than ever.

Warning bells clamoured in his head. Lucas knew he must be careful. To become enamoured of Annabelle Havenham would not suit his purpose at all. He decided he would have to forgo the pleasure of seeing her, at least for a while.

Lucas was in Annabelle's thoughts a great deal over the next few days. The morning following their curricle drive she looked for him on her morning ride, but there was no familiar figure on the skyline. She was not perturbed and guessed he was very busy at the manor. She longed to ride over to Morwood to see him, but could think of no valid reason to do so. When a week went by and there was still no sign of him, she wondered if he, too, had heard the rumours and decided that they should not be seen so much together. Perhaps he was staying away to protect her reputation. That thought gave way to another, far less comfortable one. Perhaps he did not want to raise hopes he had no intention of fulfilling.

If that were so, then Annabelle told herself sternly that she really must not care. She had gone on very comfortably before Lucas Monserrat arrived in Stanton and she would continue to do so. But it did not prevent an unfamiliar restlessness gnawing away at her and she decided to work it off by walking into Stanton to pay a visit to old Mrs Hall. However, when she reached the main street and saw Lucas coming towards her she gave him a smile of genuine pleasure. He stopped and touched his hat, his own smile putting a brooding look to flight.

'Miss Havenham, good day to you, ma'am.' His eyes fell to her basket. 'Are you shopping?'

'No, sir. I bring a few small things for Mrs Hall. I call upon her every week, if I can.'

'And you walk here alone? Should you not have a maid to accompany you?'

'In a town where I am known by everyone? I do not think it necessary.'

'And how long do you stay with Mrs Hall?'

'Long enough to catch up on all the local news.'

He grinned. 'That cannot take you very long at all in such a small place.'

'About half an hour.' She laughed up at him. 'But it is good to stay in touch with old neighbours.'

'Half an hour, you say?' He took out his watch. 'Then I shall be waiting by the market cross at eleven to escort you home.'

She was inordinately pleased at the thought and made no effort to discourage him. He touched his hat again to her as they parted.

'Until eleven, then, Miss Havenham!'

Lucas hurried back to the Red Lion, where his man was waiting for him in his room.

George Stebbing had served under Lucas in the Peninsula and at Waterloo, where he had lost an arm. When they returned to England Lucas had taken him on as his valet and had never regretted it. Lucas prided himself that he was not dependent upon any man to dress and shave him, so Stebbing's infirmity was of little consequence and like Rudd, Lucas's groom, Stebbing's loyalty to his master was absolute. Now he waited silently for Lucas's orders.

'Send a message to the manor, if you please, and tell Greenwood that I will not be there to see his man about the roof tiles until later—four, at the earliest. He can handle all the arrangements until then.'

'Very good, Major. You are going out?'

'Yes, once I have changed my coat. I'll wear the new superfine with the brass buttons, George. Can you find it for me? Hurry, man, I do not have long.'

'I saw you talking to Miss Havenham in the market, Major. Would it be the lady you are off to meet?'

'And what if I am?'

'Knowing your, er, interest in the family, sir, I have been keeping my ears open.'

'Oh?'

With his one hand Stebbing held up the blue coat for his master. Lucas shrugged himself into it and stood before the long mirror to rearrange his neck cloth.

'Miss Havenham and her father are very well thought of in Stanton, sir.'

'I am well aware of that—what is your point?'

'Business is one thing.' Stebbing dragged the clothes brush across Lucas's shoulders. 'If the family is brought down because they can't meet their obligations, well, there's no helping that.'

'But? I feel you are about to admonish me, George.'

'I wouldn't do that, sir, but…'

Lucas met his man's eyes in the mirror. 'Out

with it, man. We have known each other long enough for you to say what you think.' He added wryly, 'You are not usually so reticent.'

'Well, sir, if you wants the word with no bark on it, I don't think people here would take too kindly to your seducing Miss Havenham.'

Lucas's brows snapped together. 'Damn you, George, do you think that is my intention?'

Stebbing rubbed his chin. 'Your *intention* is to punish her father for what he did to you, sir, and ruining his daughter would be one way of doing it.'

A dull flush crept into Lucas's cheek. It was so close to the truth that he could not deny it, but until the words were spoken aloud he had not considered the enormity of what he had planned.

'I have no intention of ruining Miss Havenham,' he said at last. 'I plan to offer her marriage as a means of saving her father from total ruin. To that end I am befriending her. It will be better, when the time comes, that she does not find me totally repulsive.'

The sceptical look in his servant's eye made him look away.

'You can try that, Major, but I can't see as how she could do otherwise, once she discovers what you are about.'

Lucas went out, trying to banish Stebbing's words from his mind, but they were lodged there, niggling away. Damn George, he had it all wrong. He had no intention of *seducing* Annabelle Havenham. It was not as if he intended to bed her, then abandon her.

But you do plan to make her fall in love with you.

He twisted away from the uncomfortable thought. Hell and confound it, he had changed his plans once with regard to Samuel's daughter. He would not do so again.

Annabelle was already approaching the market cross when he arrived. Lucas schooled his face into a smile.

'Let me carry your basket for you, Miss Havenham.'

She released the wicker basket into his hand and took his arm. The High Street was busy and he knew the sight of them strolling off together like this would do nothing to halt the speculation. Let the townspeople gossip, there could be no harm in it. But while Lucas conversed pleasantly with his companion about everyday things, he found George's words would not leave his brain. She would be horrified when his plans were revealed, but she would learn to accept it. Wouldn't she?

He pushed the disturbing thoughts aside. He need not think about that. Not yet.

'Do you often walk into Stanton, Miss Havenham?'

'Not as often as I would like—there is much for me to do at Oakenroyd. Not only keeping house for my father, but running the estate, too. As he grows older he passes more responsibility on to me.'

'That must be a heavy burden.'

'No, why?' She looked at him, genuinely surprised. 'I love Oakenroyd and want the best for it and our people. Do you think administration is a task best suited to a man, Mr Monserrat?'

Her grey eyes held a laughing challenge and he could not help smiling back at her.

'I would not dare to suggest such a thing.'

'I am very glad. I take advice from Mr Telford, our lawyer, and also from the steward, but that is no more than any conscientious landowner should do.'

'Of course.'

'Our neighbours are very good, too, and are always willing to give me the benefit of their experience. We are fortunate to live amongst such good people.'

'You are indeed.' They had come to a junction and he stopped. 'Do we take the road, Miss Havenham, or is there a shorter way?'

She pointed to a narrow track.

'That is by far the quickest and the prettiest, too, so let us take that.'

The sun was warm on their backs and as they left the town the plaintive cries of a curlew carried to them from the upland pastures. They talked, although Lucas could not recall afterwards the subject. All he could remember was the sparkle in her eyes when she was animated and how much he wanted to kiss that smiling mouth.

Their path lay alongside a stream, swollen with spring rains and when the path narrowed he fell behind, enjoying the view of her confident stride, the sway of her hips that made the skirts of her muslin gown dance about her ankles. And what pretty ankles, too: neatly encased in their half-boots, above which he occasionally caught the glimpse of a silk stocking. His musings carried him off into a daydream, where he was removing those same stockings and kissing the dainty foot beneath…

'Mr Monserrat, I do not think you are listening to me.' She had stopped and turned towards him, grey eyes twinkling with amusement. 'I have addressed several remarks to you and had no reply.'

A stray curl had escaped from her bonnet and now fluttered across her cheek, the ends caressing her mouth, just as he wished to do. Without thinking he raised his finger to hook away the curl. She did not flinch, did not move at all even when his hand cupped her cheek. His body hardened. It was as much as he could do not to draw her towards him and all the while she kept looking at him. The twinkle died, replaced by a look of shy anticipation. And trust.

With an effort he quashed the desire, forced himself to remove his hand from her cheek and step back.

'I beg your pardon. I was not attending.'

'You were perhaps thinking of Morwood and all the work you have to do there?'

A smile tugged at the corners of his mouth. 'I do not think I dare tell you what I was thinking of.'

The lashes fluttered down, screening her eyes, but there was no concealing the telltale blush on her cheek. Her next words surprised him.

'I thought you were going to kiss me.'

'That would hardly be the actions of a gentleman.'

'No.' The word ended in a sigh that he could almost interpret as regret.

'Miss Havenham—Annabelle. There is so much you do not know about me.'

'We are to be neighbours, sir. I am sure we shall learn all about you in due course.'

Her comfortable tone struck a blow at his conscience. Would she ever smile at him again once she knew the truth? Would she turn from him in disgust? He squared his shoulders. That was for the future.

'You will indeed.' He offered her his arm. 'The path is wider here. Shall we walk on?'

Annabelle rested her fingers on his sleeve. Strange that she should feel so at ease now with this man. Even the moment when he had touched her cheek, when she had thought he was going to kiss her, she had not been frightened. She was a little shocked to realise just how much she had wanted him to kiss her, to compare it with that first, bruising embrace that he had forced upon her.

A pleasurable thrill ran through her. This man was dangerous, she knew it in every fibre of her being, but she could not help being drawn to him. She enjoyed his company, the way he teased but never patronised her. They laughed at the same things. Even at dinner at the Rishworths, the first time she had seen him in company and had been very much on her guard, there had been moments when something had sparked her sense of the ridiculous and she had seen a corresponding gleam of amusement in his hard eyes. Despite their disastrous beginning, she thought—hoped—they could be friends.

* * *

The next few weeks passed quietly at Oakenroyd with no visit from their new neighbour.

'I confess I am a little surprised that Mr Monserrat has not called,' said Samuel in his mild way. 'We have not seen him since the day he escorted you back from Stanton.'

'I expect he is busy with the building work at Morwood.'

Annabelle replied lightly, but she too was disappointed. Perhaps he had thought her conduct unbecoming at their last meeting. After all, she had accused him of wanting to kiss her. She had not thought him offended, but her experience of gentlemen was limited, so she could not be sure.

She went about her business as usual, consulting the steward, looking after the house and her father, paying morning calls and receiving them in return, but through it all there was a sense of something missing, that life was, dare she say it, a little *dull*. It was not that she heard nothing about Mr Monserrat. It seemed everyone in Stanton was eager to follow his progress, and because so many of the menfolk were employed upon the rebuilding of Morwood there was no want of news.

The town was buzzing with information about the amount that was being spent on new tiles for the roof and glass for the windows. Annabelle tried to be happy about the changes. After all, the house and grounds were in dire need of restoration, but she had come to look upon Morwood as her own special place. It was difficult to think of someone else owning it, changing it.

Lady Rishworth called at Oakenroyd with Celia and told her that any number of carts and wagons were passing Rishworth Lodge every day, bound for the Manor.

'And the road between Morwood and the town is to be remade,' added Celia. 'That will make our lives so much more comfortable when we go out. We won't be forever bounced around in the carriage.' She blushed, 'Oh—that is, I mean—'

Annabelle smiled at her.

'Pray do not distress yourself, Celia. Do not think that because we are presently managing without our barouche you must guard your tongue. Heavens, what a sad time we should have of it if we had to consider every word we say!'

'A very sensible view, my dear,' approved Lady Rishworth. 'And your father's fortunes will come about again with a little good management, I am sure. But to return to the subject of the roads, I am sure the new surfacing will be beneficial to everyone. What with that and the new toll road at Dyke's Ridge, travel to and from Stanton will be easier than it has ever been and that can only be good news.'

Even when Annabelle went to collect her new gown for the forthcoming assembly, Mrs Ford told her that Mr Monserrat was making himself universally popular by paying at every store, rather than using credit, which was the way with most of the large houses in the area.

'Which reminds me, Miss Havenham.' Mrs Ford gave an apologetic smile. 'There is still the bill for your winter redingote to be settled.'

Annabelle blinked, but immediately begged pardon and promised to pay all outstanding bills by the end of the week.

'Oh, there is no hurry,' the dressmaker replied hastily. 'I know I can rely upon you, but in these difficult times it is perhaps best to be beforehand in the world.'

Annabelle left with her new gown, but also with a sense of unease. She had visited the dressmaker hundreds of times over the years and money had never been mentioned. Now it seemed she thought Miss Havenham of Oakenroyd might not be able to pay her way.

Annabelle was still frowning over the idea when she reached home and learned that Mr Telford was closeted with her father. She knocked on the study door and went in.

'I beg your pardon, Papa, may I speak with you both?'

'Of course. Come in, my dear, come in.'

'I wanted to talk to you about our…financial situation. I hope you do not mind, Papa? I was in Stanton today, with Mrs Ford, and something she said…'

'Ah.' Samuel shook his head and gave a long, despondent sigh. 'People are apprehensive that because we are retrenching we will not meet our obligations.'

'Is that all?' she said, relieved. 'Everyone is anxious, of course, but they have no cause to be. We shall continue with our present economies for as long as is necessary.' She saw a look pass between them and was immediately on her guard. 'What is it? Has something occurred?'

Her father appeared to shrink in his chair, looking very tired.

'Telford, perhaps you would explain?'

'Of course, sir.' The lawyer stood before the fireplace, his hands clasped behind his back. 'Miss Havenham, I called today to inform your father that the mortgage on Oakenroyd has been sold to another party. At present that is all I know. There is no change to the terms, or the interest rates, but I thought it best to forewarn you. Very often, in cases such as this, the new lender will ask for more favourable terms.'

'But how can this be?' She looked up, a frown creasing her brow. 'We have a contract.'

'As with all such contracts, Miss Havenham, the lender has the right to give notice and increase the rate whenever he wishes.'

'And what of the borrower's rights?' she demanded.

'The borrower has the right to settle at any time.'

'Then I suppose we must be prepared to find another lender.'

'That is what I have been trying to do, Miss Havenham,' came the solemn reply. 'The problem is that the mortgage we secured upon Oakenroyd was a very generous one, more than the property is actually worth. I can find no one willing to match it without more security.'

'Which we cannot give.'

'Exactly, ma'am.'

'I had such hopes that the new toll road would be giving us a return by now,' murmured Samuel. 'But it is unlikely we shall see any profit on that for another year at least.'

'Could we sell our subscription?'

Mr Telford shook his head. 'Alas, I have made enquiries and there is no one willing to buy.'

'But we must not be too despondent,' said her father, trying to look cheerful. 'Telford here is a man of the law and trained to be pessimistic.

We have been told only that the mortgage has changed hands. It may be that the new lender is content to leave things as they are.'

Mr Telford looked sceptical, but when he realised Annabelle was watching him his face became a polite mask. He smiled. 'It may well be, sir.'

Chapter Six

'Good morning, Major. Your morning coffee.'

Lucas yawned and blinked as his man opened the shutters and threw back the curtains around the bed.

'Damn you, George, take it away again. I'll get up in an hour!'

George Stebbing took no notice of his master's angry mutter. During their time in the army they had seen many rough times together and the bond between the two men was stronger than just that of master and servant. Now he stood by the bed, the coffee in his hand.

'I thought you'd want to get to the manor early today, sir, seeing as how you are engaged to attend the assembly this evening.'

Lucas groaned. 'Did I really agree to go?'

George chuckled. 'Aye, sir. You said it would be useful to do the pretty with the local bigwigs.'

'I must have been foxed.'

'Very likely,' agreed George with distressing candour. 'But best to stay on good terms with your neighbours, get them on your side for when—'

'Yes, George, that will do!' Abruptly Lucas sat up and his man held out the coffee cup.

'I've ordered hot water for when you return from the manor, so you can bathe before you get ready for the assembly.'

Bowing to the inevitable, Lucas drank his coffee and thought of all he had to do today. There was a meeting with his builder at the manor, then he had to instruct the gardener he had engaged. Most of the grounds close to the house would be unusable until the building work was finished, but the fellow could make a start by repairing the walls around the kitchen garden and replacing the cold frames. He would also need to make himself familiar with the woodland, where there was a deal of work to be done. Perhaps he would take the man with him to start thinning out the trees in the park. Lucas knew there was no need for him to do any of the work himself, but he liked the physical effort, and he was determined to involve himself in the resurrection of Morwood Manor. It had been his dream for the past five-and-twenty years.

Lucas returned much later in the day, hot, dirty and tired. He was not looking forward to the evening assembly at the Red Lion, but it was almost an obligation, especially since he was staying at the inn. There could be no excuse for his staying away. Besides, George was right, he needed to be on good terms with these people if he was going to live at Morwood, and when the truth came out, there would be some who would take Havenham's part. Better to have as many allies at his back as he could before that time.

His thoughts went back to Annabelle. She would most probably be there tonight. It would be the first time they had met for three weeks. Lucas could not deny he had been avoiding her. The lady had shown herself willing to be friends and it would have been very easy to accept Samuel's invitation to take pot luck at Oakenroyd and pay court to her—after all, that was his plan, was it not? But the deception irked him, it pricked at his conscience. He was no Lothario and it was Samuel Havenham he intended to punish, not his daughter.

Even that was proving difficult enough. Over the years he had envisaged Samuel as a hard, ruthless man, not the gentle scholar who had wel-

comed him so warmly to Oakenroyd, and Lucas
had to harden his heart against any sympathy. He
must not weaken. Justice must be done and he
would exact his revenge. Annabelle would suffer as a consequence of that. She would be a ca-
sualty of war. Harsh, but it could not be helped.
And once he had brought Samuel Havenham to
his knees, it would be in Annabelle's power to
save her father from complete ruin. That, surely,
must be some comfort to her.

Lucas thrust aside the unpleasant suspicion
that it would be no comfort at all.

The Assembly Rooms were already crowded
when Annabelle and her father arrived. She had
half-expected Mr Keighley to offer his carriage
again, but in the end it was Sir John and Lady
Rishworth who collected them and promised to
see them safely home again afterwards. Belle
was wearing her new green muslin embroidered
with tiny yellow flowers. She knew the pale colour suited her and brought out a greenish hue in
her eyes. She was also pleased at the effect of the
yellow ribbon threaded through her curls. She
could not compete with Celia and Lizzie when
it came to beauty, but she thought she was looking her best and experienced a little thrill of anticipation for the evening ahead.

Sir John carried her father off to the card room

where old Dr Bennett was waiting for them. Belle watched him go without a qualm. Despite the debts he had run up in Harrogate she knew the stakes agreed between the gentlemen of Stanton would be negligible and she could relax as she accompanied Lady Rishworth and Celia into the ballroom, where the country dances were already in progress.

'The usual complaint, not enough single gentlemen,' remarked Celia, looking about her. 'At least, not enough single gentlemen in want of a wife.' She brightened. 'But Mr Keighley is here, dancing with Lizzie Scanlon, so you at least will have a partner tonight, Belle!'

Annabelle blushed and disclaimed, but she did hope that Mr Keighley would ask her to be his partner for the next dance. She prayed her smile did not look too forced when he carried Celia off instead, and she was obliged to sit on the benches, her foot tapping to the lively music.

'So you *are* here, Belle.' Lizzie Scanlon flopped down in the seat Celia had vacated and fanned herself vigorously. 'Mama wondered if you might not come tonight, in the circumstances—'

'What circumstances?'

'Should I not have said anything?' Lizzie

frowned slightly. 'It is all over Stanton that you have had to retrench.'

'Well, that is no secret,' said Annabelle. 'And I see nothing to be ashamed of in the fact that we are living within our means.'

'Oh, no, no, of course not,' replied Lizzie hastily. 'But it has somehow got out that your father is on the verge of ruin and you are going to sell Oakenroyd.'

'Good heavens, it is not as bad as that!' exclaimed Annabelle, shocked.

'Oh.' Lizzie managed to look relieved and embarrassed at the same time. 'Well, I am very glad to hear that it is no more than malicious gossip, Annabelle. I beg your pardon, I did not mean to offend.'

Annabelle smiled at her old friend.

'You did not, Lizzie, and it explains some of the comments I have heard in the town recently.' And Mrs Ford's behaviour in presenting her bill so promptly, but Annabelle kept that to herself. 'I wonder who could have started such a rumour?'

'I have no idea, but you know how these things spread,' Lizzie continued with alarming frankness. 'It could be why Mr Keighley is not so attentive to you this evening. You weren't engaged to him, were you, Belle?'

'No, no, of course not.'

Nor likely to be, now, she thought, watching him stand up for a second dance with Celia Rishworth. Well, she could bear the loss. And it saved her making the decision about whether to accept him.

As the evening progressed there was no shortage of dancing partners for Annabelle. Mr Scanlon led her out for her first dance and he was followed by several other gentlemen, husbands or fathers of her many acquaintances. After a particularly lively jig she was glad to sit out for a while to recover her breath.

Her eyes moved around the room and almost immediately fell upon Lucas Monserrat. He had just come in and was standing by the door, surveying the company. Her heart gave a little flutter. His height was above the average, but it was the width of those powerful shoulders that drew one's attention. He looked quite magnificent in the dark coat and snowy waistcoat with his black hair brushed back from his brow and gleaming like ebony. With his harsh features and those dark eyes beneath fierce black brows he could not be considered handsome but he was… Stunning, she thought. He quite took her breath away.

His gaze swept the room and she looked down, not wanting him to know she had been watching him. How different she felt now from that first, unfortunate meeting. Then he had seemed cruel, bent upon humiliating her, but his behaviour since that time had been unexceptional. Lucas. She realised she had been thinking of him as Lucas since he had escorted her home from Stanton three weeks ago. A tremor of self-doubt shook her. That was the last time they had met and she wondered if he, too, was deterred by the rumours of her father's financial trouble. However, when she looked up again he was crossing the room towards her. Annabelle's heart lifted.

A bow, a few words and Lucas was leading her on to the dance floor. She forced her hand to rest lightly upon his, but even so she could feel the knotted muscle beneath the sleeve, the coiled strength of the man. She risked a glance at him, noted the contracted brows that gave his face such a harsh look. Could he be nervous attending his first assembly? She felt it her duty to try to put him at his ease.

'I am so glad you decided to come, Mr Monserrat. These monthly gatherings are the highlight of our social life in Stanton.'

'It is certainly popular,' he replied, expertly guiding her through the crowd to take their places.

'Anyone can buy a ticket, all we ask is that the gentlemen have a good coat and the ladies a suitable gown.' She looked up at him suddenly.

'You will find several people here who work for you—Elias Greenwood, for example. I hope that does not make you uncomfortable?'

'Not in the least, why should it?'

'I am not sure. I do not feel you are at ease here.'

His brows rose, as if she had caught him out, then he smiled and that disturbing look disappeared.

'I beg your pardon. My thoughts were elsewhere, which was most impolite of me. Now I am completely at your service.'

The musicians struck up the first notes and the dancing commenced.

'I—*we*,' she corrected herself quickly. 'We have not seen you for a few weeks, Mr Monserrat.'

'I have been very busy at the Manor.'

'I thought as much,' she said, relieved. 'Is all going well?'

'Very well, but slowly. Much of the old building is unsafe and needs to be pulled down before we can rebuild. I do not see the house being finished before the spring.'

That did not surprise her. The Manor was in a parlous state. When the dance brought them back together she asked him if he intended to remain at the Red Lion.

'No, I have other plans.'

She saw again that harsh look descend, but could not think that she had said anything untoward. They finished the movement in silence and she had nothing to do but to concentrate upon her steps. Her partner was an elegant dancer, light on his feet for such a powerful man, and she enjoyed dancing with him, acutely aware of the light clasp of his hand, gently but expertly guiding her through the figures. He was smiling, but it was a society smile, it did not reach his eyes. She thought perhaps she had offended him in some way, although she had no idea how. Her pleasure in the dance was diminished.

They made their final salute and he led her in silence from the dance floor. She spotted her father and Dr Bennett at the side of the room and drew her partner's attention to the fact. He escorted her to them and bowed politely when her father introduced him to the aged doctor.

'Monserrat, Monserrat,' mused Dr Bennett. 'Not a local name, that.'

'No, sir.'

'Pity, thought I knew you from somewhere.' The doctor stared up at him short-sightedly. 'You look familiar, though. Remind me of someone...'

'I do not think so.' Lucas gave a tight little smile and with a nod he moved off.

Doctor Bennett waved a hand at his departing back.

'Can't quite put my finger on it. Ah well, it will come to me eventually, it usually does. I remember the same thing happening at Knaresborough last year.'

'Ah, Knaresborough,' declared her father. 'Such a lively place. Haven't been there for years. Where did you stay, the George? That used to be the most fashionable hotel…'

Annabelle left her father and his elderly companion to their reminiscences. As she wandered through the ballroom she thought about her dance with Lucas. It seemed at the end that he could not wait to get away from her. Perhaps it was those wicked rumours, after all.

A young man begged her to partner him for the last dance before the interval and she gladly accepted. As they took their places she noted that Lucas was leading out Lizzie Scanlon, whose pale beauty was enhanced by her partner's dark colouring. Quickly she looked away, shaken by a stab of jealousy. He was free to dance with whomsoever he wished and with the current rumours she thought bleakly that she was fortunate he had sought her hand for even one dance.

Later Annabelle made her way to the refreshment table and found Mr Keighley there, helping himself to a glass of punch. He looked startled when he saw her. Like a trapped rabbit, she thought angrily, convinced now that he had been avoiding her. She marched up to the table, allowing him no escape, and he was obliged to acknowledge her.

She smiled and held out her glass to be filled.

'We have not seen you at Oakenroyd recently, Mr Keighley. My father has missed your visits.'

'Ah.' His eyes darted swiftly around the room. He looked anywhere rather than directly at her. 'I have been busy of late. But I should be delighted to keep him company at any time, if you are engaged elsewhere.'

The implication was all too clear. Annabelle drew herself up.

'You do not need to avoid me, sir,' she said quietly. 'Let me assure you that you have aroused no expectations of anything other than friendship between us.'

He relaxed visibly at that and the hunted expression was replaced by a smile.

'I am heartily relieved to hear you say so, Miss Havenham. It was never my intention to do so, but I was afraid you may have thought...'

She remembered the way he had sought her out, how he had hinted at a union. To see him struggling thus to disclaim was embarrassing and deeply insulting. But if he thought she was penniless she could understand his reluctance to ally himself to her. Now she lifted her chin.

'You need say no more, Mr Keighley. I understand perfectly. But please feel free to call upon my father at any time. He would appreciate your company.' After the slightest pause she ended, 'You have my word I shall not embarrass you.'

'My dear Miss Havenham, I never meant—'

She turned and walked off before he could embarrass her or himself further. With dismay she felt the angry tears rising and blinked them away. She would have to find a quiet corner to compose herself.

The Red Lion was an old hostelry and had been altered and extended many times over the years, so there were numerous shadowed alcoves and hidden nooks in the twisting corridors. Annabelle slipped out of the ballroom and made her way to one such alcove on the far side of the stairs. It was mercifully empty at present, for the assembly was well underway and everyone was either in the ballroom, at supper or playing cards. She sank down on the bench at the back of the recess, where she was screened from the view of anyone passing to or from the main rooms.

Annabelle stripped off her gloves and took out her handkerchief. A rogue tear had rolled on to her cheek and she quickly wiped it away. She was not upset at having lost a suitor. After all, she had never really wanted to marry Mr

Keighley, but the manner of his going hurt her
pride. She chided herself upon her sensibility.
This snub was not important, she must regain
her composure and return to the ballroom before
her father missed her. Poor Papa, she hoped he
would never learn of these malicious rumours.

She was wiping her eyes and did not notice the
shadow fall across the alcove, was not aware of
anyone's presence until she heard Lucas's deep
voice.

'I saw you leave the ballroom. Are you un-
well, Miss Havenham?'

'No, no. I w-wanted a little air.'

To her consternation he sat down beside her.

'I do not believe that is all.' His keen eyes
searched her face. 'You have been crying.'

'No.'

'Yes.' He gently cupped her chin and turned
her face towards him. 'Your eyes are even now
full of tears. Tell me what has upset you.'

She freed herself. His sympathy would indeed
make her weep if she did not look away.

'I am merely being foolish,' she said, thread-
ing her handkerchief through her restless fingers. 'There have been rumours.' Her glance slid
back towards him. He was silent, waiting for
her to continue. She ran her tongue around her
lips, suddenly nervous. 'Rumours that we—that

my father—cannot meet his obligations.' She frowned. 'Who would start such a report?'

He did not reply, merely continued to look at her, his harsh face inscrutable.

'Several persons this evening have distanced themselves from us because of such talk.' She looked down and added quietly, 'I wondered if that was why you had kept away from…from me.'

'Would it matter to you, if that was the reason?'

She raised her head and met his eyes, determined to be honest.

'Yes. I thought better of you than that.'

'And Keighley? I saw you talking to him. I thought he might have upset you.'

'He was avoiding me tonight. It was all the more noticeable because he had been growing very particular in his attentions. I cannot deny I am disappointed in him, not for myself but for my father, who will miss his company if he cannot bring himself to visit Oakenroyd. It is very lowering to know one's only suitor is so easily discouraged.'

She tried to sound light-hearted, but even to her own ears these last words sounded sadly flat. To her dismay the tears spilled over. Her handkerchief was too damp to be of use so she lifted her gloves to wipe her face, but Lucas stopped her.

'No, satin will not do it. Allow me.'

Again he used his fingers to tilt her face up towards him and applied his own fine linen handkerchief to her cheeks.

'There.' He smiled into her eyes, his face only inches from her own. He said softly, 'You should not cry, Belle.'

'I am not normally so lachrymose,' she managed, unable to look away. 'I—'

He lowered his head and kissed her open mouth. For a moment he hovered there, his touch light as a feather, as if unsure how to proceed. Annabelle remained quite still, afraid that if she moved he would release her, and she knew, she *knew* she did not want him to do that. His arms slid around her and she leaned into him as his kiss deepened and he pulled her on to his lap, cradling her head against his shoulder as he kissed her with a thoroughness that made her tremble right down to her toes. She felt flushed with excitement and there was an ache tugging at her thighs.

When at last he released her mouth she dragged in a ragged breath, but it caught in her throat as she felt his lips on her neck, then on the soft swell of her breast. Her head was thrown back against his shoulder and she arched upwards, offering her body to his caresses. The blood was singing in her veins, she had never felt so alive before. Annabelle put her hand to his cheek, slid her fingers into his hair and gently drew his face closer so that he could kiss her again and this time she responded, her mouth working against his. But then the rest of her body was bereft. Her breasts tingled, ached for his touch, and when she felt his fingers sliding over them a little groan of satisfaction trembled in her throat.

What might have happened, what other delightful sensations he might have awakened in her she would never know. A door slammed somewhere below, and Lucas raised his head. He was still cradling her and she clung to him, burying her face in his neck, breathing in the mixture of soap and spices and clean linen that overlay the male scent of him, the familiar scent she remembered from the first time she had been in his arms. Now it filled her senses and made her feel weak with a longing she did not understand.

Raucous voices sounded on the stairs, getting closer. Lucas's chest rose and fell on a sigh. They both knew the moment was over. Reluctantly Annabelle sat up, trying to order her thoughts.

'If we are discovered now, there will be hell to pay.'

It did not need Lucas's hushed whisper to tell

her that. If she was found here her reputation would be ruined. How could she have been so thoughtless? What was it about this man? He only had to touch her and she melted into his arms, counting the world well lost.

Annabelle slid from his lap to the bench, but he kept his arm about her and they remained there, silent and still, listening to the voices and the thud of heavy feet on the stairs. There was a sudden swelling of music and chatter as someone opened a door. Then it was gone, the voices had disappeared and they were alone again.

'I must go—'

As she rose he caught her hand.

'Belle, I need to tell you—'

She looked back at him. Even in the shadows his face was ashen. He looked as shaken as she was by their encounter.

'Tell me what?'

'About me.'

She shook her head. 'There is no time. I will be missed.' She squeezed his hand, but his fingers did not relax their grip.

'Forgive me, Belle.'

For what, for kissing her when she was only too willing to be kissed?

'There is nothing to forgive.'

'Do not think too badly of me.'

'I do not.' She gave him a puzzled smile. 'Please, you must release me.'

He looked as if he would say more, but she dared not stay longer. Tugging her hand away, she hurried off.

Lucas did not stir. He heard her soft footsteps as she crossed the landing, the sudden rise and fall of the music as she slipped into the ballroom. His hands clenched into two hard fists. Hell and damnation, what was he about? He had spent the past couple of weeks avoiding the chit because he could not square it with his conscience to befriend her while he was plotting her father's ruin, and here he was now making love to her!

He wished to heaven he had not come to the assembly. He should have stayed away, continued with his plotting and his planning until it was time to spring his trap and take his revenge. By coming here tonight he was once again prey to doubts. Samuel Havenham had greeted him in such a genial manner it was very difficult to hate him. Difficult, but not impossible.

But Annabelle—he looked up at the ceiling, exhaling slowly. He could not deny the attraction, she fired his blood but it was more than that. He had admired her spirit at their very first meeting, the way she handled that brute of a horse and since then he had enjoyed being with her, making her laugh, seeing her eyes light up when something amused her. He liked her. He wanted her to be happy, and he wanted to banish that sad shadow he had seen in her eyes tonight, even when he was the one to put it there.

He had not thought of Annabelle when he dropped the first hints about Havenham's impending ruin, but the rumours were hurting her. Fool that he was, he should have known they would. She had left the ballroom with her head high, but his keen glance had detected the unnatural glitter in her eyes and he had followed, wanting to comfort her.

Lucas dropped his head in his hands. It had all seemed so simple before he came here, and even in those early weeks after he purchased Morwood he had but one goal: to ruin Havenham. Annabelle had seemed at first just one more weapon he could use against the man, but since then he had come to know her and if there was some way he could save her from any pain he would be glad to do so.

As he opened his eyes, his gaze alighted upon Annabelle's discarded gloves lying at his feet. She had forgotten to pick them up in her hurry to get away. He scooped them up and lifted them to his face. There was a faint trace of scent about them, a hint of orange blossom and a touch of citrus. He recognised it as Annabelle's perfume and breathed it in.

Perhaps he would delay his plans a little. After all, there was no hurry. He had waited this long, a little longer wouldn't make much difference. He was clutching at straws and he knew it. However long he waited to exact his revenge she would be hurt by it and she would blame him. Perhaps he should talk to her, explain why he had to do this. Would she understand? He rose and prepared himself to return to the ballroom. He had to try. He must arrange to see her. Alone.

Annabelle realised as soon as she returned to the ballroom that she had left her gloves behind. She dare not go back for them and could only hope that no one would notice. That seemed quite possible, for everyone was in a boisterous mood now, joining in the country dances with such spirit and laughter that the old building positively rocked with their enjoyment.

Her body was still in shock after her encounter with Lucas, but she was determined not to allow it to show. She desperately wanted to sit down and go over every kiss, every touch but she dared not do so here. Such an indulgence must wait until she was alone. She thought perhaps she would make herself stay awake all night to think about it and relive those delicious sensations, but for now she must put it from her mind and dancing would help her to do that.

Annabelle returned to the dance floor, thankful that her wide acquaintance meant she could find plenty of partners. It did not matter to her whether they were very young men or contemporaries of her father, she was just happy to dance, forcing herself to concentrate upon the steps. The room was very warm. The windows were thrown wide to allow in the night air, but even so by midnight Annabelle's cheeks were glowing and she laughingly excused herself from dancing and sought the cool breeze by one of the open windows. She was staring out at the night, fanning herself vigorously when a familiar deep voice murmured in her ear.

'I thought you were determined to dance your shoes into ribbons.'

She looked around to find Lucas behind her. He was smiling and she suddenly found it hard to breathe, but even so she could not resist smiling back.

'Who knows when I may have the opportunity to dance again?' she said lightly.

'You could hold a ball at Oakenroyd.'

She shook her head. 'Papa would not enjoy it. He would feel it was his duty as host to be in place until every last guest had gone and that would tire him too much. His health is not good, you see. He was very ill a few years ago and it has left him with a weakness.'

'So you do not entertain.'

'We hold dinners and the occasional card party, but I must look to others for dancing.' She smiled brightly. 'But you are not to be pitying me, sir. I do not repine. My life is very full, I assure you.'

'I am glad of it.' A waiter passed close to them, bearing a tray and he reached out to scoop two full glasses. 'Would you like a little wine?'

'Thank you.'

She reached for the glass and her fingers slid over his as she took it from him. Touching his skin revived memories of their recent embraces and sent little shock waves running through her arm. Afraid she might drop the glass, she brought up her other hand, only to find she was now cradling Lucas's fingers as well as the glass between her hands. It felt incredibly intimate and her cheeks began to burn.

'Oh, I beg your pardon.'

'No need for that.' He extricated himself from her grasp, but kept his smiling eyes upon her. His look caressed her and she felt like a cat basking in the sun. She wanted to purr with happiness. She resisted the urge to smile foolishly up at him and instead said quietly, 'Did—did you see my gloves, sir? I think I dropped them…'

'You did.' He patted his breast. 'I have them safe, but I do not think it would be wise for me to return them here, do you?'

The smile deepened and set her heart hammering once more. It was exhilarating, thrilling, but the tumult of emotions unnerved her. She sipped her wine and looked out of the window at the velvet darkness.

'Meet me tomorrow,' he said quietly. 'Come to the boathouse in the morning and I will return your gloves to you.'

An assignation. The warm glow that had enveloped her vanished. After what had occurred, did he think she would put herself into such a situation? Shaking her head, she turned towards him.

'You know I cannot do that.'

'Can't you?'

He was gazing down at her, the fire in his black eyes burning into her very soul. All around them the big room buzzed with chatter and noise yet they seemed to be in a little bubble, cut off from the rest of the world. Beyond Lucas everything was blurred and distorted, yet he was so very clear. She could see every minute stitch on his coat, every detail of the intricate embroidery on his waistcoat and the complicated folds of his neckcloth. The bubble enclosed them. Belle felt its pressure on her back, pushing her towards him. He loomed over her, enveloping her in his animal presence. She blinked, trying to break the spell with a shaky laugh.

'I know you are teasing me, Mr Monserrat. You may return them tomorrow, if you wish. To Oakenroyd.'

'And may we talk there, privately?'

'If you wish.'

To disguise her shaking hand she finished her wine and put the glass down on the window sill. With a slight shock she realised the dancing had ended and the musicians were packing away their instruments. 'It—it is late. I must find my father.'

'I will take you to him.'

She allowed him to pull her hand on to his arm. No one was in any hurry to leave and they had to thread their way between the chattering guests to reach her father, who was still sitting with Dr Bennett. Elias Greenwood stood nearby with his pregnant wife, the Scanlons and the Rishworths were in a little group with Mr Keighley, while Mrs Kensley was gossiping with one of her cronies a short distance away. To Belle's overstretched nerves it seemed that they were all looking at her. Would they know from her heightened colour, her glowing cheeks how much she enjoyed Lucas's company? Would they know he had kissed her?

'Ah, my dear, I was about to send a man to find you.' Her father beamed as she came up, while Dr Bennett merely acknowledged them with a sleepy nod.

'I am here now, Father, as you see. I have been t-talking with Mr Monserrat.'

'Ah yes.' Her father looked up, his bright eyes twinkling. 'You still here, sir? I thought you might have taken to your bed hours ago, for young Greenwood over there tells me you are spending every waking hour at Burnt Acres.'

Dr Bennett shot up in his chair. 'Burnt Acres!' he cried. 'That's it.'

'No, no, Bennett, that is *not* it,' Samuel said gently. 'I should have called it Morwood, to give it its proper title.'

'No, no, but your calling it Burnt Acres re-minded me!' Dr Bennett waved his stick towards Lucas. 'I know now where I have seen you be-fore, sirrah!'

Lucas froze.

Not now, he thought desperately. *Not now, not here.*

'I was doctor to Mrs Blackstone, the poor lady who perished in the fire at Morwood. And it has come to me now, sir.' The old doctor was chuckling, his hand on Havenham's arm. Lucas could not move. He felt as if he was on the edge of a cliff and it was crumbling away beneath his feet. The truth would out now. There was no going back. He remained impassive as the doctor's twinkling eyes came back to him.

'You are Maria Blackstone's son. You have the very look of her, my boy!'

His quavering voice, made shrill with age, carried around that part of the room and everyone stopped talking. All eyes turned towards Lucas.

He could deny it, of course, but even as the thought crossed his mind he could see recognition dawning in Havenham's eyes. The old man was remembering the ten-year-old boy he had known and finding a resemblance in the man now standing before him. And from the tail of his eye Lucas could see Annabelle. She was still beside him, but regarding him with bewilderment.

As well she might. There was no way he could save her pain now, but perhaps it was for the best. He had been in danger of becoming too entangled with the lady. He straightened his shoulders.

'Yes, Doctor,' he said coolly. 'I believe I do look like my mother. I am Lucas Monserrat Blackstone.'

Chapter Seven

Silence followed his announcement. Lucas observed the reactions of those around him. Some had not even been born when Morwood had burned to the ground twenty-five years ago and for the rest it was only a distant memory. Not for them the terrifying nightmares that still haunted his sleep, the guilt that he had survived while his mother had perished in the inferno. He watched Samuel Havenham, alert for any sign of unease or guilt, but although the old man looked shocked at first, the next moment he was smiling, as if genuinely pleased with the news.

'My boy, this is delightful, quite delightful! How did I not know you? I of all people should have seen the resemblance to your poor, dear mother. But I said to Belle that you looked familiar, did I not, my love?' She nodded silently while her father continued to shake his head in wonder. 'So you have come back to Morwood, sir. That is very good, very good. But why change your name—did you think your old friends would not want to know you? Why, my boy, nothing could be further from the truth.'

Lucas looked away, uncomfortable with the memories that surfaced. The Samuel of his early childhood had been a big, genial man who had always treated Lucas kindly when they met, but no amount of words could absolve him of the one heinous act that Lucas was bent on avenging. However, for now he must answer coolly.

'Monserrat was my mother's family name.'

'Ah…' Samuel had a faraway look in his eye. 'She would never talk of her Spanish family. That is why I did not recognise the name, but I still rebuke myself for not recognising you, Lucas—may I call you that?'

It was intolerable. The daughter had already breached his defences, he could not let the old man become too familiar. He must focus on his goal, keep his distance.

'I shall of course be reverting to the name Blackstone now,' he said curtly.

That, at least, would be a relief. He had every right to use his mother's name and it had served to remind him of the task he had set himself, but he was glad to be done with the deceit.

With a bow he excused himself and left the room. Behind him the chatter was beginning again and he had no doubt of the subject. Let them conjecture. They would all know soon enough why he was here.

'Well, who would have thought it?' Lady Rishworth settled herself in the corner of her carriage and pulled her skirts close, making room for her daughter and her husband to sit beside her. 'I suppose we must all get used to calling him Mr Blackstone now. What say you, Mr Havenham?'

'I am sure we will grow accustomed in time, as we will grow accustomed to having Morwood occupied again.'

Annabelle heard the wistful note in her father's voice and put it down to fatigue. The evening had been a long one.

'But how is it that no one recognised him?' asked Celia. 'Is he changed so very much, Mama?'

'Goodness, yes,' said her mama. 'He was only a child when he left here. But now I think of it he was always a very dark little boy, rather on the thin side. Mr Havenham may remember him better, being close neighbours.'

'The pity of it is that I don't,' Samuel confessed. 'I wish he had made himself known to us at the start. I really cannot see why he should come here under another name.'

'Perhaps he did not want to be the object of pity,' suggested Annabelle.

'Aye, that is very likely,' agreed Sir John, squashed into the far corner of the carriage. 'He wouldn't want to be gawped at by all and sundry and reminded of his past.'

'Was it so bad then, Papa?' Celia asked her father.

'Yes, a very bad business. Mrs Blackstone perished in the fire. There was some talk that she had locked the door to her rooms. Her husband was severely burned trying to rescue her. He died a few days later and their son was taken off to live with relatives somewhere in the south.'

'He must have done well for himself if he can afford to buy back Morwood,' remarked Lady Rishworth.

'And he is spending a fortune on rebuilding it,' added Sir John. 'The family sold the place to pay off the creditors, and from what I remember there was not that much left for the boy's inheritance.'

'I wouldn't want to live at Morwood,' said Celia, shuddering. 'They say it is haunted.'

Annabelle felt obliged to respond to this. 'Nonsense,' she said. 'The ruins are—were— a sad place, to be sure, but I have never seen any sign of a ghost. I hope Mr Mon—I mean Mr Blackstone will make a very comfortable home there.'

'And there is another good thing to come out of this,' chuckled her father, squeezing her arm. 'This revelation is just what is needed to take everyone's attention away from our attempts to economise!'

The assembly gave Annabelle a great deal to think about when she retired to her bed that night, but although she frowned a little over the disclosure of Lucas's real identity her thoughts kept returning to the moment he had taken her in his arms and kissed her. In the whole course of her life no other man had ever done more than press a chaste salute upon her fingers, yet Lucas had kissed her at their very first meeting, and now he had done so again. Just thinking about it set her body on fire and brought on that strange ache deep inside. Her head was full of him. Even during the short journey home, when she had been talking with the Rishworths, her mind had been reliving their meetings, remembering the shock of his touch, the warmth in his eyes. She feared she was besotted.

She had never known a man like him—his manners could be abrupt, but when he exerted himself he was a charming companion. He had left the assembly without taking his leave of her, but he still had her gloves. He had not actually *said* he would call upon her in the morning, but as she settled down to sleep Annabelle found herself hoping very much that he would do so.

Lucas was the first thought in her head when Annabelle awoke the following morning to bright sunshine. She rang for Becky, her maid, and bade her pull out her new morning gown of sprigged muslin. As soon as breakfast was over she took her tambour frame and seated herself in the window of the morning room, which had an excellent view over the approach to the house.

The clock ticked away the hours. She exchanged her embroidery for a book, but still no visitor came. By three o'clock she decided she would wait in no longer and instead would take Apollo for a gallop on the moor.

The next day followed the same pattern, and the next. Lucas did not call. Other visitors came, though, including Lady Rishworth and Celia, to talk over the assembly.

Annabelle invited the ladies to take tea with her and she joined in their conversation as best she could, but there was such a lot to conceal that she feared she was poor company. Her only satisfaction was when Lady Rishworth announced that Mr Keighley had offered for Lizzie Scanlon and been accepted, she could respond with unfeigned delight for her friend's good fortune.

Annabelle might tell herself that she had no hope now of Lucas calling on her, but when the bell pealed at the front door two days later she stopped in her tracks as she crossed the hall, almost trembling with anticipation. She waited, her spirits soaring, only to sink again when she saw the visitor.

'Mr Telford, good day to you, sir. This is not your usual day to visit Papa, so I hope there is nothing amiss.'

'I hope so too,' he replied soberly. 'Your father summoned me here urgently. Perhaps you know the reason?'

'No, he has said nothing to me.' She frowned. 'Papa is in the study. I will go with you to see him.'

At first her father was reluctant for her to remain, and this made Annabelle even more anxious.

'Please, Papa, allow me to stay. Whatever is troubling you, it cannot be worse than my imaginings, should you send me away. Dear Papa, let there be no secrets between us.'

He looked undecided for a moment, but then relented and waved her to a chair.

'Very well, sit down, my love, and you, Mr Telford, please take a seat.' He picked up a crisp paper and held it out to the lawyer. 'I received this letter today. It was delivered express.'

Annabelle watched with growing impatience as Mr Telford read the letter. At last he put it down and, taking out a handkerchief, he began to polish his spectacles.

'Well?' It was as much as she could do not to reach over and snatch the letter from the desk. 'What does it say?'

'It is from Messrs Powell & Son, your neighbour's lawyers in London. First of all, Mr Monserrat wishes to be known in future as Blackstone.' He looked over the top of his glasses at Samuel.

'Yes, yes, we know that. He is the son of the previous owner,' said Annabelle. 'He told us so at the assembly. Surely that is not the only reason for the letter?'

'No, indeed, Miss Havenham.' He picked up the paper again. 'They say they have been instructed to inform you—'

'Instructed?' Annabelle broke in. 'Does that mean that Mr Blackstone has spoken to them in person?'

Her spirits lifted a little. If that was the case, then perhaps Lucas was in London. That could be the reason he had not called upon her.

'Not necessarily,' said Mr Telford cautiously. 'As far as I am aware Mr Blackstone is still at the Red Lion. No doubt he communicated with his lawyers by letter.' He went back to the paper in his hand. 'They have been instructed to inform you that Mr, er, Blackstone holds the mortgage on Oakenroyd.'

'Really?' Annabelle's anxiety began to lessen. 'If that is all....'

'Not quite.' The lawyer studied the letter again carefully before continuing in his driest, most impersonal tone, 'He is giving notice that the whole amount, plus the interest, must be paid by Michaelmas.'

She frowned. 'I don't understand, why should he do that?'

Her father shrugged. 'Perhaps he needs the money himself.'

'But, Papa, even if the harvest is exceptionally good we would not be able to repay half such a sum.'

'We must find another lender.' Her father sighed. 'What do you say, Telford?'

The lawyer looked grim, the corners of his mouth turning down.

'You know I have already been making enquiries, but so far to no avail. You will recall, Mr Havenham, that when we raised the original mortgage eighteen months ago we calculated a sum to include the improvements you wished to make.'

'Of course. With the harvest failing it was important that there was work for the men to do.'

'Unfortunately there has not been sufficient time for those improvements to add to the value of your estate, sir. We agreed at the time the lender was being very generous, lending much more than the property was worth, and at such a good rate, too.'

Annabelle broke in, saying slowly, 'Are you saying, Mr Telford, that others may not be willing to lend us the same amount?'

'I fear that will be the case, ma'am, especially in the current climate. I will continue to enquire, but I fear there is no one in Stanton with such a sum to spare.'

Behind his desk her father was sitting silently, his face grey with worry. Annabelle turned back to the lawyer. 'Please do so, Mr Telford,' she told him. 'And if that is not successful, then you must try London again.'

'As you wish, Miss Havenham.'

Her father pushed himself up from his chair. 'Aye, do your best for us, Telford. But I don't need to tell you that, I know you will do so.'

'I will, of course, sir, but interest rates are higher now, too. It will be no good raising the capital if you cannot afford to repay it.'

The lawyer took his leave and her father returned to his chair behind the desk. 'I am very sorry, Belle. First Morwood, now this. I should have done better for you, invested more wisely...'

'No one could foresee that the war would be followed by quite such a bad summer, Papa.' She came around the desk to drop a kiss upon his forehead. 'It is nearly time for dinner. Let us go and change and forget about all these worries for a little while.'

But of course they could not. Dinner was a quiet affair, both of them caught up in their own thoughts, but when they retired to the drawing room at the end of the evening Annabelle could bear it no longer.

'I have been thinking and thinking about that letter, Papa. If it is from the lawyers, then perhaps they have not discussed it fully with Lu— Mr Blackstone. I cannot believe he knows just how difficult it will be for us to settle with him by the end of September.'

'I admit I had not thought him an unreasonable man, my dear.'

'Write to him, Papa. Invite him to come here to discuss the matter with you, face-to-face. I am sure once you have explained everything we can come to an amicable arrangement.'

'Yes, perhaps I should.' Her father brightened

perceptibly. 'I am sure we could raise half the capital by September, perhaps that will suffice.' He thought about it for a few moments more. 'Yes, yes, that is what I shall do. First thing in the morning I will write to Mr Blackstone.'

Lucas sipped his coffee as he read Samuel Havenham's carefully penned letter. This was it. This was the moment he had anticipated for so many years, the chance for revenge, and to make sure Samuel Havenham knew just why he was doing this. He sent a note back, advising Havenham that he would call upon him at four o'clock. Lucas told himself he needed time to visit Morwood first and see the progress there. If part of him wanted to put off the visit to Oakenroyd, he would not acknowledge it.

He arrived promptly, the longcase clock in the hall chiming the hour as Gibson led him across to the drawing room where Annabelle was sitting with her father.

'Mr Blackstone.' Samuel rose to meet him. 'So good of you to call. Do sit down.'

Lucas hesitated. 'I think perhaps we should go to your study, sir. We have business to discuss.'

'There is nothing that cannot be discussed in front of my daughter, sir.'

The knot in Lucas's gut tightened. Annabelle

was regarding him with those clear grey eyes and he had to remind himself that she was the enemy. He could not spare her.

'Very well.' He stripped off his gloves. 'You have received the letter from my lawyers, I take it.'

'I have, sir. It arrived yesterday. That is what I wish to discuss with you.'

'I thought I had made my instructions perfectly clear to Mr Powell. The mortgage on Oakenroyd is to be terminated at Michaelmas.'

'That is less than six months, Mr…Blackstone,' said Annabelle.

He noted how she stumbled over his name. 'I am aware of that.'

'You must know that to settle with you we will have to borrow money from elsewhere,' explained Samuel. 'It is very difficult at present.'

'Impossible for you, I should imagine, when all of Stanton knows your situation.'

His callous tone brought Annabelle's eyes upon him. He dared not look at her, but could imagine the reproach in them only too well.

'Did you spread the rumours, then, about our financial troubles?' she asked quietly.

'Let us say I have made no effort to deny them.'

He set his jaw. That made him sound like a scoundrel, but this was what he had worked for.

It was a war and there was no room for sentiment. He must concentrate. Samuel was speaking again.

'Mr Blackstone, I do not think you quite understand. It is unlikely that I shall have the funds to pay you back by the end of September. If we could come to some arrangement, say a part-payment?'

'No. I must be paid in full, sir. I will not take a penny less than I am owed.'

Annabelle spread her hands. 'But if we cannot pay…'

Now he turned his head, forced himself to meet her eyes and kept his own countenance impassive. 'Then you must leave Oakenroyd.'

Annabelle put her hands to her cheeks. Surely this could not be happening? The passionate lover, the gently teasing dance partner was gone, replaced by a harsh, implacable stranger.

'But why?' she whispered. 'Why are you doing this?'

'Morwood will not be habitable until the spring. I need somewhere else to live.'

'And for that you would take our home?'

'A mortgage is a business arrangement, Miss Havenham, nothing more, nothing less.'

'No.' She jumped up. It did not make sense. 'There *must* be more to it than that. If it were merely business, it would not matter to you where we found the money to repay you, but you have deliberately made it impossible for us to find any help in Stanton. Why should that be, Mr Blackwood?'

His lips thinned. She saw the muscle working in his jaw, as if he was struggling to control his temper.

'Miss Havenham, I suggest you retire and allow me to discuss this with your father.'

'Do you think I would leave Papa to face this alone?' She crossed to the sofa and sat down beside her father, slipping her hand through his arm. 'If you are so determined to take Oaken-royd, I think we have a right to know the reason for it.'

His eyes were hard and black as jet beneath the lowering brows.

'Very well, Miss Havenham,' he said at last, his voice as harsh as his countenance. 'You shall have the reason. When I was ten years old I learned what it was to lose not only my home, but my parents, too.'

'Yes, I am aware of that, but—'

'Are you also aware that it was your father's doing?' he broke in roughly. 'He killed them.'

Chapter Eight

Annabelle thought she might faint. There was a rushing sound in her ears and a pain in her head, behind her eyes. She was looking at Lucas, but it was as if he was at the end of a long, black tunnel. She leaned against her father's arm and when she spoke her voice seemed to come from a great distance.

'That cannot be true.'

'Oh, it is true,' growled Lucas. 'Your father came to Morwood for dinner that evening. He had a row with *my* father, who threw him out, but he came back at midnight and set fire to Morwood. I escaped unharmed, but my mother perished, and my father died soon after, horribly burned from his attempts to save her. Well, Havenham, do you deny it?'

Belle looked at her father. His eyes were full of tears.

'I have blamed myself often for your mother's death, my boy, but you must believe I had nothing to do with the fire.'

'Don't lie to me,' snarled Lucas. 'I *saw* you! My bedroom window was open and when I heard a noise I looked out. The fire had taken hold by then and I saw you running away from the house.'

'No, no, it was not I,' said Samuel. 'A poacher or an intruder, perhaps.'

'In white stockings and knee breeches?' His lip curled. 'No one believed me. The magistrate ruled it was an accident, but I have lived with the memory of that night for five-and-twenty years. I know what I saw.' He walked to the door. 'I always planned to make you pay for your crimes, Havenham, and now you shall do so.' He stopped, his fingers curled around the door handle. 'And by the way, I have acquired certain vowels of yours, Mr Havenham, from a gentleman in Harrogate. Your IOUs for three thousand pounds. Those too must be paid by Michaelmas.'

He went out, leaving only a horrified silence behind him.

Annabelle listened to his footsteps retreating across the hall, heard the soft thud of the main door as he left the building.

'Papa?' She gently squeezed her father's arm. 'Papa, tell me what this is all about.'

He shook his head, his eyes still bright with unshed tears.

'Please, Papa.'

He took a long, shuddering breath. 'I will, my love, but you must remember this all happened so long ago. Years before I met your mother.'

She nodded and waited patiently until he began to speak.

'Jonas Blackstone and I had been neighbours, if not close friends, for many years. When he brought Maria to England she was already his wife and he had forced her to give up all connection with her past. All we knew was that she was from Spain—that is why I never recognised the Monserrat name.

'My father had just died and I returned from the Grand Tour to take up residence at Oakenroyd. Maria and I met occasionally and found ourselves falling in love. Perhaps it was inevitable. She was a sensitive, intelligent woman and I was much more of a scholar than Jonas, who was impatient of learning and preferred to be active. Maria bore Jonas one child, a son.'

'Lucas?'

'Yes.' He turned and gripped Belle's hand. 'Let me tell you now, my love, Maria was never unfaithful to her husband. Never. I loved her—

worshipped her—and she, I believe, loved me. It was implied in a look, a gesture, but we never spoke of it. She gave me the picture, you see. The watercolour of Morwood. I treasured it, knowing she had painted it herself. But I never did more than kiss her fingers. We existed thus for years, until Lucas was ten years old. By then life for Maria was becoming intolerable. Jonas had always been a hard man, but as he grew older he became a cruel one, prone to jealousy and fits of drunken rage, when he would become violent. I urged Maria to bring Lucas and run away with me. We could fly to the Continent and live as man and wife. Maria loved me, I am sure of it, but she was very loyal to Jonas and reluctant to break her marriage vows, so all I could do was watch and wait and assure her I was there if she needed me.

'On the night of the fire I called at Morwood. Lucas and his cousin had been out hunting and one of their dogs had got lost and ended up at Oakenroyd. I could have sent him back with a servant, but to tell you the truth I wanted an excuse to call and see Maria, so I put the dog in my gig and drove over. I had been about to sit down to my dinner, so I was already dressed for it and Maria invited me to stay and dine with them. Blackstone was in one of his black moods. She told me he had been drinking all day and she was nervous of him. When the meal did not meet with his approval he flew into a rage.' Samuel rubbed a hand across his eyes. 'There were others there—Jonas's widowed sister and her son, who is a few years older than Lucas, I think. Maria sent the boys to bed, and her sister, too, but I remained, because I was anxious for her safety. When Jonas threatened to take a horse-whip to her I stopped him, knocked him down. It was a fluke, he was so much stronger than I, but he was drunk, I suppose...

'That was the last straw for Maria. She agreed to leave him. I wanted her to collect Lucas and fly with me immediately, but she would not. She said there were matters that must be attended to first. I think she was afraid that once she had gone Jonas would take out his anger upon his sister and her boy. She promised to come to Oakenroyd in the morning. I protested, but she insisted I go. She told me she would lock her door so Jonas couldn't reach her.' He dropped his head in his hands. 'God forgive me, I thought she would be safe enough. Blackstone was almost paralysed with drink, he could barely stand. I thought he would eventually collapse into a drunken stupor and sleep for hours. I drew him out of the house, to give Maria time to get to her room. He had realised by then that I was in love with Maria

and he began to rage, calling her all manner of
names and swearing he would never let her go.

'As soon as I was sure Maria was safely upstairs I went back home to put my house in order
and prepare to leave the country. The last time
I saw Jonas his servants were helping him back
into the house. There was a great deal to do at
Oakenroyd, for I did not know when I would be
in England again. I was still in my study in the
early hours when a servant came to tell me that
Morwood was ablaze.'

'Lucas says he saw you,' Annabelle reminded
him.

Samuel shook his head. 'He is wrong. What
reason would I have for burning Morwood? It
saddens me to say it, but I think it much more
likely that it was Jonas he saw that night. He was
ranting when he followed me outside. He said,
"No one shall have her if I cannot!" I took no
notice of him, thought it was merely his drunken
posturing. If I had known—'

He broke off, his hands covering his face, and
Annabelle sat beside him, not knowing how to
comfort him. At last he raised his head.

'Lucas is wrong, also, to think no one believed him. Sir Angus, who was magistrate at
the time, came to see me a few days after the
fire to tell me of his allegations. Of course my
servants vouched for me and Sir Angus admit-

ted that he, too, suspected Jonas of starting the fire. He was well aware of Blackstone's temper and knew he was capable of terrible violence when roused, but Jonas was dead by then and the boy gone away, so we decided to say nothing. We thought it kinder to let everyone think it had been an accident.'

'Why did you not tell him that today, Papa, why let him think you are to blame?'

He looked at her sadly. 'Nay, my love, he would not have believed me. And besides, how could I suggest to him that his own father had started that fire?'

'And for this he would ruin us.' Annabelle drew back, clasping her hands together. 'You must write to him, Father. You must tell him your side of the story.'

'What good will it do? Sir Angus died several years ago and the young man is unlikely to believe the word of my servants over what he thinks he saw with his own eyes.'

'Please, Papa. I cannot bear that anyone should think you guilty of such a crime.'

'Very well.' Samuel stood up. 'I will write to him, in a day or two, when he has had an opportunity to think things over.'

She looked up. 'And do you think then he might change his mind about calling in the loans?'

For a long moment her father stared at her. 'No, my dear,' he said at last. 'I don't for a moment think that he will change his mind about that.'

It was the hottest day of the year so far. The June sun shone down from a cloudless blue sky and there was only the slightest breeze to cool the air. Usually Annabelle loved the summer, but as she rode Apollo at breakneck speed across the park she barely noticed the weather. It was three days since Lucas had called upon them, three days when she had spent hours with her father, discussing what was to be done, going over the indentures with Mr Telford and coming back to the same conclusion. If they could not raise the money to pay off Lucas Blackstone, then they would have to leave Oakenroyd at Michaelmas. They engaged Mr Telford to make enquiries on their behalf, but Samuel seemed resigned to his fate. Belle had never felt so at odds with her father. She felt a mixture of dismay and anger at his calm acceptance of their situation and when she had walked into his study after breakfast that morning and learned he had not yet written to Lucas she gave vent to her exasperation.

'My dear sir, I sometimes think you are glad that this is happening to us!' As soon as the words were uttered she was sorry for them, appalled at her outburst. Thankfully there were no servants present to hear her and she immediately dropped to her knees beside her father's chair and begged his pardon. Samuel merely shook his head.

'No, no, you are right to feel aggrieved, my love. I am not *glad* this has happened, but neither am I surprised. The guilt of poor Maria's death has weighed heavily upon my soul all these years and I have always thought I should be called to account for not doing more to help her.'

'My dear sir, what could you have done? Your faith has always been very strong and you know that to intervene between a man and his wife would go against everything you hold dear.'

His hands trembled in a futile gesture.

'But I knew that Jonas was becoming more tyrannical. If I had spoken to Maria more openly, pressed her more urgently to fly with me…she might well be alive now.'

A tiny blade, small but painful, twisted in Annabelle's heart. She gave a rueful smile. 'But then, *I* might not.'

Her father turned to her, saying quickly, 'You must not think I was not truly attached to your mother, Belle. I loved her very much indeed, but when she died, and then Edwin, I felt, somehow, that I was paying the price for not saving Maria, and possibly for loving her, too. I bought Morwood, you see, as a memorial to Maria and because I could not bear to see anyone else living there. But the memories were too painful for me. I went there rarely, and after Edwin died, not at all.' He sighed. 'I have so much to regret.'

'No, no, that is not true,' said Belle vehemently. 'You are a good man, Papa, you have done nothing wrong, save spend a little too freely and that is a very common fault.' She took his hands. 'Please, Papa, write to Mr Blackstone. It may not do any good, but we have to try!'

He regarded her for a long moment, sadness in his gentle eyes, but at last he squeezed her hands.

'I have been very selfish, wallowing in my self-pity, have I not, my love? Very well, I shall write the letter now, for your sake.'

Annabelle had offered to sit beside him and help him with the letter, but he had sent her away, saying he was better left alone, so she had ridden Apollo up on to the moors to work off some of her frustration in exercise. Keeping the big horse under control took all her concentration for the first part of her ride, but once Apollo had settled down her mind returned again to her most pressing problem: the treacherous behaviour of Lucas Blackstone. She could not come to terms with his betrayal. She had trusted him, and in her heart she still could not believe he would really carry out his threat to ruin her father. The doubt niggled away at her. If she could just see him, talk to him… The woods that marked the edge of the Morwood estate were ahead of her, their leaves forming a solid wall in varying shades of green, contrasting strongly with the rocky brown moorland around her.

Apollo slowed as they galloped towards the edge of the moor. He had learned that they turned back once they reached the road, but today Belle kicked him on and guided him on to the carriage-way that led to Morwood Manor. The house was still encased in a web of scaffolding and the ac-tivity was greater than ever, despite the burning sun. Elias Greenwood was standing before the house and he turned as she trotted up, one hand raised to shield his eyes.

'Miss Belle, we haven't seen you here for some time.'

His smiling greeting surprised her, until she realised that he did not know of Lucas's visit to Oakenroyd. If Lucas had told anyone in Stan-ton about his plans to ruin her father, then word would have spread rapidly. Perhaps he thought he was doing them a kindness. Again the con-tradiction. It did not make sense.

'Good day to you, Elias. Is Mr Blackstone here today?'

'Nay, ma'am, he's gone.' He moved closer,

saying confidentially, 'And I'm glad of it, too, for he's been worrying me, Miss Havenham, and that's a fact. For the past couple of days he's been here, behaving like a man possessed. He'd arrive early in the morning, strip off his coat and involve himself in all the most physical tasks, felling trees, carrying stone, never seen anything like it.'

'But he has left now?'

'Aye, miss. Rode off a while since.'

'Back to Stanton?' she asked. 'I did not see him on the road.'

Elias shrugged. 'I weren't taking that much notice, but I think he went into Home Wood.'

With a nod and a smile she turned Apollo and cantered off across the park. The shade of the trees would be a welcome relief from the hot sun, but as she rode along the new carriageway Belle realised she had no idea where in the wood Lucas might be. She halted and remained very still, straining her ears listening for any sounds of woodcutting, but everything was silent. Sitting very straight in the saddle, she squared her shoulders. She had come this far, she would find Lucas now, and she would talk to him. She made first for the lake and felt a little spurt of satisfaction when she spotted Sultan quietly cropping grass by the old bridge. There was no sign of Lucas. Her gaze shifted to the lake, where something was disturbing the mirrored surface. Someone was in the water and moving steadily towards the boathouse.

Annabelle slipped to the ground and loosely tethered Apollo beside the dilapidated bridge. She crossed it carefully, holding her breath until she was safely on the far bank. The swimmer was still cutting through the water, so she made her way to the boathouse. It had to be Lucas, she told herself. No one else would dare to be here.

She was at the foot of the boathouse steps just as he reached the bank. He looked up then and saw her.

'What in hell's name are you doing here?'

She put up her chin, hoping she would sound braver than she felt. 'I came to see you.'

He raised his brows, then he put his hands on the bank and hauled himself out of the water. 'Well, now you can see me.'

Belle gasped. It had not occurred to her that he would be naked. He stood before her, black hair plastered to his head and his body glistening in the sunlight.

Poseidon, she thought wildly. *Poseidon rising from the ocean.*

She swallowed, her eyes taking in every inch of that muscled body, the powerful shoulders, the shadow of dark hair across his chest that tapered down to—

She forced herself to look away. 'Th-that is not what I meant.' Despite her efforts to sound calm her voice shook.

'No, I thought not.'

He began to walk up the stone stairs. Belle followed him, keeping her eyes on the steps, where his bare feet left a wet imprint.

'I wanted to talk to you,' she said.

'Did your father send you to plead with me?'

'No!'

He disappeared through the door at the top of the stairs. Belle hesitated, but when she saw him pick up a towel and wrap it around his waist she summoned up her courage and stepped into the room. It looked different to the way she remembered. Cleaner. As if someone had taken a broom to it.

'No,' she said again. 'I came because I wanted to understand.'

'I thought I had explained myself perfectly clearly.'

'You blame my father for the fire at Morwood.'

'I blame him for the death of my parents.'

'He did not do it.'

'How do you know? You were not even born then!'

'Papa told me, and he would not lie.'

He glared at her, then picked up another towel

and began to rub his head. 'Go away, Miss Havenham. You will only compromise yourself by being here.'

'I thought…' She clasped her hands, squeezing until her knuckles gleamed white, forcing out the words. 'I thought we were friends.'

'How could we ever be that?'

'No. Of course not.' There was a constriction in her throat and she swallowed to remove it so she could continue. 'Was it all a trick, then? A ruse to get closer to my father?'

'Yes. No! Console yourself with the fact that I would have spared you this if I could. It is your father I want to punish, not you.'

Her hands crept up to her cheeks. She closed her eyes. 'If you foreclose, then you may well kill him.'

'An eye for an eye, madam. Your father is a good church man. He will understand that.'

'How can you be so cold about ruining a man's life?'

He cursed beneath his breath and turned, slamming one fist upon the small table beside him.

'I have had years to think about it, madam. Five-and-twenty years, in fact. This gives me no pleasure, but I will have justice done!'

She met his eyes and saw so much anger and pain in them it frightened her more than his physical presence. She began to back away. His lip curled.

'Aye, you'd be wise to remove yourself from here, Miss Havenham. Being alone with a naked man will do your reputation no good at all.'

'I will go.' She bit her lip. 'But first, I want you to tell me—did you…did you deliberately set out to trap Papa at Harrogate? Did you trick him into playing cards?'

His brows drew together. 'No, of course not.' When she did not move or speak he continued, 'I lived very modestly while I was in the army. The little that was left from the sale of Morwood was invested for me, and added to that was a small inheritance from the elderly relatives who had taken me in, so when I sold out I set people on to find out all I could about Samuel Havenham and I instructed my lawyers to buy up his debts. The mortgage was a piece of good fortune, since the amount outstanding far exceeds the value of the property. Then I learned Samuel had lost a great deal of money at the gaming tables, so I bought up his notes of hand. There, now you have it. You may hate me for what I am doing, Miss Havenham, but I am no scoundrel. I used no stratagems to trap your father, he did that himself. Now, will you go and leave me in peace?' His hands moved to the towel at his waist. 'Or perhaps you would like to finish what we started at the assembly?'

His barb hit home. Belle felt hot tears cramming her throat and she turned and fled, his savage laughter following her down the stairs.

'I am leaving Stanton tomorrow and shall not be back until September.'

Lucas was at Morwood with Elias Greenwood. He did not doubt the man would be glad to see the back of him for a while. He had been spending far too much time at the manor over the past few days, working like a demon to rid himself of the image of Annabelle's horror-stricken face during that last meeting at Oakenroyd. Then, when he thought he had at last buried the memory she had turned up at the lake, her sweet innocence pricking, nay, stabbing at his conscience. Now he shrugged himself into his coat as he issued final instructions to Elias.

'I think we have covered everything, but if you have any problems you can write to me at Mr Powell's office in London. You have his address?'

'Aye, sir.'

'Very well.' He mounted Sultan and took a last look at the house encased in its cage of scaffolding. 'I hope to see a great deal of progress upon my return.'

'Aye, that you will, sir,' said Elias, grinning up at him. 'As long as the weather don't slow us up too much.'

Lucas rode back to the Red Lion. George would have everything packed up in readiness for an early start in the morning. One more dinner in Stanton and he would be off. He had business with his lawyers in London and invitations from friends that could not be ignored. He would spend the summer in Brighton, there was always plenty to occupy him there, and of course there was a visit to a discreet little house in Downing Street that must be paid. He turned his thoughts to the ripe young beauty waiting for him there.

He had met Nancy soon after he left the army. Arriving in London in the aftermath of Waterloo, he learned from Mr Powell that the small sum he had left with him fifteen years ago when he had first joined up had grown into a considerable fortune. Nancy had been only too willing to help him spend it and he had set her up as his mistress with her own apartment and a generous allowance. But he had no illusions about her fidelity. Nancy was fond of him, but only as long as he had money to spend on her and he was well aware that during his long absence she would have been taking presents from other men in return for her favours. Even when he had been in town on leave she had been unwilling or unable to remain faithful.

Lucas was surprised how little he cared. It was time he paid her off. After all he would not be spending much time in London in the future. A diamond bracelet should be sufficient. And he would tell Powell to pay her rent until the end of the summer. That should give her time to find another protector.

Unbidden, the image of Annabelle rose in his mind. Would she, too, have found a man to protect her by the time he returned? He had done his best to put a spoke in that wheel, by making it known that she had no fortune. It had certainly discouraged Keighley, and surely no man would be tempted to take her to wife without a dowry, would they?

He remembered how she had felt in his arms, soft, pliant, eagerly returning his kisses. A man might well forgo a dowry for such a partner. Angrily he thrust away the thought and dug his heels into Sultan's flanks. The horse bucked a little, indignant at being so roughly treated, but soon settled into his long stride and Lucas forced himself to concentrate on keeping Sultan steady and looking out for rabbit holes as he rode back to the inn, where he found George Stebbing waiting for him.

'Dinner is ready for you, Major, when you are.

And this arrived.' He handed Lucas a sealed letter. 'Came just after you left this morning, sir.'

Lucas turned it over. He did not recognise the handwriting or the seal. Quickly he broke it open. It was from Oakenroyd. His eyes travelled over the first few lines but no further. His mouth twisted as he refolded the letter and threw it into his writing box, which stood open on a side table.

'It can wait,' he said shortly. 'It is not important.'

Chapter Nine

Annabelle waited each morning for the post, hoping there would be a letter from Mr Telford with some good news. Summer dragged on and the lawyer's infrequent correspondence brought only disappointment. She ventured into Stanton only when it was necessary. As soon as Mr Telford had started making local enquiries, trying to find someone to loan them the money they needed, the word had spread that Mr Havenham was indeed in dire financial straits and was selling Oakenroyd. Annabelle saw to it that every outstanding bill was paid and refused to take any further credit, even where it was offered, but she found the sympathy very hard to bear. Most was genuine, like the Rishworths, the Scanlons and old Mrs Hall. Even the dressmaker, Mrs Ford, offered to help her in any way possible. One or two, like Mrs Kensley, smiled and uttered sympathetic noises, but there was no mistaking the cruel gleam of satisfaction in their eyes at her father's misfortune.

Belle rode Apollo over the estate, taking a keen interest in the harvest this year, but in her heart she knew that even if it was the best ever it would still not be enough to pay the debts they owed. Samuel's letter to Lucas had received no reply. She wondered if he had even read it and concluded sadly that he had not.

Worst of all was the fact that despite all Lucas had done she missed him. She kept busy, tried not to think of him, but in unguarded moments the memory would return of those precious moments at the assembly, of being cradled in his arms and being kissed by him. Every detail was etched into her mind, the butterfly touch of that kiss, the gentle caresses that had aroused in her such desire that just the thought of it made her shiver.

She had been in a fair way to losing her heart to him and still found it hard to relate that loving man to the cruel monster who was determined to ruin her father. Even now she remembered his words as he held her hand.

'Do not think too badly of me.'

And the truth was, she did not think badly of him. Even that painful meeting at the boathouse, when he had taunted her so cruelly, had not left her totally despondent. He had told her that he had merely bought up her father's debts; he had had no hand in creating them. She could understand his quest for vengeance, even if it was unjust, and deep in her heart burned a little flame of hope that he would change his mind, that he would prove himself to be the honest, honourable man she believed him to be.

At the end of August Annabelle received two pieces of news. The first was that the wheat harvest had been a good one, the second that Lucas Blackstone was back.

Her steward told her about the harvest, but it was Celia Rishworth who brought Annabelle the news of Lucas's return. She had come to Oakenroyd to take tea and celebrate Annabelle's birthday and was happy to regale her friend with all the latest gossip from Stanton.

'Mama and I were in Mrs Ford's yesterday, collecting our gowns ready for Lizzie's wedding to Mr Keighley and we saw Mr Blackstone's curricle outside the Red Lion.' Celia took another small bite of the rich fruit cake Cook had made for the occasion. 'His groom was following on with that big black hunter of his and he had a baggage waggon, too. Such a to-do as there was, with servants running here, there and everywhere. He had any number of corded trunks carried into the Lion.'

'So it would appear he is staying for a while.'

'Oh, yes, Papa spoke to him only this morning and he declared he is going to remain in Stanton now until Morwood is finished. Strange, though, I cannot think that he will want to remain at an *inn* for all those months, can you?'

Annabelle gave an evasive answer and distracted her friend by asking about the arrangements for Lizzie's wedding.

'Oh, everything is quite ready now,' exclaimed Celia. 'Lizzie is very excited by the idea of being Mrs Keighley and they are off to Italy for their honeymoon...'

Annabelle knew much of this already, but she nodded and allowed Celia to chatter on, preferring it to any further talk of Lucas Blackstone.

When Celia had gone Annabelle joined her father for a quiet dinner together and when he bemoaned the fact that it was only the two of them she was quick to reassure him. He shook his head, looking very sad.

'To have this business of my debts hanging over us, I am afraid I am not very good company for you on your birthday, my love.'

'Nonsense, you are all the company I want,' she told him. 'Look, I am wearing the pearl eardrops you gave me. Do they not look well? Now, let Gibson help you to some of the chicken, Papa, for it is very good, and afterwards you shall hear everything Celia Rishworth told me about the improvements her father is making to the lodge…'

She was at pains to keep him entertained throughout the meal, but she knew he was fretting over the loss of Oakenroyd, and when it was time for her to retire he took her hand and held it tightly.

'Bless you, Belle. I do not know what I would do without you.'

'Nor I you, Papa.' She leaned over his chair to drop a kiss upon his forehead. 'Tomorrow I plan to take some flowers to Mama's grave before breakfast. Shall you come with me?'

He shook his head. 'I think not, my love.'

'I was going to walk into Stanton, but we could take the gig, if you prefer.'

'It is not that.' He raised his hand as if warding off some dark thought. 'You go, my love. I shall visit her grave another day.'

She had hoped that by the morning he would have changed his mind, but it was not the case, so she put on her chip-straw bonnet, gathered some of the brightest blooms from the garden and set off for Stanton church.

It was a beautiful morning, only a few high clouds dotted about the blue sky as she walked into the town. The church was in the centre of Stanton, an ancient stone building with a square tower surrounded by a large graveyard. She had deliberately set out early in the hope that she would not meet anyone. Everything was quiet and peaceful, bathed in the morning sunshine and the grass still wet with dew. Annabelle slipped into the churchyard and made her way between the graves, thankful for the solitude. A movement to her right startled her and she looked across to see Lucas only yards away. Her heart was thumping wildly. She was certain the graveyard had been empty and could only suppose that he had been hidden by the ornate pedestal tomb that stood between them.

Annabelle hesitated. She wanted to turn and run, but that would be cowardly. Surely he would not dare to accost her in this holy place? Squaring her shoulders, she walked on towards her mother's grave and pretended not to notice him. He touched his hat.

'Good day to you, Miss Havenham.'

She could not ignore him now, but she refused to be intimidated, despite the rapid tattoo beating against her ribs. 'I did not think you a God-fearing man, Mr Blackstone.'

'Then that shows how little you know me.'

He made no move to follow her, but to her consternation he watched her as she bent to place her flowers at the base of the simple headstone that marked her mother's grave. She knelt down, pulling away the weeds that threatened to creep over the headstone, tracing her fingers over the carved lettering as she uttered up a silent prayer for her mother. Then she offered up a second prayer for her father and herself.

Lucas was still watching her from the side of the path when she returned. 'Your mother's grave?' He began to walk alongside her.

'Yes. She died when I was a baby. I never knew her.'

'My mother died when I was ten.'

'Yes, of course—I am so sorry, that must have been very hard for you.'

'Spare me your sympathy, madam. I have no need of it.'

'It seems you are very much in need of it, since you are so eaten up by hatred.'

'I want justice, nothing more.'

'Did you read my father's letter to you?'

'Not yet.'

'Not yet? It has been months!'

'I have no need to read it, I know the truth.'

'You were a little boy—'

He turned on her with a snarl. 'Are you saying I should not believe the evidence of my own eyes?'

'I think you are mistaken,' she replied, holding her ground. 'There were others at Morwood that night in knee breeches and white stockings, were there not? Well?' she challenged him.

'Only my father and my cousin Hugh. I have discounted them.'

She shook her head in disbelief. 'And you think my gentle father could be guilty of such a crime?'

'Damn you, I do not *think,* I know!' He turned on his heel and strode away.

Annabelle remained rooted to the spot, shocked by the violence she had seen in his face. She was saddened, too, by the pain she had seen there and by the thought of that little boy losing both his parents in such a terrifying ordeal.

She watched him march out through the lych-gate and on an impulse she turned and went back to the monument where she had first seen him. As she suspected, it was the tomb of the Blackstone family, with the names of Maria and Jonas Blackstone carved into the stone beneath a long line of ancestors.

Annabelle told no one of her meeting with Lucas, but it stayed with her through the evening and long into the night. For five-and-twenty years he had believed her father responsible for the fire that killed his parents. Even if he read her father's letter, it was unlikely that he would change his mind now. But she was her father's daughter and Samuel Havenham was a great believer in the goodness of human nature, so she, too, believed it might happen. She had to hope. But even if Lucas could be brought to believe Samuel was innocent, she knew now he was not the Lucas Monserrat who had captured her heart, the one who had brought her alive with his kisses. That man was an impostor, a charade conjured up to beguile her.

That Lucas was gone for ever.

'Mr Blackstone to see you.'

Annabelle was in the morning room, setting stitches in her embroidery when Gibson made his announcement and it caused her to prick her finger.

'Surely he wants to see my father.'

'He asked for you, Miss Havenham.'

'Oh. Then you had better show him in, Gibson.'

She set aside her embroidery and rose, absently putting the punctured finger to her lips as she waited for her visitor.

The first thing Lucas saw as he entered the room was Belle with one finger pushed against her full, cherry-red lips. He did not for a moment think she was trying to entice him, but it was a damned alluring image, and it shook him to realise just how much he had missed her during the months he had been away. He put his hat and riding crop down carefully upon a chair and stood, stripping off his gloves while he pulled himself together.

She watched him for some moments before saying with a touch of haughty impatience, 'How can I help you, Mr Blackstone?'

'You can tell me if your father has any hope of paying me off at the end of the month.'

Her brows rose. 'Surely that is a question you should put to him.'

'Let us not play games, Miss Havenham, I am well aware that you are in your father's confidence.'

Her eyes slid away from his. 'No.' She uttered the word quietly, no longer aloof. 'I fear we will lose Oakenroyd.'

That was the answer he was expecting. He had worked hard these past two years to make sure of it. He moved across to the empty hearth and turned to face her. 'Then I have a solution for you.'

Her eyes flew to his face again and he had to steel himself not to weaken when he saw the naked hope there. He cleared his throat. 'Marry me.'

Silence.

'I—I beg your pardon?' The words came out in a husky whisper.

'I said marry me. As my wife you can continue to live at Oakenroyd, at least until Morwood is completed, when we would make that our home. And your father could spend the rest of his days here. You have my word on that. There will be no need for anyone to know the financial details of our arrangement. As far as our neighbours are concerned they may think it a marriage of convenience, but nothing out of the ordinary.'

She sank down on to a chair. Her face was as white as the muslin fichu about her neck.

'I—I do not understand.'

'At Michaelmas Oakenroyd will be mine. That is four weeks' time. There is time for us to marry before that, then you and your father can carry on here, as before.'

'But you will be master.'

'Yes.'

'And this is part of your plan for revenge?'

It was his turn to look away. He found he could not meet those clear grey eyes.

She continued quietly, 'Your plan is to take from Papa the things he loves most.'

That had indeed been his original plan, but not any more. He would not be taking anything from the old man, save the knowledge that he had got away with murder. She should be grateful for that.

'Your father would lose nothing. He would continue to live here, as would you.'

'But I would be your wife.'

By God, she was scorning him! He heard the contempt in her voice, saw the disdainful curl of her lip. He might as well have offered her a *carte blanche*.

'You will not find me ungenerous,' he said coldly. 'You will still be mistress here. And there is Morwood Manor to be furnished and decorated. You may have a free hand to do with it as you wish.'

The colour returned to her cheek, matched by an angry sparkle in her eyes. She rose, drawing herself up to her full if diminutive height.

'You think I care for such things when you have ruined my father? Goodbye, Mr Blackstone.'

As she walked past him he caught her wrist.

'Be careful, madam. I think rather I am saving your father. His life will not change a jot.'

She tried to pull herself free, but he held on, drawing her close. Beneath his fingers her pulse was racing, but she regarded him fearlessly, a haughty curl to her lip.

'What, you expect him to share a house with you, knowing you think him a murderer? And his daughter is to sacrifice herself for this privilege?'

He frowned. 'I am offering you a solution to your problems, madam,' he snapped. 'If you do not accept, then at Michaelmas you and your father will have to find somewhere new to live, and on a fraction of the income you now enjoy. I do not see you have a choice.'

Her eyes positively flashed at that, sparks of green fire flew at him. She tore herself from his grasp. 'I will not be part of your petty revenge. I would rather *starve* than marry you!'

'Then starve, madam.' Angrily he thrust his hands into his gloves. 'It is your choice, but you might wish to discuss it with your father.' He walked to the chair to collect his hat and his riding crop. 'The offer remains upon the table for the rest of the week. After that—' He reached into his jacket and pulled out a package, which he tossed on to the side table. 'Your gloves, Miss Havenham. I thought you should have them back. It might be some time before you can afford to buy another pair.'

Chapter Ten

Annabelle remained on her feet until the door closed behind him. Only then did she collapse on to a chair, trembling. How dare he, *how dare he* add this insult to the rest? She would not cry, this was beyond tears.

When the trembling ceased she went into the gardens, but even there it was impossible to think clearly. The heady perfume of the roses, the beautifully scythed lawns, every scent, every image combined to bring home to her just what she would lose in a few weeks' time.

Unless I marry Lucas Blackstone.

That was a price she would not pay, but even as she told herself so another voice told her she must at least consider it. Her decision would affect not only her life but her father's, and everyone at Oakenroyd. She could remain mistress here, her father's comfort would be assured.

And the alternative?

She exhaled and looked up, staring at the cloudless blue sky. It was all very well for her to choose to live in penury, but could she expect her father to do so? His health was not good. What if he became ill? There would be doctors' bills, medicines. Could she risk his health when all that was asked of her was that she marry Lucas Blackstone? The irony was that before the truth of his identity was known, before she had learned his outrageous plans for revenge, she would have been only too pleased to comply.

Belle went into the house to look for her father. She found him in his library, reading. He roused himself when she came in, greeting her with a kindly smile.

'My love, have you come to tell me it is time for luncheon already?'

'No, dear Papa, we have a while yet, but I wanted to talk to you.'

'That sounds serious.'

'It is. I presume there has been no further news from Mr Telford?'

'No way out of our difficulties, if that is what you mean. But there is some good news. Telford tells me that Blackstone has written to assure him that he means to keep on all the staff at

Oakenroyd, if they wish to remain. Everything is to continue just as it is. So that will be a comfort, will it not? I was very much afraid that my improvident spending would mean they would all be turned off.'

She tried to smile. 'That is indeed a relief, sir.' She took a chair opposite him. 'Papa, what if…' She clasped her hands together. 'What if there was a way we could keep Oakenroyd?'

He gave a wistful smile. 'Ah, if only.'

She took a deep breath. 'Papa, what if I were to marry Mr Blackstone?'

There, she had said it.

'Marry Lucas Blackstone? What is this, my love?'

'He came here this morning and—and made me an offer. He said if I married him then we could carry on living here, as before. Of course, when Morwood is finished he and I would move there, but you would be able to live on here, as you have always done.' She stopped and waited for him to speak.

'Do you *want* to marry him, Belle?'

She looked away. 'No. No, not this way.'

'Then you must not do so.'

'But, Papa, have you thought where we shall go, how we shall live?'

'Yes, as a matter of fact, I have,' he said, surprising her. 'Sir John Rishworth has offered us a house in Stanton. Croft Cottage. It is a small place, I believe, but big enough for us both and one servant, which is all we will be able to afford. And it is on the High Street, so we will be able to walk wherever we need to. We shall still be near our friends. And the vicar has promised to put some work my way. There are one or two boys locally who need help with their studies. What with that and the small annuity you have from your mother, I think we shall go on very well.'

'Oh, Papa.' She put her face in her hands. 'That we should come to this.'

'It is not so very bad, my love. If everything had been sold on the open market then it would not have covered what I owe. It could have been the debtors' prison for me. Mr Blackstone is being very generous—'

'Generous! How can you say that, when he is taking everything we have?'

'He has done nothing illegal, my dear,' he said gently. 'And he thinks he has cause…'

'If only we could prove to him that he is wrong.'

'Mayhap he will realise that in time.'

She said slowly, 'If I married him I would have funds, I could search for witnesses.'

'Do you think he would let you do that?'

'I—I don't know. He wants to marry me as

part of his revenge against you.' She moved from her chair and knelt at her father's side. 'Could you live with him, Papa, knowing how he thought of you?'

'Could *you?*' he countered.

She nodded. 'If I had to, if it meant you could keep the comforts you have known.'

'You must not do that for me, Belle. You know I feel myself in part responsible for Maria's death. If I had only been stronger—' He sighed, his shoulders drooping. 'My conscience tells me this retribution is not wholly undeserved—'

'Papa, no! My dear sir, we have discussed this.'

'I have lived with it on my conscience for five-and-twenty years, my love. Jonas was ranting that night. If I had stayed—'

'You did what you thought right at the time, Papa.'

'I did, God forgive me.'

'And if I accept Mr Blackstone's offer we can keep Oakenroyd—'

He raised his hand to stop her. 'That is not a good reason for marriage, my love. Do you remember when you were a little girl, I bought a lark from a pedlar in Stanton? It had a very elegant cage, finely wrought from silver wire.'

'Yes, I remember.' She nodded. 'You put the cage in the garden and opened the door. The lark flew away and we never saw it again, although later I thought I heard it singing in the woods.'

'Which is as it should be. We have no right to imprison any creature, no matter how beautiful the cage.' He put his hand on her head. 'That is what you would be if you married Lucas Blackstone merely to save Oakenroyd. A bird in a gilded cage. I would not wish that for you, Belle.'

Lucas ran up the stairs to his room at the Red Lion, calling for his man.

'Are there any letters for me?' he asked, stripping off his gloves.

'No, sir. Was you expecting something?'

Lucas cursed silently. The week was up, he had expected to have a response from Annabelle Havenham by now. Devil take it, what was wrong with the chit? He was offering her a way out of all her difficulties. And it was not as if she was repelled by him. She had been keen enough for his embraces that night of the assembly!

'Miss Scanlon and Mr Keighley was married this morning,' said his valet, waiting to carry away his coat for a brushing. 'The church bells was ringing all morning. I'm surprised you didn't hear 'em at Morwood.'

Of course, Annabelle was a close friend of the Scanlons, she might still be celebrating with the family. Lucas looked at the clock. There were some hours yet. She was making him sweat, but he had no doubt she would give in. After all, what choice did she have? He took a solitary dinner in his rooms, then busied himself with paperwork, determinedly keeping his mind off the ticking clock, but at midnight he was forced to face the truth.

She had refused him.

On the twenty-eighth of September, Annabelle entered Stanton church on her father's arm, her head held high. Tomorrow was Michaelmas, so this was the last time they would occupy the closed box set aside for the owner of Oakenroyd. Her father patted her hand and supported her, dignified, as always. She kept her eyes fixed upon the parson throughout the service, but she was aware of the stares, the whispers. It was of course common knowledge now that her father was unable to pay his debts and had been obliged to sell up. Samuel had refused to let it be known that the crisis had been forced upon them by Lucas Blackstone. It would only cause difficulties, he said, if their friends had to choose between them and their new neighbour, and most could not afford to fall out with Lucas, who was now a major landowner in the area.

They could not afford to take anyone with them to Croft Cottage except Abel, her father's valet, who had begged to be allowed to accompany them and had offered to act as their general manservant. It had fallen to Annabelle to explain this to the staff at Oakenroyd and to tell them that the new owner was willing to employ them all. She advised them all to remain, since work was still scarce in the area. The hardest to convince had been Clegg, her groom. He had been shocked when she had told him they were giving up all the horses and it had taken some time to persuade him that they would not be able to afford such a luxury. He had been mutinous and at first determined to quit Oakenroyd, but Annabelle persuaded him to stay.

'This has always been your home,' she told him. 'Mr Blackstone has assured us that he means to be a fair employer and I would have you give him as good service as you have always given us.' It had cost her no small effort to say this, but it was her father's wish that they should make an honourable and dignified exit. Clegg had shaken his head, and she had seen the glint of tears in his eyes as he addressed her.

'I shall be that sorry to see you go, Miss Belle. I wish there was some way I could help you.'

It was then that she had given in to one small temptation.

'There is something you could do, Clegg. You could take Apollo to market for me. Not here, out of the area.' She knew that everything should be left for Lucas, that he had bought the whole, but she could not bear to see her beloved horse in his hands. She would leave the money for him, instead. 'Find a good home for him, Clegg, and if Mr Blackstone should enquire you may tell him that you were following my orders.'

Clegg had told her yesterday that he had sold the grey to a gentleman from Halifax who was looking for a hunter and with this she had to be satisfied. It was a small comfort, but it was something.

It was not until the service was over that she realised Lucas Blackstone was present. It was the first time she had seen him in church. He had not been present at Lizzie's wedding to Mr Keighley, for which she had been profoundly grateful. Had he come now to gloat over their misfortune? She hoped not. She made her way out of the church, her hand resting lightly upon her father's arm. The bright sunshine was encouraging the parishioners to congregate in the churchyard. Her father wanted to speak to Sir John Rishworth and they were on their way to join them when Mrs Kensley detained her. Reluctantly Annabelle let her father walk on ahead.

'So tomorrow you quit Oakenroyd, Miss Havenham. How sad you must be.'

'We must bear it as we can,' replied Annabelle.

The widow moved a little closer, saying confidentially, 'I had not thought Mr Havenham addicted to gambling, but—'

'There is no addiction, Mrs Kensley.'

'Oh? I understood it was debts he accrued at Harrogate last year...'

'I am afraid your sources have misled you,' replied Annabelle, keeping her temper in check. 'It was the recent war and the bad harvests that have proved so disastrous.'

'As they have for so many families,' said a deep voice.

Belle looked up to find Lucas at her side.

'Perhaps it would have been more appropriate if the sermon today had been on the subject of prodigality,' tittered Mrs Kensley. 'It behoves us all to live within our means, is that not so, Mr Blackstone?'

'Indeed,' he retorted. 'As it behoves us to be charitable to those who fall upon hard times.' He gave a little bow. 'Good day to you, madam, we will detain you no longer.'

The widow's eyes snapped angrily, but thus dismissed, she could only move away.

'If you had married me you would have been spared this humiliation,' he muttered when the widow was gone.

'You would have replaced it with a worse one.' She turned and walked on, but he stayed at her side.

'Would it be so bad, to be my wife?'

'Yes, while you believe my father to be a murderer.'

'I *know* him to be one.'

She stopped. 'You know nothing of the kind.'

'How can you be sure? You were not even born.'

'I know my father. Have you still not read his letter?'

'No.'

'His manservant vouches for him. He was at Oakenroyd when the fire was started.'

'Servants can be bought.'

'You are determined to believe him guilty. Excuse me—'

'Belle!' He caught her arm as she went to walk away. 'I do not want this for you.' He ground out the words, his jaw clenched. 'I have not been able to get you out of my mind. Poverty will destroy you, but it is not too late. Marry me.'

She looked up and met his burning gaze steadily. 'That would destroy me even more surely.'

Annabelle and her father moved into Croft Cottage the next day. It was indeed small, but

Annabelle cheerfully asserted that with a little work it would be very comfortable. The little room overlooking the street would make a cosy sitting room, and the small dining parlour beside it could also be used as a study for her father. They had brought very little from Oakenroyd, a few trunks of private possessions, but they were sanguine. After all there was no room for more.

The Rishworths were the first to visit them and Sir John made a point of taking Annabelle to one side and saying quietly, 'I know, my dear, that you and your father will feel this change of circumstance keenly, but it does not alter the respect in which you are held in Stanton. I would like you to know that if ever you or your father feel in need of support or protection, you can call upon me.'

Annabelle was touched by his kindness and by that of the numerous friends who called upon them over the next few weeks, many bringing small gifts, useful things such as food or candles. The sort of items Annabelle would have included in the baskets she gave to the poor and needy at Oakenroyd. She thought wryly how much more difficult it was to receive charity than to give it.

She was kept busy with all the little tasks she had previously left to her servants. Abel proved himself very useful and between them they shared all the household tasks, leaving her father free to sit in his study and receive callers, read from the few books he had brought with him and to tutor the occasional student sent to him by the vicar.

Housework had the charm of novelty, but Annabelle knew it would not last. Of all the tasks that fell to her lot, she most enjoyed the shopping. Each day she would take her basket and sally forth to the market to buy their food. She was gratified and a little surprised to find everyone so friendly. There were exceptions, of course, but she ignored them where she could and refused to be cast down by the occasional snub. After all, it was no more than they had expected.

She often saw the servants from Oakenroyd in Stanton. At first they were a little embarrassed to talk to her, but when they realised she was genuinely happy to meet them they relaxed and told her what was going on at the house. With mixed feelings she discovered that Lucas was proving a good master, exacting but fair. He had only brought in two servants of his own, both of whom had been with him since his army days. His one-armed valet, Stebbing, who was generally considered an easy-going fellow and the other was Rudd, his groom. She learned that Clegg had been reluctant to share the stables at first, but Mr Blackstone had purchased a couple of first-class hunters and he was also intending to set up his own carriage, so in the end Clegg was grateful for the extra hands.

And Mr Blackstone was making improvements to the house, too. The draughty windows in Mrs Wicklow's rooms were being replaced and Cook was to have a new range in the kitchen, which pleased him mightily. Belle was glad, for their sake, that everything was going well at Oakenroyd, although she was a little rueful that the staff could change their allegiance so readily. But she refused to be bitter. She would follow her father's example and be thankful for the life she had, rather than regret the one she had lost.

There was little time to repine. In fact, there was very little leisure time at all, but occasionally she managed to get away and enjoy a walk in the lanes surrounding the town. She avoided the paths leading to Morwood or Oakenroyd, but enjoyed exploring the countryside on the other side of Stanton. One of her favourite walks was to Oldroyd Farm, where she would buy her eggs, cheese and milk. With the new toll road around Dyke's Ridge to take the traffic, the old road was hardly used now, save for the weekly visit of the teamster with his string of packhorses bringing goods to Stanton market. She enjoyed the solitude, but wished she could persuade her father to walk with her occasionally. Since moving to

Croft Cottage he rarely went out, save to church on a Sunday. It was true he had plenty of visitors and the tutoring of two young scholars filled some of his days, but she feared his inactivity was not beneficial to his health.

She considered this as she returned from Old-royd Farm one morning. It was a bright autumn day with a fresh breeze tugging at her skirts. The sun was shining on the rocky outcrop above Dyke's Ridge and there was an orangey-gold tint to the grass in the high pastures. It was just such a day as her father would enjoy, but her entreaties could not coax him out of the house. She suspected that for all his cheerful demeanour he was missing his life at Oakenroyd and that hurt her more than all her own deprivations.

A movement on the highway caught her eye. A rider on a grey horse. As she watched he left the road and came galloping down across the fields towards her. At first she thought nothing of it. It was just someone enjoying the fine weather. Then she stopped. There was something familiar about the gait of that horse. She strained her eyes to see and as the rider drew closer her breath caught in her throat. Lucas Blackstone. And she recognised his horse.

All the careful control and meek submission to her fate that she had been practising for the past weeks disappeared, replaced by a burning resentment. As soon as he was close enough she addressed him in a voice shaking with anger. 'Where did you get Apollo?'

He touched his hat to her. 'Good day to you, Miss Havenham.' He stressed the greeting, reminding her of her own lack, but she was beyond courtesy.

'I sold him.' She ground out the words. 'I left you the money for him.'

'I know.' He dismounted. 'It was the devil of a job to get Clegg to tell me who had bought him and it cost me something to get him back.' He patted the grey's neck. 'I think he is glad to be home, though.'

Apollo recognised her and came closer. She could not help but put up her hand to stroke the velvet muzzle. All at once she was overcome with homesickness.

'I saw you from the toll road,' Lucas continued. 'Since I now own your father's subscription I thought I should show some interest in it.' She kept her attention on stroking Apollo's head. He pushed against her, gently lipping her shawl, searching for titbits. 'I have not had the opportunity to take that road since I drove you there. Do you remember?' She did not reply and after a few moments he said, 'Perhaps you would allow me to drive you again.'

'I think not.'

Turning away, she resumed her walk. Lucas fell into step beside her, the big grey clip-clopping behind them.

'Or we could ride out together. I will lend Apollo to you.'

She bit her lip. 'Thank you, but no. I do not ride any more.'

'Ah, your riding habit is at Oakenroyd, is it not? Your room there is still as you left it.'

'You would do better to clear it out. I have no use for any of it now.'

'No, it shall stay. I still hope that one day you will return.'

'Never.'

He halted and caught her arm. 'Never is a long time, Belle.'

His touch, the use of her pet name, cut through the last vestige of her control. She flung away from him, dropping her basket. The eggs and milk spilled unheeded over the path.

'Why will you not leave me alone?' she cried. 'Why do you persist in punishing me?'

'I do not want to punish you. You are not responsible for your father's actions.'

'And no more are you for yours!' she flashed back at him.

'What do you mean by that?'

She was beyond anger now. She would no longer put up with his taunts. No matter what her father said, Lucas should know the truth.

'Jonas Blackstone was a drunkard and jealous of anyone who came near your mother. She was going to leave him, to run away with my father—but you would know that if you had read my father's letter. But what he did *not* put in his letter was that Jonas understood their intentions that night and he raged about it, declared he would never let Maria leave him. You told us your window was open that night, did you not hear him say that?'

'He was angry. If, *if* he said that, he did not mean it.'

'And it is not true that no one listened to you,' she continued angrily. 'The magistrate came to see my father, to question him. *His* opinion was that if the fire was started by anyone it was your father. Everyone knew his violent temper, many had suffered from it, but since he was dead they decided to say nothing, to save *you* from disgrace and embarrassment.'

He stared at her, his face grey, his hands clenching and unclenching at his side. 'They are lying.'

'Are they?' she flung at him. 'Why should everyone be lying save you? If you had read my father's letter you would have seen that all the facts were there, such as they are. The old magistrate is dead now, so it is merely the memory of one ten-year-old boy against my father's word. How *dare* you expect me to believe you rather than him!' She put her hands against his chest and pushed him away from her. 'Go away,' she screamed. 'Go away and leave me in peace!'

Unsettled by this outburst, Apollo snorted nervously and backed away. Annabelle dashed a hand across her eyes.

'You had best look to your horse,' she muttered, her anger spent. 'It is a long walk back to Oakenroyd from here and I do not want you anywhere near me.'

She turned, blinking away the tears so that she could see to collect up the cheese and the now-empty milk jug. The eggs were beyond redemption. The wind whipped at her shawl and she pulled it tight about her, keeping her eyes fixed on the ground until she heard him mount up and ride away.

'Please, Belle, you must come! With Lizzie away on her honeymoon you are my only friend. I shall not enjoy the assembly half as much if you are not there.'

Annabelle found herself subjected to Celia's pleading gaze. 'I have no ticket...'

'I asked Papa to buy one for you,' said Celia. 'And if you say you have nothing to wear I shall bring you one of my gowns. And,' concluded her friend triumphantly, 'Papa saw Dr Bennett earlier today and he is coming here to play chess with Mr Havenham tonight, so you see, there is really no excuse for you not to come with me.'

'It would appear not,' said Annabelle with a reluctant smile. 'Save that I do not want to go.'

'That is nonsense, when you love dancing so much!'

She shook her head, thinking of her meeting with Lucas on the old road yesterday.

'Mr Blackstone might be there.'

'I can understand why you might not want to see him,' said Celia, who really understood nothing, since Annabelle had told her nothing. 'But he is not coming. He told Papa as much last night. There was a meeting of the toll-road subscribers, you see, and Mama charged Papa *particularly* with a message for Mr Blackstone.' She laughed. 'I think they would like me to form an alliance there, but for my part I would rather not. Although his fortune may be very handsome, the same cannot be said for his countenance, can it? Far too craggy, and so *brown,* from all those years fighting in Spain. And his manner, too, he is always very abrupt when he speaks to one, and he looks so severe.' She reached out and took Annabelle's hands. 'But let us not think of him. There will be so many of your old friends who want to see you. Do say you will come, Belle. Mama says we will collect you in the carriage, so you do not have to enter the Red Lion on your own—I know there is a separate entrance and stairs for the assembly rooms but still, the tap-room is the haunt for some rather rough persons and Mama knows your father will be happier if you are escorted.'

'You leave me no option,' Annabelle capitulated. 'And since I now live so close I can always slip away before the end if I wish to do so.'

That made Celia laugh out loud. 'You, leave a dance early, Belle? You are always the one who wants to stay to the very end!'

Chapter Eleven

Having decided to attend the assembly, Annabelle pulled out the newest of the few evening gowns she had brought with her. It was the green muslin she had worn to the last assembly and immediately it brought back memories of Lucas. She resolutely pushed them aside, but when she looked for a pair of gloves to wear the only ones suitable were the lemon satin, and she could not bring herself to wear them again. The past weeks at Croft Cottage had taken their toll of her hands, which were not quite so soft and white as they had been, but that could not be helped. It was honest toil and, since the assemblies were for everyone in and around Stanton, many of those dancing tonight would have hands even more chapped and rough than hers.

Annabelle had been obliged to let her maid go

when they had moved to Croft Cottage, but she was becoming quite adept at putting up her own hair. When she regarded herself in the little mirror on her dressing table she was quite pleased with the result and liked the way the soft brown curls danced about her head when she moved. She might no longer be mistress of Oakenroyd, but she was still passably pretty and hopefully would not lack for partners tonight.

Annabelle entered the assembly rooms as part of the Rishworths' party, prepared to remain firmly in the background, but she was greeted warmly by those already gathered in the rooms, several people going out of their way to enquire after her health and that of her father.

'And why should you not be so well received?' demanded Lady Rishworth, when Annabelle remarked upon it. 'You and Mr Havenham have always been highly respected. That has not changed, not amongst your true friends, and you have many of those.'

Reassured, Belle linked arms with Celia and they went off to join their young friends. As they passed Mrs Kensley, the widow stepped in their path.

'Miss Rishworth, good evening—and Miss Havenham, how good to see you have not allowed your reverses to stop you from enjoying yourself.'

'As you see, ma'am,' said Annabelle, coolly.

'And your friend Miss Scanlon—Mrs Keighley, I *should* say—is away on her honeymoon now,' continued the widow, the smile she gave them not quite reaching her eyes. 'And we all thought Keighley had you in mind for his life partner, Miss Havenham.' She patted Belle's hand, saying as she walked away, 'How sad that the loss of a fortune should mean the loss of one's suitors, too.'

'Yes, but your husband had to die to get away from you!' muttered Celia, rigid with fury.

Annabelle shushed her, but the widow was already out of earshot.

'Odious woman, how dare she say such things to you?'

'It is no more than the truth, after all,' said Belle quietly. 'And it is not as if I was ever enamoured of Mr Keighley, so I have lost nothing.'

'No, and as Mama said, your true friends will not desert you.'

That certainly seemed to be the case. Many gentlemen of her acquaintance were happy to partner her on the dance floor, as well as several of Oakenroyd's tenants, who had previously been too diffident to ask their landlord's daughter to stand up with them. One of these was Elias

Greenwood, whose wife was so near her confinement that she would only watch the dancers from the benches at the side of the room.

Once Annabelle had enquired after his family, she could not resist asking Elias how work was progressing at Morwood.

'Coming on a treat, miss. T'would do your heart good to see the place. 'Tis going to be a grand house when it's finished and no mistake. I am sorry that you cannot ride over and see it for yourself, although I am sure Mr Blackstone would fetch you. Perhaps I could ask him for you...'

Hastily Annabelle declined the offer and was glad that the energetic dance made further conversation impossible.

The mood in the assembly was very merry. The hard work of the harvest was over and everyone was determined to enjoy themselves. As the evening went on and glasses of wine and punch were imbibed, the atmosphere became even more boisterous.

'Are you glad you came, Belle?' asked Celia when they were sitting down together during a break in the dancing.

'Very much,' replied Annabelle, fanning herself.

It was true. For a while she had been able to

forget the constraints of her new life and lose herself in the dancing, but her friend's next words brought back all her anxieties.

'Good heavens, Mr Blackstone has arrived and he has a friend with him.' Celia sat up, her eyes shining with speculation. 'A military gentleman, too. How handsome he looks in his regimentals.'

Through the shifting crowd Annabelle could just see Lucas's black form and, beside him, a fair-haired man in a red coat.

'He is limping slightly,' observed Celia. 'A wounded war hero, perhaps.'

'That makes him even more interesting,' agreed Annabelle, a laugh in her voice.

Her amusement fled, however, when the two gentlemen came towards them. She made to leave, but Celia clamped her hand on her arm, forcing her to remain in her place and muttering a command to her to smile. She tried to comply, but with Lucas towering over her and the memory of their last encounter still fresh in her mind, it was all she could do not to run away.

'Miss Rishworth, Miss Havenham. Allow me to present my cousin to you, Captain Hugh Duggan.'

Lucas stood back as soon as he had made the introduction, allowing his cousin to do all the talking. Hugh was good at that. He was five years older than Lucas and was always a great favourite at parties. His charming manners and ready smiles might grate upon Lucas, but the ladies seemed to like it. Even now Miss Rishworth was engaging Hugh in conversation, and Annabelle had her eyes fixed upon Hugh's handsome face as if she was captivated by his every word. Damn him.

'So you are staying at Oakenroyd, Captain Duggan,' said Celia, making great play with her fan.

'I am indeed.' Hugh cast a laughing glance at Lucas. 'I decided to visit my cousin and arrived in Stanton today, expecting to put up here at the Red Lion, only to find that Lucas has bought Oakenroyd!'

'Yes, it was Miss Havenham's home until very recently,' put in Celia, in case their new acquaintance should say anything untoward.

'Indeed?' Hugh turned his charming smile upon Annabelle. 'Of course. Havenham. I should have remembered the name. I was used to visit Lucas's family when they lived at Morwood, you see. That is why I came to Stanton. I heard my cousin had bought the old place and was curious to see what he is doing to it. Then to find he owns Oakenroyd as well. It is a charming house,

Miss Havenham. You must be sad to leave it. But you are still living locally?'

'Yes, we live in Stanton now. At Croft Cottage.'

'A cottage?' Hugh laughed. 'How romantic. I hope I may be allowed to visit you there.'

Lucas waited to hear no more; he excused himself and walked away. His cousin no longer needed him, he had the sort of easy-going nature that allowed him to fit in anywhere.

Hugh had arrived earlier that day while Lucas was at Morwood, and had already established himself in a guest room by the time Lucas returned to Oakenroyd. Lucas could hardly blame Gibson. The butler had understood from George Stebbing that Hugh was his cousin and had raised no demur about his staying. And of course there *was* no problem about it. If Lucas had been there to meet him he would have been obliged to put him up, even though he had never felt less like company in his life.

Yesterday he had ridden back from Oldroyd Farm, barely able to see for the blind rage that had overtaken him. Annabelle was wrong. She had made the most outrageous allegations against his father in an attempt to protect her own. How dared she accuse Jonas of setting fire to his own house! If she had seen him, when he lay dying from the burns he had suffered trying to save his wife, she would know it was ridiculous to suggest any such thing.

Lucas had stormed back to Oakenroyd and spent the rest of the day in a black mood, unable to settle to anything. That night his sleep was disturbed by dreams, nightmares that took him back to that awful night twenty-five years ago, the shouts, the screams, the awful roar of the flames and the smell of burning. The memory had followed him into wakefulness today, as had Annabelle's accusations.

Samuel's letter was still in the side drawer of his travelling writing box. As soon as he was dressed Lucas went to the study and took it out. It was pristine, since he had done little more than break the seal before shutting it away. He read it through from beginning to end. The tone was measured, scholarly, like its author and Lucas quickly dismissed it as Samuel's attempt to justify himself. But he forced himself to re-read it, to calmly consider the arguments.

It was then that the doubts had begun. Memories he had suppressed for so many years, the arguments, his mother's tears, locked doors, blows. The voices arguing beneath his window on the night of the fire.

Damn you, Havenham, she's my wife! No one shall have her if I cannot...

No! It could not be true. Lucas had taken himself off to Morwood after breakfast, throwing himself into the work there to try and forget, but when he had arrived back at Oakenroyd he was confronted by another reminder of the past. His cousin Hugh Duggan, urbane, smiling, confident of his welcome. It had been an effort to be hospitable and Lucas had decided that coming to the assembly was preferable to sitting alone with his cousin all night.

Having introduced Hugh to several acquaintances, he now felt at liberty to take himself off to the card room where he need not make idle chit-chat with anyone.

The presence of Captain Duggan certainly brought a little buzz of excitement into the assembly rooms. His red coat stood out boldly amongst the general blacks and browns and when he announced laughingly that his intention was to dance with every young lady in the room, Annabelle was aware of a positive *frisson* of anticipation running through the ladies gathered about her. Watching him as he worked his way through the little group, she thought his constant smiles and ready charm a little disingenuous, but no one else seemed to think there was anything wanting. She concluded sadly that her nature was somewhat contrary. How else could she account for the fact that she preferred harsher features and a rather more abrupt manner? Quickly she buried all thoughts of Lucas Blackstone. She was done with him and would not allow him to hurt her again.

Belle turned her thoughts to the entertainment on offer for the evening. Since she was here she would dance and dance and think of nothing else. The tears, the regrets would be banished for a few short hours. Surely she could allow herself that small respite? There were plenty of partners willing to oblige her, including Captain Duggan, who proved to be an excellent dancer. That particular set was followed by a short interval and she allowed him to carry her off to the refreshment table where they were soon joined by a number of young ladies.

'Do you make a long stay in Stanton, Captain?' asked one, rather breathlessly.

'That depends upon how long Blackstone will have me.'

'Surely he would not throw you out,' declared Celia. 'He is your cousin, is he not?'

'He is, Miss Rishworth. His father was my mother's brother, and after my own father died, Mother and I often stayed at Morwood. Blackstone and I were very close, as children, but after the fire he went to live with other relatives and we lost touch. Even though I am his heir I did not see him again until a couple of years ago, in Brussels.'

'Ah, you were at Waterloo together,' exclaimed Celia. 'How exciting that must have been.'

'It was,' he agreed. 'But we were not *together* as such. That is, we were not in the same regiment. My cousin was in the guards, a major. I was merely a lowly captain of infantry. However, it was fortunate for me that he was there. He rescued me from the battlefield, you know, when I had been struck down. Recognised me amongst the fallen and carried me to safety. Hoisted me on his own shoulders to do it, too.' He tapped his leg. 'I'd taken a bullet through the thigh. Dashed lucky not to lose the whole leg, and it's left me with a slight limp, but as you can all bear witness, it don't affect me when I dance.'

He gave a merry laugh and the ladies gathered around him, only too willing to sympathise and admire his bravery. Belle smiled to herself. Captain Duggan positively *basked* in their attentions. She slipped away unnoticed and went off to join Lady Rishworth until the dancing commenced again.

Lucas spent a couple of hours in the card room where he lost heavily, wandering back to the ballroom in time to see Hugh dancing with Celia Rishworth. Annabelle was dancing too, partnered by Henry Blundell, the bookseller. He wondered if Hugh had danced with her. If not, he would certainly do so before the evening was out. Hugh made a point of dancing with all the pretty girls at any party, and even though she was wearing a gown he had seen before and with her hair dressed with a simple ribbon, Lucas thought Annabelle Havenham very pretty.

Watching her, Lucas did not think she was enjoying herself. Her smile was forced and the enticing sparkle had gone from her eyes. Had he caused that change in her? He kept his distance, remembering her distress yesterday, but he could not look away as the dance ended and Blundell escorted his partner from the floor. He disliked the way the bookseller had his hand on her back, as if he owned her. And he was leaning over her, far too close. Lucas's brows snapped together. The fellow would never have taken such liberties when she was mistress of Oakenroyd. Did he think now she was poor she deserved any less respect? Annabelle was trying to disengage herself, even as her escort was hustling her towards the door. The flush on Blundell's cheek told its own tale. Confound it, the man was drunk.

Lucas shouldered his way through the crowd. 'Ah, there you are, Miss Havenham. Have you forgotten that you promised me this next dance?'

He stepped into the couple's path and they

were obliged to stop. Annabelle was biting her lip and looking as if she was caught between the devil and the deep sea. Lucas thought wryly that he could guess which one of those disasters she thought him to be. But at least he was not drunk, nor did he have lecherous intentions towards her—at least, not at that moment—so he stepped up, intimidating the bookseller with his superior height and weight.

Belle had not been enjoying Henry Blundell's attentions, but how she wished it had been anyone other than Lucas who had stepped in to help her. His being in the room was painful enough, but to have him standing so close, his powerful presence enveloping her, brought back every hurt he had inflicted, as well as memories of his embrace, which she found even more agonising, knowing that it had meant nothing to him and everything to her. She owed him nothing. If he could rid her of Mr Blundell, then all the better, but she would not remain in his presence a moment longer than necessary.

'Oh, right, yes. Of course.' Blundell released his fair partner and stepped back, mumbling something about misunderstanding.

Lucas ignored him. He put his hand beneath Annabelle's elbow and firmly guided her away. He was determined to remain calm, but when she was so close, her scent filling his head, a madness came over him, a desire for her to realise just what she was throwing away by rejecting him. He could not resist a warning issued in arctic tones.

'You should be more careful, Miss Havenham. Men like Blundell see women in your situation as easy prey.' She did not reply, and when she pulled herself out of his grip some of his icy politeness disappeared and he rasped out, 'You should be grateful to me for rescuing you.'

Her response was low, but despite the chatter around them he heard every word.

'Do you think I can be grateful to a man who has so effectively ruined my life and that of my father?'

He flinched at her bitterness and he forgot his resolve to be coldly correct. He wanted only to strike back.

'Your father? Hah! His current situation is nothing less than he deserves.'

She stopped and swung round to face him, her eyes sparkling, cheeks flushed with anger.

'That is not true. His letter explains—'

'That damned letter was nothing more than a cowardly attempt to—'

She slapped him, hard, across the face.

Chapter Twelve

Annabelle's hand stung with the force of the blow. Her bare skin contacting with his cheek was like a pistol shot and since the orchestra had not yet struck up again, the sound caused those closest to them to turn and stare. Almost immediately they were surrounded by concerned faces.

Elias Greenwood came up, his pleasant face unusually grim and his fists clenched.

'Miss Belle, can I be of assistance?'

'Let me pass!' Sir John Rishworth pushed his way through to her. 'Madam—' his glance quickly summed up the situation '—if Blackstone has offered you an insult—'

The crowd around them continued to grow. Mr Scanlon stepped forwards, offering mute support, and Annabelle saw even more familiar faces ranged about her, willing to take her side against Lucas. This was her chance. She could denounce him, call upon them to defend her. She could ruin Lucas's good standing with his neighbours in an instant.

Even as the angry thoughts whirled through her head she knew she could not do it. Despite the good harvest, times were hard. Elias Greenwood would lose his position as Lucas's foreman and possibly his farm if he stood up for her. Nor could the townspeople afford to antagonise him. And she could not embroil Sir John in this argument. A rift between local landowners could only bring more misery for the whole area.

'It was nothing,' she said, making sure she spoke clearly enough for everyone around her to hear. 'It was a jest, a silly misunderstanding, which is now resolved.' With an effort she looked at Lucas. The angry marks of her fingers were already showing on his cheek and she could tell by the rapid rise and fall of his chest and the glitter in his eyes that he was furious, but he remained silent, which was all that was required. She turned to Sir John. 'If you will excuse me, I think I should go home.'

'Of course. I will escort you.'

He led her away. The moment was over, but there would be others, since nothing was resolved. Belle knew that every time she met Lucas Blackstone there would be conflict.

Lucas watched her walk away. His cheek burned, but that was nothing to the maelstrom of anger and self-loathing raging inside him. He deserved flogging for taunting her so and would almost have welcomed being called to account by Rishworth or one of her other champions. But she had not allowed that. She knew the damage it would do. He was humbled by her actions, while his own had not been those of a gentleman. It behoved him to beg her pardon and he would do so. He would have to do so.

The orchestra struck up and the crowd began to move away, speculating on the cause of the outburst. He heard the words 'lovers' tiff', and 'the fellow must be drunk'. Let them think what they liked and be damned to the lot of them!

'By heaven, Cousin, I never thought to see you involved in such a fracas.' Hugh Duggan was at his side, grinning. 'What did you say to her? It must have been outrageous to make her slap your face.'

'It was.' Lucas raked a hand through his hair. 'I am going back to Oakenroyd. Do you want to stay on here?'

Hugh clapped a hand on his shoulder.

'No, I will come with you. I have had enough excitement for one evening.'

When they arrived at Oakenroyd Lucas walked directly to the drawing room.

'Brandy?' He held up the decanter as Hugh followed him into the room.

'Please. Something on your mind, Cos?' he asked. 'You have been dashed quiet all evening. Then that little incident with the lady...'

'Yes, as a matter of fact.' Lucas handed a glass to Hugh and carried his own to a chair on one side of the fire. He waited until they were both seated and even then he did not speak immediately. He kept going over the words in his head, trying to find the best way to explain.

'You remember, Hugh, when Morwood burned down?'

'Aye, of course. How could I forget it?'

'I don't think it was an accident.'

Hugh clasped his hands around his glass and watched him. 'What makes you think that?' he said carefully.

'The fire was discovered in the drawing room, but by then the east wing was well alight at the opposite end of the house. There was no way the fire could have spread like that naturally.' He paused, forcing himself to keep calm. 'I saw someone that night. Someone moving around the outside of the house. And I saw the glow of a light. I thought nothing of it at the time, thought it was the light from a cigar, but it could have been a taper.' Lucas stopped again, not wanting to ask the question, but knowing he had to do so.

'Do you think it could have been my father?' When Hugh said nothing he continued, 'I have been trying to think. You remember there was an almighty row that night, after we had gone up to our rooms?'

'Yes, of course. Your father had been in a black mood all day, which was why we took ourselves off to the lake, fishing. Then Mama went up to bed, and told us we should do the same, to get out of the way.'

'That just left three people in the dining room. My father, my mother and Samuel Havenham.'

'Miss Havenham's father?'

'Yes.' He shot a glance at his cousin. 'He was in love with my mother.'

Hugh was silent for a moment, digesting this information. 'I beg your pardon, Lucas, but I have to ask you. Were they lovers?'

Lucas shook his head. 'I think not.' He bit his lip. 'But my father was not an easy man. You knew that, Hugh, you were there often enough to see it. He had a terrible temper. Your mother would take herself off to her room and we would disappear into the grounds out of the way, but

Mama—' He finished his brandy. 'She was not happy. Father had made her life a misery. Looking back, I can see it now. Havenham urged her to go abroad with him and that night she had decided she would do so. Do you think...?' He fixed his eyes upon his cousin. 'Is it possible, if my father knew this, if he was in a rage, that he would have set fire to Morwood?'

Silence hung around them. Hugh looked down at his glass, turning it between his hands.

'You said yourself my uncle was a hard man,' he said at last. 'He was not the sort to settle for anything less than perfection. If his wife was unfaithful—'

'She wasn't,' said Lucas swiftly. 'I would stake my life she would not have thought of going off with Havenham if my father had not pushed her to it.'

'But if he couldn't have her, no one would.'

Lucas looked up. 'What made you say that?'

Hugh shrugged. 'I cannot say. I think I must have overheard Uncle Jonas say as much.'

'So you think it possible he was so enraged he set fire to the house?'

'Yes,' agreed Hugh. 'It is very possible. Nay, it's likely. I am very sorry, old fellow, but there it is.'

Lucas closed his eyes. He did not want to believe it. Every fibre of his being cried out against the idea of his father as a murderer.

'It does not make sense,' he said slowly. 'Why should he work so hard to try to put out the fire? And he went back for my mother.'

'Perhaps he came to his senses once he saw the damage he had done. And thank heavens you were awake and raised the alarm,' added Hugh, 'or we might all have been burned in our beds.'

'If my mother had not locked herself in her apartments then we might have been able to save her, too,' said Lucas. 'My father tried to force the door, but he was beaten back by the flames—'

He broke off, shaking his head to dispel the memories that crowded in.

'Too late to think of that now, Cos.' Hugh rose from his chair. 'I am going to bed and I advise you to do the same. There is no point worrying over something that happened so long ago.' He put his glass down on the sideboard and walked to the door. He reached for the handle, but stopped and looked back. 'That little affair with Miss Havenham tonight, does that have anything to do with what we have been discussing?'

Lucas paused for a heartbeat.

'How could it?' he said at last. 'She was not even born when all this occurred.'

* * *

Samuel was still playing chess with Dr Bennett when Annabelle arrived home. She managed to smile when they quizzed her about leaving the assembly before the final note had been played and she retired quickly to her room, saying she was fatigued. But it was a long time before she slept. She was angry with Lucas for tormenting her, but even more angry with herself for lashing out. They could not agree, it was unlikely that they ever would, so she must find some way to avoid his company. Leaving Stanton seemed to be the only solution. Yet how could she leave? How could she take her father even further away from his friends and everything he held dear?

Annabelle awoke to the sound of the rain dripping from the eaves outside her window. The dismal weather matched her mood. Heavy cloud hung low over the town and the rain poured down steadily. She wanted only to bury her head under the bedclothes and go back to sleep, but there was work to be done, so she slipped out of bed, trying to throw off her depression. When they had lived at Oakenroyd she had ridden Apollo on many such days as this and enjoyed it, so she would not let the weather prevent her from going out.

Having to walk everywhere was taking a toll

on her shoes and she must take at least one pair to the cobbler to be mended. Wrapped in her cloak and armed with her umbrella, she set off for the cobbler's house. It was market day and despite the rain Stanton was bustling. Not only was the square filled with animals and stalls packed with local goods, but farmers and corn merchants were making their way to the Red Lion to do business, taking or placing orders and settling accounts. Belle hurried through the crowds, thankful that the pouring rain made everyone disinclined to stop and talk. Once her errand was complete she made her way back along the main street, holding the umbrella low to keep the worst of the rain from her head and shoulders.

'Miss Havenham.'

That deep, familiar voice broke into her thoughts and she stopped. She was aware of a pair of muddy top boots standing in her path. As she raised her umbrella the rest of Lucas Blackstone appeared. He was wearing a wide-brimmed hat, from which the rain dripped on to the shoulders of his caped driving coat. Even his sodden appearance could not stop her heart drumming heavily against her ribs, nor prevent the exquisitely painful yearning from enveloping her once more. In silence she tried to turn it all against him, to summon up every ounce of anger she should feel for him. He wasted no time on pleasantries, not that she wanted them.

'I came to see you. Your father said you had gone out.'

He was blunt, straight to the point. Well, she could do that, too.

'As you see, sir, and I would like to get home as soon as possible.'

'I shall not detain you long. I wanted to apologise for my behaviour last night. It was inexcusable.'

Annabelle said nothing. She glanced at the road. If she stepped off the pavement she could walk around him, but the muddy water was ankle-deep in the gutter. If he did not remove himself soon, then she would suffer that unpleasantness rather than remain in his presence a moment longer.

'I also wanted to say…' he spoke again, with obvious difficulty. 'I wanted you to know I…I could be wrong. About the fire.' For the first time she looked up into his face. What she could see of it beneath the brim of his hat appeared more rugged than ever. Haggard, even, as if he had not slept. 'I have read your father's letter and—I can see that there may be some doubt. That is all.' He stepped back. 'I shall not plague you further. Good day, Miss Havenham.'

With a slight nod he turned and strode away.

Belle watched him, her thoughts and feelings once more in a tumult. Just when she had decided he was beyond forgiveness he had surprised her with an apology and an admission that he might be mistaken.

In a daze Annabelle walked on to Croft Cottage and hung up her wet clothes. While she bustled about the little house, her thoughts careered around wildly, but they kept coming back to Lucas. Papa would be pleased to think he was willing to consider that someone else might have set fire to Morwood, but with Oakenroyd sold it would make very little difference to their circumstances. She decided to say nothing to her father. Lucas himself must speak to him. They were engaged to dine at Rishworth Lodge that evening and there was every chance Lucas would be there. If so, she would make sure he knew what was expected of him.

By late afternoon the rain had eased, but the roads were still too wet for comfort and, having refused Sir John's offer to send the carriage for them, Annabelle hired a gig to take them the mile or so out of Stanton to Rishworth Lodge. The vehicle and its sturdy pony were spattered with mud by the time Annabelle drew to a halt at the door. A lackey hastened out to take the gig to the stables, leaving Annabelle and her father to go indoors where their hostess was waiting.

'Just a snug little gathering,' Lady Rishworth announced, leading them into the drawing room. 'I have invited Mr and Mrs Scanlon to join us. They are feeling the loss of Lizzie quite desperately, but there, that is what happens when one marries off a daughter.' She glanced at Celia. 'I have invited Mr Blackstone, of course, and his cousin Captain Duggan, whom Celia insisted should be included.'

'Well, you could hardly leave him out, Mama,' remarked Celia, coming up. 'He is staying at Oakenroyd, after all.' She reached for Annabelle's hand. 'You are the first to arrive, and I am going to take you away to a corner and make you tell me just what it was Mr Blackstone said to upset you last night.'

Samuel looked up quickly. 'Upset, Belle? What is this?'

'No, no, it was all a mistake, Papa,' Annabelle was quick to reassure him. 'Mr Blackstone was funning, only I did not understand him.' She managed to laugh. 'It was a silly trifle, and I am afraid one or two people thought we had quite fallen out, but it was nothing, I assure you.'

'Well, it certainly looked to be more than nothing,' observed Celia with alarming frankness. 'You with your face as red as anything, and Mr Blackstone looking positively murderous—'

Sir John held up his hand to silence his daughter. 'Celia, you are embarrassing Miss Havenham by bringing up a subject she would much rather forget. Let us talk of more pleasant matters. Mr Havenham, I am so glad you are well enough to join us this evening. Come and sit by the fire, sir, and take a glass of mulled wine to drive off the evening chill…'

'So what was it, Belle?' Celia put her arm through Annabelle's and led her away. 'You can tell *me*. Captain Duggan was sure it was a lovers' quarrel.'

The coaxing tone in her friend's voice did not tempt Belle to confide. She smiled and shook her head, leaving Celia to her own conjectures. These would most likely run to some lurid romantic entanglement, but even that was better than confessing the truth. So Belle kept her own counsel and waited for Lucas to arrive.

Her hopes were dashed when Captain Duggan came in alone.

'My cousin sends his apologies,' he informed his host, his bluff, cheerful voice easily carrying around the drawing room. 'He is not feeling quite the thing this evening.' The captain turned to Sir John with a comical grimace and mouthed the word 'foxed'.

Belle frowned at the impropriety of such a disclosure and even Sir John's good-natured smile disappeared momentarily.

For Annabelle the evening was not a success. She enjoyed talking to Mrs Scanlon, who was eager to share news of Lizzie, whose letters home from her honeymoon were reassuringly full of her 'dearest Keighley' and the delightful time they were having in the capitals of Europe, but she found Captain Duggan's constant geniality very wearing. He was determined to be on good terms with everyone, gently flirting with the ladies and treating the gentlemen with a boisterous bonhomie that occasionally made her father wince. By eleven o'clock she had a headache, and was not at all displeased when her father indicated that he would like to go home.

Alert for his elderly friend's comfort, Sir John immediately sent for the gig and the party began to break up. As Samuel was being helped into his greatcoat, Captain Duggan came up and offered to escort them to Stanton.

'That is very kind of you, Captain,' said Samuel, 'but we would not want to take you so far out of your way.'

'Not at all, sir. As a matter of fact, that *is* my way tonight. There is a card party going forwards at the Red Lion this evening and I am invited to look in.' He grinned. 'I have booked a room there for tonight, too. I would rather not be at Oakenroyd with Blackstone so sunk in gloom. Takes after his father, you see. When we were boys we would always make ourselves scarce when Jonas was in one of his black rages.'

An uncomfortable little silence followed these unguarded revelations, but the captain did not appear to notice and cheerfully prepared to escort Annabelle and her father into Stanton. The journey was not a long one and Annabelle elected to drive, knowing that she would rather give her attention to controlling the pony than try to make small talk with Captain Duggan. When they reached the Red Lion Samuel assured him that they could manage the rest of the short journey quite safely, and with a flourish of his hat the captain took his leave of them.

'A genial enough fellow,' said Samuel as their escort disappeared through the arch and into the inn's yard. 'A little indiscreet, though. I cannot think it was quite the thing to talk about his cousin so.'

'I am sure it was not,' agreed Annabelle. 'If Mr Blackstone is not well, his cousin should be giving him his support, keeping him company.'

'Perhaps the young man does not want company. And if he has drunk a little too much—'

He spread his hands. 'Strange, though. I had not thought Blackstone a man to succumb to the bottle.'

Annabelle bit her lip, remembering Lucas's gaunt face that morning. 'Perhaps he has had some bad news.'

'Perhaps. I do hope it is nothing too serious.'

They had reached the cottage and as Belle pulled up she turned to smile fondly at her father.

'Dear Papa, you can wish him well, after all he has done to us?'

'Of course,' he said simply. 'To lose his parents at such a young age and to believe they suffered an injustice—that is a grave burden for anyone to carry. I believe Lucas Blackstone is a very troubled young man, despite his fortune.' He threw the rug from his legs. 'Ah, good. Abel has seen our arrival. He will be able to take the gig back to the livery—'

'No.' Annabelle was thinking quickly. 'No, I will take it, Papa.'

'But, my dear, it is midnight!'

'And everything is quiet in Stanton, Papa. It is but a step to the stables and this section of the street is well lit. You are very tired, Papa, let Abel put you to bed and I shall be back shortly.' She looked up and addressed the manservant, who was waiting at the open door. 'Pray look after my father, Abel. And there is no need to wait up for me, I will let myself in when I return.'

The old retainer shook his head. 'You can let yerself in, miss, but I shall sit up and wait for 'ee once I've seen the master to his bed.'

Belle could see he would not be swayed and did not waste time on further argument. She set the little pony in motion again and glanced over her shoulder. The door of Croft Cottage was closed. With a deft flick of the reins she set the pony to a trot, past the entrance to the livery stable and out of the town.

Oakenroyd was quiet. The servants had all gone to bed and the house had settled into darkness and silence. Except in the study, where Lucas was sitting in twilight with only the sullen embers of the fire and a single burning candle to lift the gloom. He had discarded his coat and neckcloth, his waistcoat was undone and he was sprawled in his chair, his long legs stretched out towards the hearth, one ankle crossed over the other. On a small table at his elbow was his empty glass and a decanter of brandy.

He knew he should go to bed, but he was not ready to face the demons waiting there for him. Thank God Hugh had taken himself off. He might not approve of Hugh's predilection for gambling and keeping low company, but he was relieved now that Hugh had elected to stay out for the night. He almost wished he had not unburdened himself to his cousin. Hugh was trying to help, but his constant reminders of little incidents that had occurred in the past, evidence of his father's temper and violent moods, only added to Lucas's misery.

Black despair pervaded everything, it added to the guilt that gnawed at him. For over twenty years he had blamed the wrong man. Bad enough that he should have done so when he was a child, but when he returned to Stanton and met Samuel Havenham again he should have recognised the goodness in him. Even before reading Samuel's letter the evidence was there. The man was too kind, too gentle. He was incapable of such a gross act of violence.

As a boy Lucas had convinced himself that Samuel had coveted Morwood, that his whole aim had been to gain possession of the land. Coming back at five-and-thirty he should have realised that nothing was further from the truth. Samuel had done nothing to Morwood. He could not even bear to visit it because of the memories it evoked. His only crime was to allow a good house to go to ruin.

And to love Maria Blackstone. Knowing his own heart, Lucas could even forgive that, now, and if his mother had returned that love it was because she had not found it with Jonas. The memories he had denied for so long loomed large to taunt Lucas. His father had rarely raised a hand to his son, but when the black rage was upon him he would take it out upon Maria. Looking back, he recalled that his mother had always been at her happiest when Jonas was away.

All day he had wrestled with the problem. The beliefs, the certainties of the past five-and-twenty years had been overturned and he had to face the idea that Jonas had started the fire at Morwood. It was a bitter blow, and the wrong he had done to the Havenhams gnawed away at his conscience.

The thought of seeing Samuel and Annabelle at Rishworth Lodge, making polite conversation with them—it was not to be borne, so he had sent Hugh with his apologies. Lucas doubted he would be missed. Annabelle at least would be relieved. He refilled his glass. One more drink and he would seek his bed. Perhaps things would look better in the morning. He dropped his head in his hands. How could things ever look better? The implication, the guilt, the stain on his family name could never be erased.

He heard the faint scrape of the door handle.

George, perhaps, come to shepherd him off to bed. He looked up.

'What the devil—!' He jumped out of his chair. 'What in hell's name are you doing here?'

Chapter Thirteen

Annabelle stood in the doorway. The last person he expected, but the one he most wanted to see. He glanced down at the decanter, beginning to question just how much he had drunk. She had closed the door now and was standing with her back against it, watching him. She was wrapped head to toe in a voluminous cloak, but even in the gloom there was no mistaking that dear face, nor the eyes that looked at him so fearlessly.

'I was anxious for you. I came to see if you were all right.'

He laughed bitterly. 'Came to gloat, more like!'

She pushed back her hood. 'I would not do that.'

'No, you would not.' He shook his head, trying to clear the fog from his brain. 'No. You cannot be here.'

'But I am.'

She moved into the light, dispelling the lingering suspicion that she was a dream, conjured up by his imagination.

'You must go.' He tried to think of the reasons why she had to leave, but his whole being wanted her to stay. At last he said, lamely, 'My cousin will be returning soon.'

'No, he won't. Captain Duggan told us he is staying at the Red Lion tonight.'

He pushed his hand through his hair. 'I must be foxed or I would not let you remain here.' He peered towards the shuttered windows, frowning. 'The house is locked up for the night. The servants are all abed. How the deuce did you get in?'

'This was my home, Lucas. I do not need servants to show me the way.'

He could not bear the fond amusement in her voice and threw himself back in his chair. 'I will have every damned lock checked in the morning.' There was the whisper of silk skirts as she came closer. He growled, 'You cannot stay here.'

'Will you call your servants to throw me out?'

'The devil I will! If anyone knew you were here alone with me—'

'Quite.'

She knelt down by the hearth and added a couple of logs to the fire. The embers immediately came to life, sending yellow flames to lick around the dry wood. It enhanced the golden glow in the room, but then, it had seemed brighter from the moment she had appeared. She remained kneeling, hands stretched out to the warmth.

She said, keeping her eyes on the fire, 'Why did you not come to Rishworth Lodge tonight?'

'I needed to think.'

'About the fire at Morwood.'

'Of course. Suddenly I am faced with a new and fearsome possibility. One I had not considered.'

'That your father started the fire.'

'That he…murdered…my mother.' It was the first time he had uttered the awful thought aloud. The words echoed around in his head, taunting him. He gripped the arms of the chair. 'It is too horrendous…even now I can hardly credit it.'

'It is no more than you asked me to believe of my own father.'

The words were softly spoken, but they hammered into him, battering his already smarting conscience. He jerked forward, resting his elbows on his knees, hands clasped tightly together.

'I was so *certain*,' he said slowly. 'I know I

saw someone, a man…and not a servant, I am sure of that.'

'But you did not see his face.'

'No.'

'Then it may not have been your father.'

'The trouble is…' he chewed his lip '…the trouble is, I can believe my father might have started the fire. He was prone to fits of rage. He rarely lost his temper with me, but the servants, my mother—'

He stopped again, rubbing a hand across his face. The memories were too painful to recall and he had to push them away before he could continue.

'My father wanted more children. He often said he regretted that I was the only one. He blamed my mother for that. Maybe…' He exhaled, a long, slow breath. 'Perhaps, if there had been more children, he would have mellowed.'

'You cannot know that.'

Lucas stared into the fire. 'He loved her,' he said at last. 'Even if he did start the fire, he died trying to rescue her.'

She reached out and covered his hands with her own. 'Then hold on to that, Lucas. Remember he tried to save her.'

'Do you know what my greatest fear is?' His gaze shifted to the pale, ringless fingers wrapped over his. 'The hatred, my thirst for vengeance—

it was all-consuming. Even when I was in the army it was there, in the background, the knowledge that some day I would come back and demand justice. In the early days I thought only that I would become an expert with a sword and challenge your father to a duel, but as I grew older I wanted a more subtle reckoning. When I sold out I was prepared to spend everything on retribution. I could see nothing else, think of nothing else. It was only when I came here that I began to realise how much pain my plans would cause.'

'But you would not abandon them.'

He shook his head. 'No, but I did change them. At first it didn't matter what you thought of me, but then I decided the revenge would be all the sweeter if I made you fall in love with me.' His lip curled in self-disgust. 'Think how that would hurt Samuel. He had already told me you were his only joy.'

She withdrew her hands and immediately he missed their warm comfort. What else did he expect? What else did he deserve?

'Is that what you meant?' she asked quietly. 'At the Red Lion, when you told me not to think badly of you?'

'By then I knew I—' He sat up, pushing his hair back from his forehead with an impatient hand. 'I knew I did not want to hurt you. I thought—foolishly—that somehow I could punish your father, but make it up to you.'

'With marriage.'

'Yes.'

She did not respond. Silence enveloped them, broken only by the spit and crackle of the fire. A burning ember fell on to the hearthstone and absently he slid from his chair to sweep it up and add another log to the fire. He remained on his knees beside her, staring into the red-hot heart of the blaze.

'I have wronged you,' he said heavily. 'You and Samuel. I have spent all these years blaming an innocent man. I refused to see what was so plain to everyone else.'

'Not everyone, Lucas. It was only Samuel and Sir Angus, the old magistrate, who suspected your father.'

'And my cousin. He has pointed out to me enough instances of my father's ungovernable rages to convince me.' He shook his head. 'And I have been so blind, determined on my revenge, no matter what the consequences.' He swallowed, resolved to conceal nothing. 'I have inherited his temper, but I am even more culpable. My revenge was not the heat of the moment, it was carried out in a cold, calculated manner. Pure wickedness. I am the worst sort of villain.'

He closed his eyes, unable to put into words

the horror of his thoughts. In his army career
he had been an exemplary officer, tough, determined, but rigidly fair. He was aghast now at
how unjust he had been in his own affairs.

'Lucas.' He felt her hand on his shoulder.
'Lucas, you are no villain. You believed you
were doing what was right.'

'How can you say that?' He shrugged her off.
'How can you defend me?'

'Because if you were truly wicked you would
not feel like this.' Her hand touched him again,
this time on his cheek. She said softly, 'You are
a good man, Lucas Blackstone, I truly believe
that.'

He opened his eyes. She was kneeling beside
him, her face just inches below his own and there
were tears in her eyes. He shook his head.

'No. I am my father's son—'

'You are your own man, Lucas. Whatever
your father was, whatever he did, it is not your
fault.'

She cupped his face, gently pulled him down
to her and kissed him. For a moment he did not
move, but her arms crept around him. She drew
him closer, her lips working against his, parting
them and deepening the kiss. It was balm to his
wounded spirit and he responded, holding her
against his heart, allowing himself to forget ev-

erything except the relief, the joy of having her in his arms.

Annabelle leaned into him, her body melted as he drew her closer. Until then she had thought only of Lucas, wanting to comfort him, to drive the tortured, haunted look from his eyes, but as his tongue moved over her own she recognised the tug of desire deep inside, reminiscent of the feelings that had overwhelmed her in the dark, shadowy alcove at the Red Lion.

When she feared he was going to stop kissing her she caught his lip between her teeth and nipped it gently. His reaction startled and thrilled her. His whole body stiffened and he pulled her even closer. He began to cover her face with kisses. She let her head fall back, offering up her throat for the light, warm touch of his mouth. His lips nibbled at her skin and she moaned softly, her body responding, aching for more.

Gently he eased her down on to the floor. The cool satin lining of her cloak was some slight comfort, though she was hardly aware of it. She cared nothing for the boards beneath her, only for the man stretching himself out at her side. He pulled on the strings of her cloak and it fell away, leaving her neck and breasts free for him to ravish with kisses and caresses that set the blood pounding through her body. She had lost weight over the past few months and instead of fitting snugly over her breast, the bodice of her gown was loose enough to allow his hand to slide over one soft swell, his thumb circling the tender nub until it hardened. She gasped, her body arching towards him. She was eager for him to run his hands over every inch of her skin although some small, disconnected area of her brain knew this was impossible—they were both fully dressed.

Even as she thought it, his hand was gathering up her skirts. His fingers trailed over the bare flesh of her thigh, moving upwards, pushing aside the filmy folds of muslin. Belle knew a moment's panic as he reached the delicate spot at the top of her thighs. The knot of desire in her belly tightened, pulling on muscles from all around her lower body. Her legs parted at the oh-so-gentle pressure of his hand and it was all she could do not to cry out with longing as his fingers gently caressed her.

She had no idea when he had unfastened his breeches, but as he moved over her she felt his flesh upon hers and instinctively her hips arched upwards, inviting him in. His fingers had prepared the way, she was hot and slick with desire. Her body flinched a little as he pushed into her, but it was a pleasurable pain and she found herself moving against him, matching his rhythm whilst returning the hot, passionate kisses that he pressed upon her mouth. She had never known anything like this, to be so close to another person, so at one.

He held her close, whispering her name, his body stroking hers, lifting her spirit until she felt as if she was flying. When he stopped kissing her she threw back her head, gasping for air. She felt such joy, such exhilaration she wanted to cry out. Her body was moving of its own accord, in unison with his, and the wave inside her was building, threatening to crest and flood her senses. Lucas gave a groan, a gasp. Belle clung on tightly, aware of him over, around, inside her. She was almost swooning, her body locked into a spasm of uncontrollable pleasure as he thrust into her again and again before collapsing down beside her, his passion spent.

Silence followed. Annabelle cradled Lucas in her arms, smoothed the dark hair from his brow and held him until his breathing steadied. Now the moment was over she was aware of how undignified they must look with their clothes in such disarray. But it did not matter, it did not matter one jot.

Until Lucas groaned and rolled away from her. 'Dear heaven, I must be more drunk than I knew.'

No gentle words of love. His tone was one of profound regret. Belle closed her eyes, determined not to cry. Carefully she sat up and pulled her skirts down into a more decorous position.

'What the hell did you think you were doing?' he demanded roughly, tucking in his shirt and fastening his breeches.

'I wanted to comfort you.'

His breath whistled out through his teeth. 'So to all the grievances your father has against me is now added your seduction. Folly! Do you not realise just what you have done?'

'I did not know how else to reach you,' she told him in a small voice.

'Oh, you reached me,' he muttered, turning to face her. 'You reached me only too well.'

The glow in his eyes and his rueful smile drove away the chill that had been forming around her heart, but it hovered, not quite banished. Something in his manner made her uneasy. He rose and held out his hand to her.

'Come, make yourself tidy, and I will take you home.'

'Then what do you propose to do?'

'Do not look so anxious, my dear, I do not intend to abandon you. Tomorrow I shall call upon your father, explain the whole, confess the full extent of my transgressions towards him… and to you, my dear. Then I shall set about putting things right. You shall return to Oakenroyd. The lawyers will handle the whole, no one need know what has occurred, save that your father has come into funds and I am restoring his former home to him. To you.'

'And what about us, Lucas?'

She had given him her hand to pull her to her feet. Now he turned the hand over and stared at it, running his thumb over the roughened skin. He released her and turned away.

'There is no "us", Belle. You have every right to demand that I marry you for what has just occurred, but you know as well as I that it would not work. There is too much between us that cannot be put right.'

Belle stared at his back. 'You d-do not want me.'

With an anguished growl he swung round. 'Want? Of course I—' Exhaling, he looked up as if searching for a solution in the dark shadows above them, then he reached out for her. He took her hands and looked at them, saying softly, 'My dear, do you not see how impossible this is? You should hate me for all I have done to you and your father. I hate myself for it, but it is more than that. My family name is ruined. By his heinous act my father has destroyed any hope I had of happiness.' He added quickly, anticipating her response, 'And before you tell me that it does not matter, that no one knows, it *does* matter, because *I* know of it and I cannot, will not allow you to share my shame.'

He looked at her then, the pain in his black eyes so angry, so deep it sliced into her heart like a knife. She clung to his hands.

'Lucas, let me help you—'

'No.' There was a finality in his voice that silenced her. 'No one can help me, especially not you, Belle. I have my father's quick temper. I know now that it destroyed him and everything he held dear. I will not risk the same thing happening to you.'

'But I don't believe—'

'It is not a question of what you believe, it is what I *know*.'

'But you have been wrong before,' she challenged him. 'There may be some other explanation.'

'I think you are clutching at straws, my dear.' He picked up her cloak and put it around her shoulders. 'How did you get here?'

'In the gig we hired to take us to Rishworth Lodge. It is in the stable yard.'

'Who knows you are here?'

'Only Clegg. He heard me arrive and is looking after the horse.'

'Good. We can trust him to say nothing. I'll have him saddle Sultan and tie him to the back of the gig. I am going to drive you home.'

Silently Belle fastened the strings of her cloak. Her hands shook a little but she managed. Everything had taken on an unreal quality, as if she was in some dream from which she would wake up very soon. Lucas put his hand in the small of her back to move her towards the door, but she resisted him. One last attempt.

'What if...what if there is a child from, from what we have done? Will you not marry me then?'

Lucas closed his eyes. Marriage. If only he could take her as his wife, but it would not work. The bitter memories he had shut out for so long rose up again to taunt him, the sadness in his mother's eyes when she looked at his father. There had been fear there, too. Why had he not recognised it at the time? He would not risk hurting Belle like that, nor any child she might be carrying. And to give them a tainted name, how could that make things any better?

'I will do all that I can to protect you, Belle. Neither you nor your child would want for anything, but marriage—no. You would come to hate me.'

'But—'

'Enough,' he broke in roughly. 'It is time to go.'

The cold chill returned at his implacable tone.

She had given herself to him and he was turning her away.

Foolish Annabelle. It was your choice, now you must pay for it.

She moved towards the door, but stopped suddenly. 'Lucas.' She raised her hand and pointed. Lying on a small table beside the door was a pistol, the long barrel gleaming dully in the dim light. 'Oh heavens, Lucas, were you—?'

Her voice trailed off and she looked up at him, aghast.

'What?' He glanced towards the little table. 'Oh, that. It is my cousin's, he was showing it to me before he went out and must have left it lying there. Damned careless of him.' He frowned at her. 'Did you think I was contemplating blowing my brains out? That is not my way, believe me.'

He escorted her out of the room and Belle kept her eyes firmly away from the wicked-looking pistol as she went past it.

The moon had almost set and there was barely enough light to see the road as Lucas drove the gig into Stanton. Annabelle was silent beside him, her thoughts dulled by everything that had occurred. He pulled up a little before the turning to the livery stable.

'You had best return the gig,' he said. 'I will wait for you here and walk you home.'

Without a word she took the reins and when he had jumped down and unfastened Sultan, she drove the gig into the livery yard and handed it over to a sleepy stable hand.

Lucas was waiting for her when she returned to the High Street, the solid shape of his horse standing silently behind him. Nothing else moved and she was glad of his escort for the short distance to Croft Cottage.

'You are coming to see my father tomorrow.'

'Yes.'

'He will forgive you,' she said confidently. 'He will tell you not to be so hard on yourself.'

'After all I have done, especially the harm I have done to you?' Lucas shook his head. 'I doubt it.' He stopped at the door of Croft Cottage.

'Do not knock,' she whispered as he raised his hand. 'I have a key.'

'Very well.' He turned to her. The lamp beside the door was behind him, and his face was in deep shadow. 'Until tomorrow. I shall insist upon seeing your father alone.'

'Of course. You will tell him what happened this evening?'

'I must.'

'And if…' She stopped to run her tongue nervously across her lips. 'If he should insist upon you marrying me?'

'He won't.'

With a nod he left her. Annabelle watched him scramble into the saddle and ride away before she let herself quietly into the house.

Annabelle was not looking forward to seeing her father the following morning, but it could not be put off. Abel had been dozing in the chair when she had let herself into the house and would be sure to tell his master that she had not come home until almost dawn, so some explanation would be required. Samuel had been both father and mother to her as she grew up and they had always been very close. They had agreed there should be no secrets between them, but even so it would be difficult to confess to him the enormity of her actions, yet she was determined that he should not learn of it from Lucas.

As soon as her father came downstairs she followed him into his study. The interview that followed was both difficult and painful, but Belle was determined to lay before her father everything that had occurred at Oakenroyd last night and to impress upon him that her visit there had been entirely her own idea. No blame should fall upon Lucas for what followed.

'It was not his fault at all, Papa. I—' She was on a low stool beside his chair, her hand resting on his arm, her head bowed because she could not bring herself to look at him. 'When he spoke of his father, he was so hurt, I just wanted to comfort him…'

'You let your kind heart run away with you, Belle.'

'Do you think I was wrong, sir? To—to give myself to him like that?'

'It was not wise, my love. In fact, I am very sorry for it, but it is not for me to judge you, when I myself had planned to run away with another man's wife.'

Her father's gentle restraint hurt Belle more than any amount of angry blustering and she reached for her handkerchief to wipe away a tear. Samuel put his hand on her hair.

'There, there, my love, it is too late to go back now. We must decide what is to be done. You say Lucas is coming to call upon me?'

'Yes, he wishes to atone for his behaviour towards you, Papa.'

'And how will he atone for his treatment of *you,* Belle? In such cases it is customary for the injured party to demand marriage. I have already advised you once against marrying Lucas Blackstone for the wrong reasons, but if you are carrying his child then that is a very different matter. Are you still opposed to marrying him?'

She looked down, the colour stealing into her cheeks. 'Not any more, Father.'

When he did not speak she looked up at him and was alarmed at how pale and grave he looked, but he was quick to assure her that he was not ill.

'You have given me a great deal to ponder, my love. Have Abel bring me a glass of wine and water, and leave me to consider all you have told me while I wait for my visitor.'

She could do no more until the two men had met. Knowing the time would pass much faster if she was busy, Annabelle went off to attend to her household duties. If all went well, in a few weeks she and her father might once again be at Oakenroyd, but for now Croft Cottage was her domain and she would have it spotless. She brushed and cleaned and polished until the little sitting room glowed and when she had finished she busied herself in the kitchen. She wanted to be at home when Lucas arrived, so she resolutely ignored her basket and the shopping list waiting for her on the table.

The morning turned to afternoon and still there was no knock at the door. The daily shopping could be delayed no longer and Belle set off for the market. She did not tarry over her purchases and when she returned she was informed by Abel that the master was closeted in his little study with Mr Blackstone. Her heart beating hard against her ribs, Belle put away her purchases and went upstairs to tidy her hair and change her gown. She wished she could know what they were saying, but she forced herself to be patient and took her embroidery to the sitting room.

She had slept very little, her thoughts too full of Lucas. She did not regret kissing him, nor anything that followed, save that he would not marry her. That he cared for her she was certain. In fact, he cared for her too much and was afraid he might hurt her, but she did not believe his temper was ungovernable. His quest for revenge had been cold and calculated, as were his plans now to make amends. She wanted to share his life, for good or ill, but he was afraid of making her unhappy. She gave a little sigh. Did he not realise that she would be wretched without him?

A heavy footstep in the hall and the banging of the front door brought her out of her reverie. She looked up in time to see Lucas's shadow fall across the window. He had gone, and without a word to her.

'Papa?' Annabelle peeped into the study. Samuel was sitting in his chair, fingers steepled and a look of profound sadness on his face. She closed the door and crossed the room. 'Papa, you have spoken with Lucas?'

'Yes. He called, as you told me he would, my love.'

'And what did he tell you?'

'He said he had been wrong, that he no longer believed I started the fire at Morwood.' Her father sighed. 'He made me a very full apology.'

'And you accepted?'

'Of course. I was very happy to do so. He is gone now to instruct his lawyer to draw up another deed of transfer for Oakenroyd. And he does not want a penny for it. In fact, he says he is going to write off the debts I incurred at Harrogate. I protested, of course, but he insisted. When all is done we shall be better off than before.'

'He is a good man, Father.'

'Yes, I think he is. He would have had us move back to Oakenroyd immediately, but I convinced him we should wait until he has seen his lawyer and everything is legally signed and settled.' He bent his kindly eyes upon her. 'We also talked about you, my love, and what occurred last night.'

She bit her lip. 'What did he say about it?'

'That he had taken advantage of you.'

'That is not true, Papa. I told you—'

'But he could have sent you away. He *should* have done so and he admitted as much to me.'

'He was not himself, Papa. I am sure he cares for me.'

'I do not doubt it.'

'Did he tell you so?' she asked hopefully.

'It was evident in the way he spoke about you.'

Samuel paused, considering his words and Belle said quietly, 'He is not his father, Papa.'

Samuel gave a long sigh. 'No, he is not Jonas, but his actions have shown him to be a hard-hearted man. I honour him for his candour in talking to me. He was very honest, very much the gentleman and has offered to make you his wife, especially if there are any…consequences of last night's encounter. However, he knows how much you mean to me and said he would let me decide the matter.'

Belle clasped her hands together. 'Well, Papa?' She fixed her eyes upon him. 'What is your decision?'

Samuel looked at her sadly.

'I witnessed Maria's suffering when she was married to Lucas's father and I was too weak to prevent it. You are all I have in the world now, Belle. I will not risk your happiness.'

'But—but what if I am with child, Papa?'

'Then we will deal with it. You might go away for the birth, or we might move far away, where we are not known. We can start a new life and pass you off as a widow with a young child.

Lucas has promised to assist in any action we decide upon.'

'How can we leave here, Papa? How can I take you away from all your friends, everything you have known?'

'We can make new friends, Belle. I would rather do that than risk your marrying a man who admits he might do you harm.' The world tilted as Annabelle listened to her father's soft voice. 'I told him no. I cannot give my consent, Belle. You must forget him.'

Chapter Fourteen

It was done. Lucas rode away from Croft Cottage with the feeling of having completed an unpleasant duty. The interview with Samuel Havenham had been every bit as painful as he had thought it would be and the outcome, too, was as he expected. Lucas had set out his case very clearly and Samuel was too fond a parent to want his daughter married to such a rogue, even if she should be carrying his child. His child. The very idea cut him deeply. That his thirst for vengeance should have caused so much damage! He had told Belle that suicide was not his way, but now he almost wished he had taken Hugh's pistol and blown his brains out before she had arrived at Oakenroyd. At least then he would not have added this final calumny to his sins. He made his way directly to Morwood. There was work aplenty there to occupy him and he was determined to finish the house, although he doubted now that he would ever live there.

Hugh was waiting for Lucas when he finally returned to Oakenroyd. He came out of the drawing room, a glass of wine in one hand, as Lucas crossed the hall.

'Ah, there you are, Cos. I almost suggested to your butler that we put dinner back, only I plan to ride into Stanton later—another little card party, you know,' he explained. 'You are very late. Is there some problem at the manor?'

'No, everything is well.' Lucas made directly for the stairs. He was in no mood for company, but he knew he would have to dine with his cousin or face more questions. 'Give me half an hour to change and I will join you.'

Lucas escaped his cousin, but it was impossible to avoid George Stebbing's censorious tongue when he saw the state of Lucas's clothes.

'If you intended to be working at Morwood, Major, you should've come here to change first. It'll take me hours to get the dirt off that coat and your waistcoat is fair ruined, and no mistake.'

'Then I shall buy another one.' Lucas felt the old soldier's shrewd gaze upon him and said roughly, 'Damn you, George, I don't pay you to criticise my actions.'

'Oho, so who's put your nose out of joint?' retorted the valet, not noticeably dashed.

'None of your business!'

'It is if it means I have to send to that London tailor o' yours for more clothes,' retorted George, taking Lucas's coat from him and eyeing it with disfavour.

Despite his black mood Lucas laughed.

'Do your best with it, George, but first you had best find me something suitable to wear for dinner with my cousin. Lord knows I would rather eat alone tonight, but I suppose I must join him.'

'It's already put out, sir, on the bed. And as for Captain Duggan…do we know how long he means to stay here?'

'No idea, why do you ask?' He saw his man hesitate and added roughly, 'Well?'

'I just can't take to him, Major, with his gambling and his bullyin' ways, but you knows that already. It ain't my place to say so, but I don't like the way he turned up here and started giving orders, as if he owns the place.'

'Well, he is my heir after all.'

George Stebbing chuckled. 'Ah, but that'll change—'

'I can assure you it won't,' snapped Lucas. He saw the man's surprised look and cursed the ability of old retainers to know all one's business.

He said tightly, 'I am giving Oakenroyd back to Samuel Havenham, but after that all acquaintance with the man and his daughter will cease. In fact, I shall be moving from Stanton just as soon it is possible to do so.'

Stebbing looked astonished and opened his mouth to speak, but Lucas's scowl made him think better of it. Having silenced his man, Lucas finished dressing and went downstairs to dine with his cousin.

He managed to keep the conversation to unexceptional topics until the covers had been removed and they were alone in the dining room, when Hugh asked him once more if he was worried about Morwood.

'Not at all. As I told you, the work is progressing to schedule.'

Hugh reached for the brandy decanter to refill his glass. 'You came back covered in dust and looking like a labourer. Surely there is no need for that.'

Lucas answered with a touch of impatience, 'I ask nothing of my people that I won't do myself.'

Hugh's lip curled. 'No, you were the same in the guards, weren't you?'

'It encourages loyalty.'

'Loyalty be damned,' scoffed Hugh. 'You were lucky your desire to be at one with your men didn't get you killed. I never found the need for such dedication.'

Lucas lifted his glass and studied the amber liquid. 'Perhaps that is why you got a bullet in your back at Waterloo, as well as the one in your leg.' He felt rather than saw Hugh's anger, and he added, 'That is what happens to detested officers in battle, is it not? They are shot by their own men. And you had not made yourself universally popular in your regiment.'

'Because I insisted on discipline—'

'I, too, believe in order, but your name was becoming a byword for flogging and hanging.' Lucas sipped at his brandy. 'I would never have helped you buy your captaincy if I had known you would turn into such a tyrant.'

Hugh shrugged. 'I had the scum of the earth in my company. It was necessary. No one ever questioned it.'

'Perhaps that was because you were betrothed to the Colonel's daughter. What happened there, by the bye?'

'She changed her mind,' said Hugh shortly. 'Dammit, Lucas, surely you do not blame me for trying to progress? If I had a fortune like you—'

'If I remember rightly, my father left you well provided for in his will, but you chose to spend it.'

His cousin's brow darkened and he looked as

if he would argue, but after an inward struggle
he thought better of it and gave a laugh.

'I was a young fool and I admit it, but let's not
dwell on the past. You are my only surviving relative, Lucas. I do not want to fall out with you.'

Lucas felt his lip start to curl. 'Don't worry, I
am not planning to disinherit you.' He filled his
glass and pushed the decanter back across the
table. 'Tell me instead how you fared last night.'

'At the Lion? Quite well. The play was not
deep, but we arranged to play again tonight—'

'I was thinking more of the Rishworths'
party.'

'The dinner was good.' He shrugged. 'The
conversation was mostly on local matters and
not much to my taste, but the young ladies were
charming enough.'

'Miss Rishworth is considered something of
a beauty.'

'Is she?' said Hugh, considering. 'I suppose
so, but as far as I can tell she will have only a
few thousand upon her marriage.'

'You want more?'

Hugh looked surprised that he should even
ask the question.

'Well, you know, Cos, one has to look to the
future.'

'Yes, the future.' Lucas sat back, the fingers of
one hand drumming a soft tattoo on the table. 'I

saw Samuel Havenham this morning. I am giving Oakenroyd back to him.'

'You are what?'

'I dispossessed him and his daughter because I thought Havenham was responsible for my mother's death. I must make reparation.'

'Of course, I understand you would want to do so, but you can't give away your property just like that!' Hugh observed Lucas's raised brows and put up his hands. 'Forgive me, of course you are at liberty to do whatever you want. You took me by surprise, that is all. Unless…' He grinned. 'Of course, you old dog, you plan to marry Annabelle Havenham, and since she will inherit everything from her father, you will be—'

'No.' The word cut across Hugh's speech like a rifle shot, silencing him. 'I have no intention of marrying Miss Havenham. Or anyone else for that matter.' His chair scraped back. 'It has been a long day. Excuse me if I retire now. Please, stay and finish your brandy—have more, if you wish, but I am going to bed.'

Lucas strode out of the room. He should not feel guilty for leaving his cousin to his own devices. He had not invited Hugh to stay—the fellow only turned up when he wanted something or his pockets were to let. Lucas had been so preoccupied that he had no idea which it was this time, but he did not doubt that Hugh would tell him at some stage. For now Lucas had his own problems and he hoped that he had drunk enough to ensure a dreamless night's sleep.

Market day in Stanton was always busy and Annabelle coaxed her father out of doors, knowing that they would see many of his old friends in the town. Apart from going to church on Sunday they had not ventured out of the house since Lucas had visited Croft Cottage, and Samuel had asked her to say nothing of Lucas's plans to reinstate them at Oakenroyd.

'Blackstone and I agreed it would be done discreetly,' he said. 'When word gets out we will say an improvement in my fortunes has made it all possible, which is no more than the truth.'

'Many in your position would want a public apology from Mr Blackstone, Papa.'

'Nay, I am as guilty as he.'

'Papa!'

'My dear, let us not forget that it was I who broke the Lord's tenth commandment. If I had not done so, then none of this would have happened. I always felt the young man was wronged, my love, and no one suspects the connection between our hard times and his purchasing Oakenroyd. I am happy for everyone to think he has generously allowed me to buy my home back from him.'

And with that Belle had to be satisfied. Such reversals were not unknown and as for her own situation, the less people speculated about the connection between her and Lucas Blackstone the better. Time would tell if there would be any physical evidence of their liaison. For now she took her father's arm and accompanied him to the market, as if nothing had changed.

The wide street before the Red Lion was bustling with activity. Many of Oakenroyd's tenants were there and they hailed Mr Havenham cheerfully, more than ready to pass the time of day with him. Annabelle left her father talking happily with a group of local farmers while she went off to make her purchases. With so many people in the town she should not have been surprised to see Lucas, yet she had not considered what she would do when they next met. He was coming towards her with his cousin beside him. Momentarily flustered, she thought of slipping between the market stalls to avoid them, but decided against it. That would be cowardly and besides, to change direction so acutely would look as if she was running away. Instead she fixed her eyes straight ahead and hoped a slight nod in passing would suffice.

If Lucas had been alone then perhaps it would

have been enough, but Captain Duggan was raising his hat to her.

'Miss Havenham, good morning to you.'

There was no help for it. She was obliged to stop, if only to exchange civilities. The captain was inclined to be talkative, and while she responded to his questions and remarks, she was very aware of Lucas standing tall and silent beside him. He had barely acknowledged her and now hovered impatiently, making it only too plain he wanted to be gone from her company. She struggled to concentrate on what the captain was saying and realised too late that she had agreed to let him take her for a drive the following day.

Lucas was looking thunderous, but she could not take any notice of that. If he had loved her, *truly* loved her, surely he would have pressed her father to allow them to marry. He did not want her, so he could hardly object to her enjoying herself with Captain Duggan.

Except there was no enjoyment in her life now. Only distraction from the nagging ache of loneliness.

Having arranged a time to call, Captain Duggan and Lucas moved on and Annabelle continued with her shopping. When she had finished she went in search of her father. She was on her way towards the Red Lion when she heard her name and turned to find Lucas striding towards her.

She waited for him to come up to her. Despite the busy market bustling all around them there was no one close enough to hear their conversation and they might as well have been alone. He stopped in front of her, irresolute. There was so much to say, yet Annabelle could not voice any of it. Perhaps it was the same for Lucas. At length he cleared his throat.

'I did not have the opportunity to say goodbye to you last week, Miss Havenham.'

Miss Havenham. So formal, after she had heard her name on his lips in the most tender of moments. It stung her to retort.

'I was in the sitting room when you left, sir, as you could have ascertained, had you wished to do so.'

'I was afraid,' he said bluntly. 'My mood was such that I might have uttered words better left unsaid.'

'And should I be grateful for that?'

He winced at her scornful tone. 'Yes. Your father and I agreed—we are both doing our best to protect you.'

Anger and misery welled up inside her. Perhaps they were right, perhaps they were protecting her, but should she not be allowed some say in her own future? Apparently not. She thought it best to remain angry, since the alternative was to give way to the threatening tears, so she waved him away.

'Let me pass. You can have nothing more to say to me.'

He caught her wrist as she tried to step around him. 'Why did you agree to drive out with my cousin? Was that to punish me?'

'Perhaps.' She would not admit she had not known what she was agreeing to.

He pulled her closer. 'Promise me one thing,' he muttered urgently. 'I have to go to London shortly, to see my lawyers and organise for Oakenroyd to be restored to your father. Promise me, while I am gone, you will do nothing…rash.'

She drew herself up. 'I think, sir,' she replied with icy calm, 'you have forfeited any right to tell me what to do.' He was still holding her, his grip like an iron band around her wrist. She said coldly, 'Please let me go now.'

'Belle!'

She hardened her heart. She had tried to help him, to comfort him, but her forgiving nature had brought her nothing but wretched unhappiness. She could not allow herself to weaken.

'Let me go!'

'Not until I—'

'So there you are, Cousin! I thought you had left without me.'

Whatever Lucas was going to say was interrupted by Captain Duggan's hearty call. Belle pulled herself free from his grasp and hurried off. Tears were not far away and she would not for the world have anyone see them.

Lucas stared after her. Blast Hugh for interrupting. Or perhaps he should be grateful. He had given his word to Samuel that he would keep away from Annabelle and give her time to forget him, yet here he was already seeking her out. Hugh came up to him, panting slightly from the exertion.

'Miss Havenham was in a hurry to get away,' he observed. 'I do hope she has not changed her mind about driving out with me tomorrow. Is that it, Lucas, did she give you a message for me?'

'No, nothing like that,' Lucas responded quickly. 'I suppose you want to borrow my curricle for your drive tomorrow?'

'Well, yes, Cos, since I have no vehicle of my own. You told me you would be working at the manor all day tomorrow, so I thought you wouldn't mind?'

'Of course not. Rudd shall harness up the greys for you.'

'Not your matched bays?'

'I allow no one to drive the bays but me.' He saw his cousin was inclined to argue and said curtly, 'It is the greys or nothing, Hugh. Take it or leave it.'

His cousin grinned. 'Oh, very well, damn you! I don't suppose anyone in this out-of-the-way place can tell the difference between the two teams.'

Annabelle can, thought Lucas. *She saw at a glance that the bays were quality.* He became aware of Hugh's arm, linked companionably through his own and another thought quickly followed: *I hope she is as good a judge of men.*

It rained heavily during the night and Annabelle wondered if Captain Duggan might be obliged to call off their proposed drive. She almost hoped he would, but at the appointed time a carriage drew up outside Croft Cottage, pulled by a pair of beautiful high-stepping greys. Stifling a sigh, she put on her bonnet and went outside.

'Good day to you, Miss Havenham. My cousin has loaned us the use of his curricle, you see, so we shall look very smart, tooling around the countryside, eh?'

Annabelle allowed him to hand her into the vehicle, her eyes flicking briefly to the empty rumble seat. She wondered if she should refuse to accompany him without a servant, but quickly dismissed the idea. This was Stanton. She had grown up here and was quite in the habit of going out alone. Pride would not allow her to consider that her reduced circumstances might make her more vulnerable.

'I thought we might take a drive to Morwood,' Captain Duggan continued. 'We can see what progress my cousin is making with the park there, what do you say to that, Miss Havenham?'

Belle forced herself to smile. She could only hope they would not see Lucas while they were there.

Captain Duggan set off down the High Street at a pace that had Annabelle clutching at the side of the curricle. She said nothing, but could not help comparing his erratic driving very unfavourably with that of his cousin and was only thankful that he did not have the bays harnessed to the centre pole.

'I did think at first that we could drive around the park at Oakenroyd,' remarked the captain as he hauled the team sharply around a bend. 'But you will be very familiar with that, and it won't be long before you are back there as mistress, will it?' He laughed. 'Oh, you need not look so surprised, ma'am, my cousin has no secrets from me. He told me the other day that he was giving Oakenroyd back to your father.'

'Yes, he has been most generous.'

'Aye, uncommonly so, although perhaps he hopes to gain your favour by this gesture.'

'I do not think so.'

'Really?'

Belle struggled to maintain her composure, but after a moment she managed to reply coolly, 'Really. My father is opposed to any alliance with Mr Blackstone.'

'Well, that is dashed good news, if you don't mind my saying so.' Belle stiffened, but he continued, quite unabashed, 'Lucas may be the richest fellow in Stanton, but I know his manners can be a little rough, and after what he did to your father I can understand Havenham setting his face against him—'

'Ah, we have arrived at Morwood,' she interrupted him, anxious to change the subject. 'I haven't seen the park for some weeks, how different it looks.'

'Aye, it always looks its best in the autumn.' He slowed the curricle and turned into the park.

Belle had forgotten how beautiful the park could be, with the leaves turning to gold upon the trees. In the distance was the manor, still surrounded by scaffolding and tiny figures of the men moving around it. One of them might well be Lucas.

'I hope Mr Blackstone will not object to our driving here.'

'Oh, I am sure he won't,' replied the captain cheerfully. 'I am his heir, after all. I was not planning to drive up to the house, unless you wish to do so, Miss Havenham?'

'No, no, not at all.'

'Good. It's little more than a building site at the moment, so there is nothing of interest there. We'll tool around the park for a while, then see what progress has been made on the woodland carriageways.'

Driving around the park with Captain Duggan was a very different experience to Belle's previous visits in Lucas's company. The captain was interested in the changes only as far as they improved the value of the estate, and despite his constant references to the happy times he had spent at Morwood, Belle was left with the impression that he saw the house and its grounds as a commodity and not a home. When they drove down to the lake his comments were fixed upon the value of the timber rather than the beauty of their surroundings. Annabelle decided that if he was trying to impress her he had failed miserably. She did not like the way he leaned against her when he had some point to make, nor his constant allusions to his 'inheritance'. She began to wish she had not accepted his invitation and she was quite relieved when it was time to turn for home.

* * *

'Well, that was very pleasant,' he declared as they drew up outside Croft Cottage. 'Shall we do this again, Miss Havenham?'

She jumped nimbly down before making her reply. 'I think not, Captain.' She smiled and tried to soften her response. 'Papa and I have a great deal to do over the next few weeks and I really will not have time for pleasure jaunts. But thank you, sir, for your time today.'

Captain Duggan did not look best pleased with his dismissal, but Belle could not help that. She hurried inside, watching from the sitting-room window as he drove away.

'Ah, Belle, my love.' Her father came in. 'Did I leave my book in here? I was reading Horace...' He smiled absently at her. 'Have you been out, my dear?'

'Yes, Papa. I told you, Captain Duggan invited me to drive out with him today.'

'Did he? How kind of him. Did you enjoy it?'

'It was very pleasant,' she replied cautiously. 'We drove around the park at Morwood. I wish you could have seen it, Papa, the trees are looking magnificent with their leaves all amber and gold.'

'Ah, yes, of course.' For a moment he looked wistful. 'And the house, how does that go on?'

She concentrated upon removing her bonnet.

'I do not know, we did not go there.' She added brightly, 'Captain Duggan sends his regards, Papa. He could not stop, since he had no groom with him to hold the horses.'

'How thoughtful of him.' He smiled. 'Captain Duggan is very different from his cousin, is he not?'

'Yes, Papa,' she said. 'Very different.'

He barely heard her for he had spotted his book lying on a chair. Murmuring to himself, he retrieved it and made his way back to his study. Belle smiled. He would shut himself away and lose himself in his books again, forgetting all about the real world for a little while. She wished she could do the same.

'There's someone in the park, Mr Blackstone.'

Lucas was on the top platform of the scaffolding with one of the masons when Elias Greenwood called up to him. He followed the man's outstretched finger. There was no mistaking his curricle and the greys that pulled it. Hugh was driving Annabelle around the park. The stab of jealousy was like a physical pain in his chest.

No one shall have her if I cannot!

He turned away, fighting against the words that rang in his head. He was not that unreasonable. He was *not* his father.

He said at last, surprised at the steadiness of

his voice, 'It's Captain Duggan and Miss Havenham.'

'Ah. Well, they're not coming this way. Looks like he is driving her down to the lake, making use of the path you've opened up there.'

'Yes.' He forced himself to take another look and was in time to see the curricle disappearing into the trees.

I did it for her, he told himself. *Why shouldn't she enjoy it, even if it is not with me?*

Elias was looking up at him, a speculative look in his eye. Lucas scowled at him.

'Well?' he barked. 'What are you waiting for? Get back to work!'

Confound it, he should not take his bad mood out on his workers. He gave his attention to the mason again, but made a mental vow that he would catch up with Greenwood before the end of the day and make sure all was well with him.

Chapter Fifteen

Lucas delayed his return to Oakenroyd until late in the day and arrived back to learn from Rudd that his cousin had not yet come in. Knowing Hugh, Lucas was pretty sure that he would be gambling at the Red Lion, but a tiny worm of jealousy gnawed at him, suggesting that he might be dining at Croft Cottage. When Lucas retired Hugh had still not returned, so he would not discover the truth until the next morning.

Being a Sunday Lucas did not rise early to go to Morwood and instead joined his cousin at the breakfast table.

'How did you like my greys?' He asked the question casually as he took his seat.

'An excellent pair and very well matched,' returned Hugh, grinning at him. 'I'd expect nothing less of cattle from your stable, Cos!'

'You certainly kept them out long enough.'

'After I dropped Miss Havenham I met up with friends and stopped to dine with them in Stanton—at the Red Lion, so your team was perfectly safe in the stables.'

'I never doubted you would look after them.' Lucas poured himself a cup of coffee. 'And did Miss Havenham enjoy the drive?'

There was a heartbeat's hesitation before Hugh answered, 'Why, yes, of course. When are you off to London?'

The change of subject was very sudden. Lucas had no idea whether that was a good sign or bad. He replied coolly, 'At the end of the week. I have much to arrange before I go.'

'You haven't changed your mind?' Hugh looked around to check that the servants had quit the room. 'About handing over Oakenroyd?'

'No. I expect everything to be settled by the end of the month.' He flicked a glance at his cousin. 'If you intend to stay on in Stanton, then you will have to take a room at the Red Lion.'

'That would be no hardship, in fact it would be more convenient for me, but I think you are fool.'

'What you think is irrelevant.'

Hugh's face darkened. 'I am all the family you have now, so it is very relevant!'

'Hell and confound it, Hugh, it was talking to you that convinced me my father—that convinced me I had been blaming the wrong man all these years!'

'Yes, that's all very well, but it doesn't—'

Lucas brought his fist down on the table, making the cups rattle in their saucers.

'I stole his house from him, Hugh!' Guilt twisted his gut. 'I even planned to take his daughter. Returning Oakenroyd to Samuel Havenham is the least I can do.' He frowned at his cousin. 'Are you afraid there will be nothing left for you?'

'No, no, of course not, but—'

'You need not worry, there is plenty in the funds, and once I have sold the manor—'

'What? You are going to—to *sell* Morwood?'

Lucas raised his eyes to meet his cousin's shocked gaze. 'Yes. It was foolish to think I could come back. I am going to sell it as soon as it is finished. Then I shall be done with this place for ever.'

'But—but you can't,' blustered Hugh. 'It is your home, and mine!'

Lucas raised his brows. 'You were an occasional visitor, Cousin, nothing more.' He rose. 'Now, if you will excuse me, I have work to do.'

The short November day was drawing to a close. Belle had accompanied her father to the church that morning, but even her prayers and silent reflection in that holy place brought her no relief from the dull ache of despair.

It will pass, she told herself as she sat by the window of Croft Cottage, her reading book open in her lap. *This misery cannot last.*

She tried to think of the future. If Lucas was as good as his word then they would shortly be returning to Oakenroyd. Her father was quietly optimistic, and despite all that had happened Belle did not doubt that Lucas intended to make reparation for the harm he had done, but nothing could turn back the clock. Nothing could make her forget him or repair the damage he had done to her heart.

Her father was dozing by the fire. Belle tried to concentrate on her book, but the silence pressed around her. She felt the confines of the small cottage more acutely than ever before. Suddenly she wanted to get away and not to the tiny bedroom upstairs. She glanced out of the window. It was overcast, but the light should last for a little while yet. She would go out.

She dropped a kiss upon her father's brow and told him of her intention, but received no more than a sleepy response. He did not even insist that she should take Abel with her, for which she was grateful. She wanted to be alone with her thoughts. She ran upstairs to collect her cloak, then slipped out of the door. Throwing her hood over her curls, she held the folds of the cloak closely about her to keep out the chill wind as she set off in the direction of the graveyard.

The evening divine service had finished and the church stood silent and dark, unlike the Red Lion opposite, where welcoming light spilled out from the windows on to the road. As she slipped through the lychgate a sudden gust of wind whispered through the trees and sent a shower of leaves across the graveyard. They danced around her skirts as she made her way to her mother's grave.

She knelt on the soft earth and stared at the headstone. How she wished her mama—that kind, gentle woman Papa had told her of—could be with her now, to advise, to comfort her. It could not be, of course. She had to be sensible, to be strong for her father, but, oh, how she wished that just for a moment there was someone who could be strong for her.

With a sigh she brushed aside the leaves that had settled around the base of the headstone and picked up the last flowers she had laid there. The withered blooms only added to her unhappiness and she closed her eyes, praying for she knew not what.

'Belle.'

She heard Lucas call her name, soft as a whisper, and thought at first she had imagined it, conjuring his voice from her own deep yearning, but she sensed his presence even before she opened her eyes and saw him standing a few yards away. She scrambled to her feet.

'I saw you from the road,' he said by way of explanation.

Following the wave of his hand she saw Sultan tethered at the gate. Lucas was coming closer. Belle knew she should turn away, but her feet were rooted to the ground. She fixed her eyes on the brittle stems crumbling in her nervous fingers.

'These are the last of the summer flowers. When I was at Oakenroyd I picked blooms from the hothouse to lay here during the winter.'

He came up to her, stopping just an arm's reach away. 'You will soon be able to do so again, you have my word on that. And you will be able to ride over the moors as you did in the past. Apollo is in the stables, waiting for you. I have not ridden him since that day you ripped up at me. Clegg exercises him, in readiness for your return to Oakenroyd.'

She shivered and pulled her cloak more closely about her. 'I must leave—'

'Don't go.' He stepped quickly around the grave and blocked her way. Belle kept her gaze lowered, but she was very aware of him standing in front of her, broad and immovable as a wall. 'I gave my word to your father that I would stay away from you.' His voice was low and rough, as if the words were forced out of him. 'I cannot help myself. I am drawn like a moth to a flame.'

'I have done nothing to attract you.'

'You drove out with my cousin yesterday. Are you not using him to make me jealous?'

'Of course not!' Belle looked up, surprised. The suggestion would have been laughable if she had not felt so desolate. She raised her chin. 'I do not play games. Unlike…'

'Unlike me,' he finished for her. 'I deserve your censure. I could only wish—' He looked up at the darkening sky and exhaled. 'I rode into Stanton tonight because I wanted to see you one last time, even if it was only your shadow at the window of Croft Cottage.'

'Lucas, please—'

She put out her hand to stop him and he caught it, drawing it closer until it was pressed against his heart.

'I am going to London shortly to see my lawyer. I do not intend to return to Stanton, so I will not trouble you again.'

She shook her head. She should have run away when she first saw him. She should certainly not have allowed him to touch her. Now the bonds that held her to him had wound around her heart again.

'It is not your presence that troubles me, Lucas.' She risked looking up. His face was in shadow, but she could feel his pain, for it mirrored her own. She said quietly, 'When you are away I feel as if a part of me is missing.'

Something between an oath and a sigh escaped him and he pulled her close, holding her so tightly that she was pressed to his chest and could hear his heart thudding against her cheek.

'You will recover,' he muttered into her hair. 'You must.'

'I do not think I want to.'

'Foolish talk, my love.' He let her go, but only so he could take her hand and lead her across the graveyard to the raised tomb that held the remains of his family. 'Look here,' he said. 'This is why I cannot marry you. I am the son of a murderer, Belle.'

'No,' she whispered.

'Yes!' He pulled her round, his hands gripping her shoulders. 'I love you to distraction, Belle, but I have my father's temper—it has already brought you and your father close to ruin. What if it should spill over into violence?'

'If I am willing to take the risk—'

'I am not, and neither is your father. Come, it is almost dark and you must go home.' He read rebellion in her face and gave her a little shake. 'You told me once that your father rarely demands your obedience, but when he does you are happy to give it.'

'You remember that?'

A ghost of a smile flickered across his features. 'I remember everything you have said to me. But you must go now. Obey your father and stay away from me.'

He began to walk her back towards the gate. Hot tears sprang up, clogging her throat. Despite all that had happened she could not believe he would ever harm her. He stopped at the lychgate.

'I can go no further with you.'

'Then, will you kiss me, just once more?'

She was begging him, but she did not care. When he lowered his head to kiss her, Belle returned his embrace with a desperate fervour. Her lips parted, she tangled her tongue with his, desperate to show him just how much she cared. His arms tightened and she felt his body harden. They were spinning into that heady passion in which all sense of time and place is lost. It was not too late, if he would admit how much he loved her, she was sure they could convince Papa to let them marry. If she was willing to take the risk, then why should they not agree? For a moment hope flared in Belle. Then, slowly, resolutely, Lucas drew back. He moved his hands to her shoulders and gently but firmly pushed her away.

They were standing in the shadow of the lychgate; above them the small roof was a solid square of black against the darkening sky. Lucas sighed.

'They rest the coffins here before they carry them to the grave. The villagers believe it is bad luck for lovers to stop here on their way to be married. Appropriate, then, that we should take our last leave of each other here.'

The tiny flicker of hope died. Belle's shoulders sagged. She blinked back her tears as Lucas lifted her hand to his lips for one final salute.

She clung to him, her heart breaking. Summoning every ounce of will power, she forced herself to speak. 'There is something I must tell you, Lucas. I am not with child.'

The wind filled the silence around them with a sigh.

'You are sure?' he said at last.

She nodded. 'Yes. I am sure.'

'Then we must be thankful for that.'

Must we? Annabelle caught her lip between her teeth. Now, when Lucas was gone, she would have nothing of him at all to fill the aching void where her heart had been.

As he disengaged his fingers he said quietly, 'God be with you, Belle, now and always.'

Hot tears welled up, filling her throat as well as her eyes. Silently, she turned and fled.

Lucas watched her go, not taking his eyes from her until she had hurried unhindered past the lighted windows of the Red Lion and become a mere shadow flitting down the High Street, disappearing at last through the door of the mean little cottage that, because of him, she and her father had been forced to call home. He untied Sultan's reins and scrambled into the saddle. Well, at least he could rectify that. He could reinstate them at Oakenroyd. They would take their place in Stanton society again and he would disappear from their lives for ever. Belle was still young, in time she would forget him and be happy again. He had to believe that. After a final glance at the now-deserted street he turned and rode back to Oakenroyd.

As the sound of the horse's hooves faded, a figure broke away from the black shadows of the inn's arched entrance opposite the church. Hugh Duggan stepped into the street and watched his cousin disappear into the night.

Annabelle slept badly and awoke little refreshed, but there was no time for moping. With December approaching she was obliged to make

the best use of the short winter days. To offset
her restlessness she set Abel to chopping wood
for the fire while she went off as soon as it was
light to fetch more milk and eggs from Oldroyd
Farm. There were a few townspeople in the
street, including Mrs Kensley, who barely gave
her a nod in passing. Since they had moved into
Croft Cottage she had tried to patronise Belle
and her father. Now Belle acknowledged a small
but quite reprehensible glimmer of satisfaction
as she imagined the lady's consternation and dis-
pleasure once they were reinstated at Oakenroyd.

If Lucas kept his promise.

The thought occurred only to be dismissed.
She had no doubt that Lucas would honour his
word to her father and she drew comfort from
this, although she drew none from the knowledge that he would also honour his word not to
return to Stanton.

Henry Blundell was standing in the doorway
of his booksellers as she passed and although he
touched his hat as he wished her a good morning, she had to steel herself to ignore his leering
stare. She would order her books from London
once they were back at Oakenroyd. There was
no doubt that she would enjoy being back in her
old home and she would have the means to in-
dulge her interests once again, but she knew that

no amount of money would dispel the desperate loneliness she now felt.

The road to the farm was muddy and uneven and she raised her eyes to the toll road curling around the ridge to the north and watched the coaches bowling along. Traffic had increased in recent months and she thought perhaps there was now a chance that the subscribers would begin to see a return for their investment. That would be good for the town. Her sharp eyes picked out a rider on the top road and even at this distance she recognised Captain Duggan. He was riding slowly and she quickly put down her head and hurried on to Oldroyd. She did not wish him to recognise her and come riding down to meet her, full of hearty goodwill and gallant phrases, for she felt very vulnerable and alone on this desolate stretch of road.

The memory reared up of Lucas galloping towards her, mounted upon her beloved Apollo. She closed her eyes for a moment, shaking her head to dispel the image. Would she ever be free of him? Everywhere she went around Stanton there were memories waiting to pounce on her. Perhaps, when they were settled once more at Oakenroyd, she would travel. She had always wanted to go abroad. But she could not leave her father, so for the moment she was trapped. She remembered her father's story of the lark in the gilded cage. Well, she thought, in an attempt at humour, at least she would be miserable in comfort.

Chapter Sixteen

The days dragged on and nothing was heard from Lucas. Annabelle busied herself with the chores and housework around the little cottage while her father continued to give lessons to his students or read his books in his study. An improvement in the weather towards the end of the week encouraged Belle to put on her cloak and take a walk once she had completed her morning tasks. She had heard that Elias Greenwood's wife had given birth to a healthy baby girl and she decided she would walk to the farm to see the mother and child. She regretted that she could not take a basket, as she had done in the past, but she hoped that Mrs Greenwood would still be pleased to see her.

She had not gone far when she heard her name

and looked up to see Captain Duggan hurrying towards her.

'Miss Havenham, I was hoping I might see you! You are on an errand?' She hesitated, and he rushed on. 'I need your help, madam, with my cousin.'

'Mr Blackstone? Is he ill?'

He spread his hands. 'He is…not himself, Miss Havenham. He is asking for you.'

'Yes, of course.' The Greenwoods were forgotten. Belle started forwards, as if she would run all the way to Oakenroyd, then stopped. 'I should tell my father—'

'I will go back and explain. You are dressed for walking, ma'am, and I am sure you would prefer to keep moving. Continue out of the town and I will hire a gig once I have spoken to your father. I shall soon overtake you on the road.'

He was strangely agitated and would wait no longer, but dashed off in the direction of Croft Cottage. Belle stared after him. Lucas must be in a very bad way to make his cousin so anxious. Remembering Lucas's black mood the other night, she began to hurry along the road towards Oakenroyd, praying she would not be too late.

'…and that's it.' Lucas closed the ledger and handed it over to Elias Greenwood together with a large purse. 'This should cover anything you need. Have the tradesmen send their bills to my London address and keep a tally for me of all that you spend. Stebbing will be back in a couple of weeks to check on progress.'

'You are not coming back, sir?'

'No, not for some time.' Lucas busied himself with tidying Samuel's desk. He had never really come to think of anything at Oakenroyd as his. He picked up a much smaller purse and held it out, saying awkwardly, 'This is for you. Buy something pretty for Mrs Greenwood and that new baby of yours.'

'That's very good of you, sir—'

'Aye, well, enough of that.' Lucas waved aside his thanks. 'You have my attorney's direction in London, you can send word there if you need me, but the work is progressing well enough, I do not foresee a problem.'

'Not until we are in a position to decorate the house and lay out the gardens,' Elias pointed out. 'I ain't sure I could do that for you.'

'No, of course. That will not be necessary.'

Lucas hoped by that time the house would no longer be his responsibility, but he did not want to share that thought. There would be speculation enough when it became known that he was selling Morwood. He wanted to be far away before that occurred.

He dismissed Elias and left the study, sending a footman running to fetch his man. The hall was gloomy, but a cheerful fire awaited him in the drawing room and by the time Lucas had poured himself a brandy Stebbing had come in, closing the door quietly behind him.

'Is everything packed in readiness for the morning, George?'

'Aye, Major, we leave the house exactly as we found it, as you instructed. I haven't told the staff you ain't coming back, but I think they knows something's up.' He scratched his head, musing on this vexed question for a moment. 'Anyway, they've been told to continue here as normal until they hear from you.'

'Good. And Captain Duggan?'

'He packed his things and left this morning, just before you got back from Morwood with Elias Greenwood.'

'Then we are all done.' Lucas walked to the window and stared out. The short winter day was fading and the low sun cast long shadows across the valley before him. He could see the outline of the moors above the trees at the edge of the park. Beyond that lay Morwood. Soon to be sold, to pass out of his family for the second time. The last time.

'Where shall we go, George, when we have settled all this with the lawyers? What say you we try America?'

'That's an awful lot of water to cross, Major. I thought you was planning to make your home hereabouts.'

'Not any more.' He turned to find his servant eyeing him anxiously. Lucas forced a smile. 'I've been a damned fool, George.'

'As so many have been before you, sir.'

'Is that supposed to make me feel better?'

George Stebbing gave him a slow grin. 'Nay, Major, 'tis only to tell you that you're not alone.'

Lucas shook his head. He felt more alone now than he had ever done. He emptied his glass and returned to the sideboard to refill it, saying as he crossed the room, 'I have a fancy to book a passage and leave this cursed island behind me. What do you say, will you and Rudd come with me?'

'Aye, Major, you know we'd follow thee to the ends of the earth, if you asked it.'

Lucas looked around. 'I know that tone, George. Out with it, man, what is your objection?'

'Only that you was so set upon making your home at Morwood, sir.'

'That is no longer the case.'

'And…' Stebbing coughed. 'Miss Havenham, Major?'

Lucas's jaw tightened. 'Not that it is any of your business, but she will be moving back here, with her father. We shall not see her again.' He saw the speculative look in his servant's eyes and swore roundly. 'Damn you, George, it is for the best.'

'Is it, now?' murmured Stebbing, not noticeably abashed. 'Best for who, I wonder?'

Lucas's eyes narrowed, but before he could retort he was interrupted by a light knocking on the door and Gibson entered.

'I am sorry to disturb you, sir, but a note has just been delivered and it says it is urgent…'

The butler came across the room, holding out a silver tray upon which lay a folded paper. Lucas gave it a perfunctory glance. It was in his mind to send the butler away with his damned notes, but he picked up the letter and broke the seal. His eyes scanned the untidy writing once, then again.

'Thank you, Gibson. That will be all.'

'Trouble, Major?' asked Stebbing, when the butler had retired.

'What makes you say that?'

The man rubbed his nose, saying reflectively, 'I've seen that black look o' yours before, Major.'

After a brief hesitation Lucas held out the letter. George took it and read it aloud.

'"Miss H. is waitin' for you at the Boar's Head. Come alone. Tell no one."' He handed it back, frowning.

'That's my cousin's writing,' said Lucas. He

turned the paper over and studied the wax seal. 'He wrote it here. What is the damn fool up to now?'

'Whatever it is I don't like the sound of it,' muttered George. 'The Boar's Head is a ram-shackle place, used by drovers mostly, their last stop before they cross the moor to Oxenhope.'

Lucas refolded the note and propped it on the mantelshelf. 'Send a message to the stables to have the bays harnessed to my curricle.'

'You ain't going alone, Major!'

Lucas fixed his hard eyes on the old soldier. 'What do you think?'

'Is Mr Blackstone not at Oakenroyd?'

Annabelle asked the question as Captain Duggan swung the gig around a bend and away from the road to her old home. She had been in such a ferment of anxiety that she had not hesitated to climb up into the gig when Captain Duggan pulled up beside her.

'No.'

'Is he hurt, then?' she asked quickly. 'Has he had a riding accident? This road leads nowhere but to the moors.' When he did not answer her, she said more sharply, 'Where are we going, Captain Duggan?'

He glanced towards her, giving her a dis-tracted smile.

'There is an inn further on; we will find my cousin there. You know how he has been recently, I am afraid for his safety...'

He let the words hang and a chill ran down Belle's spine. She remembered the pistol lying on the sideboard the night she had visited Oakenroyd. Annabelle kept her eyes on the road as it wound upwards and the green pastures were replaced by a much bleaker landscape. The moors stretched ahead of them while to each side was only rough grazing land with a few sheep like white dots in the distance. At last she saw the gable of a stone building at the side of the road. An inn, with a number of outbuildings surrounding it. The substantial nature of the property argued a large hostelry, but as they drove up she could see that the painted sign was cracked and faded and the buildings were run-down, with grass and weeds growing between the cobbles.

'Is this where he is?' she asked, frowning.

'Aye. The Boar's Head.'

'But I don't understand. What would bring him here? How did you know—?'

'I'll explain all that later,' he interrupted her, bringing the gig to a halt on the cobbles. 'Let us go in and pray we are not too late!'

His urgent tone was not lost on Annabelle. As soon as the gig stopped she jumped down. A barrel-chested man with iron-grey hair ran out to grab the horse's head and Captain Duggan picked up a small leather case from the gig and followed her into the inn. The weather-beaten door led into a dark low-beamed passage. To the right was what Belle took to be the taproom. It held a long table and benches and a couple of barrels stood in one corner with a trestle table before them. It was empty save for a slatternly woman in a grey gown, who disappeared through a door at the back of the room even as Belle looked in.

'This way, Miss Havenham.'

Captain Duggan opened a door to the left and ushered her inside. She found herself in a much smaller chamber with a single table in one corner. As the door clicked shut a presentiment of danger came over Belle.

'What is this? Where is Lucas?'

'Ah, well, I may have misled you a little there, Miss Havenham. We will have to wait for him. Won't you sit by the fire?'

She started back towards the door. 'No, I will not. I want to go back to Stanton immediately.'

'I'm afraid that is not possible.' He grabbed her arm and pulled her towards the hearth, where a sullen fire smoked fitfully. 'Now please sit down, Miss Havenham.'

He pushed her down into one of the wooden armchairs that flanked the fireplace. Belle was thoroughly alarmed, but she was determined not to let it show. She said coldly, 'Please tell me why you have brought me here.'

'I already have,' he said, placing the leather case upon the table. 'We are waiting for my cousin.'

'I don't understand. Why should he want to come to this inn?'

'Because you are here.' He sat down opposite her, smiling at her confusion. 'I needed to get my cousin alone, you see, and you are in the nature of the, er, bait.'

She shook her head.

'You are wrong, Captain Duggan. Mr Blackstone has sworn to stay away from me. He will not come.'

'We must hope you are wrong, madam, for I cannot let you go back to Stanton if he does not turn up. You would spoil my plans.'

'Plans?' Through her fear came the thought that she must keep him talking. 'How can I affect your plans?'

The door opened and the grey-haired man looked in. 'I've stabled yer horse and put the gig out o' sight, Cap'n, like you asked, and sent the boy off on the pony with yer note—'

Hugh cursed him savagely. 'Damn you, Strutt, don't come in without knocking!'

'Damme, 'tis my ale house and I'll do as I please.'

'Not when I am paying you!'

Scowling, the landlord made to withdraw, but the captain stopped him. 'No, wait. Now you are here, send in some wine and something to eat.' When the man had gone, Hugh was once more smiling and urbane. He said apologetically, 'We may have to wait here for some time. You see, I had the note already written, to summon Lucas, but I could not risk sending it until I had you safe.'

Belle lifted her head and looked at him steadily. 'Captain Duggan, I fear you are under a misapprehension. Mr Blackstone is nothing to me.'

'That may be so, ma'am, but he cares for *you* a great deal. Why else would he be willing to give up everything? Much can be forgiven a man in love, Miss Havenham, but I cannot let him do this. I have to stop him.'

'This is surely something you should take up with your cousin, sir—'

'I have tried, but he won't listen to me.'

'Then I cannot help you.' She thought sadly of that last kiss, how he had put her away from him. 'I have no influence with him.'

'No?' Again that cold smile. 'I think you will

find he will co-operate, once he knows what I plan to do with you if he refuses.'

The curricle bowled along the road to Stanton at breakneck speed. The bays were fresh and Lucas was obliged to give all his attention to keeping them steady. It was growing very dark now with only the last ragged shreds of daylight on the western horizon. The lamps on the curricle burned with a dull glow, but Lucas knew that if anyone was in his way he would be upon them before they could see his lights. He tore into the little town and brought the team to a plunging halt at Croft Cottage. Rudd ran to the bays' heads while Lucas jumped down and rapped urgently upon the door. It was opened immediately by Samuel's man, a worried look upon his face.

'The master saw you pull up, sir. If you would like to come in.'

Samuel was waiting for him in the sitting room. 'Belle?'

The old man spoke the single word almost as soon as Lucas entered, his face so white and creased with worry that Lucas's worst fears were realised. He shook his head.

'Tell me when you saw her last, Mr Havenham.'

'At noon. We had a little soup together.'

'And you have heard nothing since?'

'No. She told me she was going for a walk, but she would never be gone so long without letting me know. I was about to send a note to Rishworth Lodge, to see…'

'I pray you will not do that yet.'

The old man fixed his anxious eyes upon him. 'Do you know where she is?'

'I think so. I am on my way there now.'

'Bring her back safely, my boy.'

The old man put out his hand and Lucas gripped it. 'I will, sir, if it is humanly possible.'

Samuel kept hold of his fingers. 'If only I could come with you,' he said. 'If only I were not so *weak!*' He looked up at Lucas. 'She needs someone younger and stronger than I to look after her. My boy, if you bring her back—'

'*When* I bring her back we will discuss it.' Lucas put his hand on the old man's shoulder. 'Do not give up hope, sir!'

Chapter Seventeen

Darkness closed in and still Belle was a prisoner in the parlour of the Boar's Head. Hugh Duggan had taken her cloak from her and roped her to a chair. She wasted no time on tears. All her pleading and protestations had not moved her captor who, to every fresh argument she put forwards, merely said, 'We will wait for Blackstone to arrive.'

Hugh bade her eat a little of the food brought into them by a shambling hulk of a youth that he introduced to her as Zac, one of the landlord's sons. It was poor fare and she had no appetite, but she forced herself to swallow a few mouthfuls. Whatever was going to happen to her, she did not want to be distracted by hunger. She refused the wine, but took a cup of small beer, which she sipped cautiously. As the evening wore on Captain Duggan became increasingly agitated. Candles were brought in and the shutters closed, but they were not barred and the captain peeped out through them every time his perambulations around the room brought him to the window.

'What if he does not come?' she asked at last. There was no clock in the room and Belle had no idea how long she had been confined. Hugh was biting his thumb as he turned to look at her. 'Well?' she persisted, her nerves so stretched she no longer cared if she angered him. 'Do you propose to kill me?'

She was steeling herself for his answer, determined not to show any fear, when there was the unmistakable sound of an arrival. He moved the shutter an inch to peer out.

'He's here.' He closed the shutter and turned to Belle, a triumphant smile on his face. 'Now, let us see how much he values you!'

There was a rumble of voices, then the door burst open and Lucas appeared, the shoulders of his caped driving coat almost filling the opening. Belle was torn between relief at his being there and sheer terror that he had walked into a trap. His hard eyes swept the room, resting only briefly on her before he fixed them upon Captain Duggan. It was impossible to read his expression, his countenance as hard and impassive as stone. He strolled into the room, stripping off his gloves. The landlord followed him and Belle went cold when she saw the heavy shotgun in his hands.

'What the deuce is this about, Cousin?' Lucas demanded.

'You've come alone?'

Lucas spread his hands. 'What does it look like?'

Duggan looked past him to the landlord, who nodded.

'Aye, Cap'n. My lads is outside, watching. There was no one with him.'

'Very well. Let us get down to business.'

'Will you let me untie Miss Havenham first?'

'No. When we have finished and you have done as I order you, I will release her. Until then she remains a prisoner. And Strutt will remain, too, with the shotgun, in case you try anything clever. First of all I would like you to empty your pockets, I have no doubt that you have at least one pistol hidden away.' When Lucas did not move, he continued in a silky voice that sent shivers running through Belle, 'Make no mistake, Cos, it is Miss Havenham who will suffer if you do not comply. Strutt has no qualms about harming a woman.'

'I can believe it.' Lucas flicked a cold glance at the landlord, who waved the shotgun at him.

'Nay, sirs, I'm a respectable innkeeper these days, but that don't mean I won't use this if I have to, if I needs to protect my property.'

Lucas ignored his interjection and addressed his cousin. 'How did you light upon this place?'

'I met Strutt in the Red Lion. I had been playing cards there and booked a room for the night, do you remember? Well, there being no lightskirts to entertain me once the gaming tables were finished and no gin shop in Stanton, I went down to the taproom for a tankard of ale and fell into conversation. I recognised Strutt as a bad lot almost immediately, although of course I didn't know then that I would need to make use of his hostelry and his, er, skills.'

'And just when did you plan all this?' asked Lucas.

'Only this week. I had to work quickly. I couldn't let you go to London. Once you had signed the papers I would have lost everything. But we are straying from the point, Cos. Your firearms, please. Now.'

'And if I don't?' Lucas jerked his head towards the door. 'If I am not mistaken, there are voices in the taproom—would you risk a shot in here?'

Hugh turned to the landlord with a snarl. 'Hell and damnation, Strutt, I told you to shut the inn.'

'Ho, and how suspicious would *that* be! 'Tis only a couple of packmen. The boys'll deal with them if necessary. And, yes, sir, to answer your question, I *would* risk a shot, if needs be, the story being that I was aiming to kill an intruder and hit the young lady instead. Would *you* be willing to risk that?'

So she was being used to force Lucas's hand. Belle strained against the ropes, but they would not give at all. She watched in dismay as Lucas drew a long-nosed pistol from his pocket and handed it to Hugh.

'There,' he growled. 'Now will you tell me what it is you want?'

Hugh inspected the pistol. 'A Manton. I should have guessed you would bring a duelling pistol. And loaded too.' He levelled it at Lucas. 'I want my inheritance, Cousin.'

'You are still my heir, nothing has changed.'

'Yes, but for how long?' He glanced towards Belle. 'I saw the two of you, in the churchyard on Sunday night. How long before you and your wife have a child to supplant me?'

Lucas said quietly, 'Hugh, that will never happen.'

'No? I cannot take that chance, Cousin. I hoped you might be cut down at Waterloo, but you survived unmarked. Of course, I didn't know then just what a wealthy man you had become. I have been thinking since I came here what a disaster it would be for me if you was to have an heir and cut me out of the succession.'

'Then let me make over something to you now,' said Lucas. 'We will agree a sum—'

'Oh, no, I want it all. Everything. It is mine by right. You see, it was bad enough when you told me you were going to give away Oakenroyd. That wouldn't be right, after you had put so much of your fortune into acquiring the place.'

'But I have promised it to Samuel Havenham.'

Hugh's lip curled. 'That foolish old man don't deserve it. You told me yourself it cost you a great deal to secure that property. But *then* you told me you were going to sell Morwood. I can't let you do that, Lucas. It was my home.'

'Nonsense, you and your mother visited once a year, if that.'

'It was my *home*,' Hugh repeated, his face contorting with anger. 'You don't think I could ever regard that damp hovel of my mother's as my rightful place, do you?'

Lucas glanced at the landlord, leaning against the door with the shotgun resting in his hands.

'Very well, Hugh, we can talk about all this, but we don't need Miss Havenham here. She is no part of this, let me send her home.'

The captain shook his head, a cunning gleam in his eyes.

'Oh, no, she is my trump card, Lucas. As long as I have her then you will do as I say.'

'Is my word not good enough for you?'

'I regret not. Neither of you will leave this room until you have signed everything over to me.' He went over to the table and, placing the pistol down, he opened the leather case and took out a sheaf of papers. 'You will need a pen. Strutt, where is it, and the ink?'

'There on the mantelpiece, Cap'n.'

Lucas watched his cousin fetch the tarnished silver inkwell and pens, followed by a branched candlestick which he put in the centre of the table. He began straightening the papers with obsessive care, placing everything just so. A tiny thread of fear ran through Lucas. There was something irrational about Hugh's behaviour and that made him all the more dangerous. He risked a glance at Annabelle. Cold rage went through him when he saw how she was bound, but it would do no good to show it yet. Her eyes were upon him. She opened her mouth to speak and he gave a little shake of his head. It was best if she did not draw attention to herself. Hugh picked up the pistol again.

'Sit down, Lucas. I want you to know what you are signing.'

Lucas glanced at the landlord, still standing by the door. 'Is it really necessary for him to be here?' When Hugh hesitated, he added, 'This is family business, Cousin.'

'Very well.' Hugh waved the landlord away. 'Wait outside until I call you. Now, Cousin, come and sign these papers.'

Lucas strolled to the table. Not by the flicker of an eyelid would he show alarm, but he had never known his cousin so unsettled. Now he said calmly, 'Not before I have read them.'

He sat down and picked up the first sheet, conscious that Hugh was pacing around him, the loaded duelling pistol clutched in one hand.

'Read away, Cos. I spent a great deal of time drawing up these documents. So helpful of you to leave all your papers in the study at Oakenroyd. I was able to see exactly what you were planning to do.'

'You went through my desk?'

'Of course. While you spent your days at Morwood I had time to copy out your instructions to Powell & Son, merely changing a few of the details, such as removing Samuel Havenham's name and replacing it with mine own. I have even explained your sudden generosity. You are ashamed of the shabby way your father treated me and have decided to make reparation.'

Lucas held up one of the documents. 'This is an indenture for Havenham's gaming debts.'

'Of course. I told you, Lucas, I will not allow you to dispose of my inheritance.'

'But the debts are worthless. Samuel cannot pay.'

'That is no longer your concern, Cousin.'

Lucas cursed silently. That indenture would put Belle and Samuel in his power, with the threat of the debtors' prison looming over them. He glanced at Annabelle, pale and silent in her chair.

'I will sign Oakenroyd over to you, Hugh, and Morwood too, if that is what you want. But let me burn this,' he said quietly. 'Havenham has no money to pay. I never intended—'

Hugh snatched the paper from his hand and slammed it down on the desk.

'If you didn't intend to collect then you should have destroyed it,' he snarled. 'Now sign them all.'

'And if I refuse?' Lucas watched him carefully.

'I shall have you killed. As you say, I am still your heir, so it will all come to me anyway. But before that you will see what happens to the lady.' Hugh walked over to Belle and stretched out one hand to touch her cheek. Angrily she batted him away. 'Strutt is outside with his sons. Four of them. I am sure they would all enjoy a tumble, once I have finished with her.'

Lucas remembered the tales he had heard of his cousin's behaviour in the army. He knew he was not bluffing. 'And if I sign, I have your word you will release Miss Havenham?'

'Of course.'

'Lucas, please don't do it,' cried Belle, struggling against her bonds. 'I don't believe—'

'Quiet!' Hugh lashed out, the back of his hand catching Belle's face. Her head snapped back.

Lucas was on his feet in an instant, but Hugh stepped behind her chair, levelling the Manton at him.

'Back, Cousin, *back,* or I will put a bullet through you, and what will happen to your precious little lady then? I shall have no further reason to keep her safe, will I?'

Lucas glanced at Belle. She had a trickle of blood on her lip.

'I should have left you to die on the battlefield at Waterloo,' he growled.

'Aye, 'tis what I would have done, had our positions been reversed.' Hugh waved the pistol. 'Now sign, before I lose all patience with you.'

Lucas had to choose, and quickly. If it were only himself he thought he might be able to overpower Hugh, but with Belle a prisoner and the landlord just outside the door the risks were too great. Signing over both properties would seriously diminish his fortune, but there might be enough left to pay off that damned indenture, if Hugh chose to use it against Havenham. He had caused the man enough harm, he must now do what he could to protect him.

He picked up the pen and dipped it into the ink. Quickly he scrawled his signature on each of the papers.

'Excellent.' Hugh reached out and took the pen from his fingers. 'Strutt!' he shouted. 'Strutt, come in here and bring your boys. I need two of you to make your marks here.' He turned back to Lucas, smiling. 'You see, Cousin, all legal and watertight, witnessed by a respectable property owner and his son.'

Lucas pushed back his chair and got up. As the landlord and his loutish boys came in he walked over to Belle and began to untie her.

'Forgive me,' he muttered. 'This is my fault. Whatever I have done in the past you have my word that I will look after you and your father.'

'Brave words, Cousin, but foolish,' said Hugh, gathering up the signed papers. 'Tie them up, Strutt.'

Two pairs of heavy hands grabbed Lucas. A noose was thrown over his shoulders and pulled tight, binding his arms to his sides. He could only watch helplessly as Strutt seized Annabelle and began to bind her in a similar fashion.

'Careful,' ordered Hugh, 'I want no marks on their wrists.'

'You damned villain,' cried Lucas, struggling. 'You gave your word.'

'Did you really think I would let you go?' Hugh sneered. 'You always were a chivalrous fool, Lucas.'

'Damn you, I signed your papers!'

'And very useful they will be, too, but I would still prefer to have you out of the way. Do you really think I am a fool? If I let you live, you will go to the court and challenge me.'

'But it will look mighty suspicious if I am murdered so soon after signing everything over to you.'

'I know. That is why you and Miss Havenham are going to have a little, er, accident.'

'So what are you planning?'

Lucas wanted to keep him talking. They had roped his body, but he was quietly confident that, given time, he would be able to free himself.

'I told you, an accident.' Hugh picked up Belle's cloak and threw it around her shoulders. 'I guessed my note would make you come in haste and you would bring the curricle, but I am so pleased you brought your bays, too. It will add so much more credence to the story. You were taking Miss Havenham for a drive in your curricle along Dyke's Ridge, showing off, no doubt, and took the bend a little too fast.'

Belle looked up. 'But I came looking for Lucas, Papa knows that.' She trailed off, her eyes darkening. 'You did not tell him.'

'Of course not, but I wanted you to be seen walking alone out of Stanton. Everyone will think Lucas picked you up on the road.' He looked up, a sudden smile lighting his face. 'They might even think you were eloping, especially when Samuel explains to everyone that he had forbidden the banns. But you need not worry, Cos, as new lord of Morwood Manor I shall give you a decent burial in the family tomb.'

'So it is to be murder, is it?' Lucas taunted him. 'You just cannot wait to climb into my shoes.'

Hugh swung round, the smile replaced instantly by a ferocious scowl. 'I have waited five-and-twenty years for what is rightfully mine!'

'Oh?' Lucas raised his brows. 'And how do you work that out?

'You were meant to die in the fire. As the next male relative, I would have inherited.' He was pacing up and down, staring before him, his face contorted in rage. 'You should have burned like your mother. I thought you were asleep, like everyone else in the house. That was my mistake, but it is not one I shall make again.'

'A mistake?' said Lucas sharply, his brows snapping together. 'What do you mean, a mistake? What do you know about the fire?'

Hugh giggled. 'Have you not guessed? I started it. I went downstairs after your mother had locked herself in her room. It was late. Havenham had gone and your father staggered in. He wouldn't let the servants put him to bed, but went into the dining room to get another brandy. I followed him.' Duggan's lip trembled. He put a hand up to his ear, saying plaintively, 'He c-cuffed me. He had no reason to be angry with *me,* but he railed and ranted. He t-told me it was time I went home. Morwood *was* my home.' His face twisted. 'He was going to throw me out.'

'When my father was angry he was prone to say things he did not mean.'

'He should not have been angry with *me*. It wasn't my fault your mother was going to leave him. I thought it would be a good thing. I told him if she left Morwood and took you with her then he would have *me* and I would be his son. We could go fishing together. And hunting. All the things I could only do at Morwood, because Mama was too poor to bring me up as she should! But, no. He s-said—' Hugh stopped, his mouth working as he relived his memories. 'He said I was out of my mind. So I showed him. While he was snoring at the dining table I started a fire in the library. I didn't want to cross the hall in case any of the servants heard me, so I climbed out of the window and went round to the west wing and set fire to the hangings in the drawing room. Everything was so dry, it was easy. Then I hid myself in the woods to watch. Once the servants began milling about outside I came back to join them.' He giggled again. 'No one even noticed.'

Lucas stepped back and leaned against the table, momentarily stunned. '*You* started the fire at Morwood? And you let me believe it was my own father.'

Sheer animal rage filled him. Bound as he was, he wanted to hurl himself at Hugh, to bite and tear at him, even if he died in the attempt, but from the corner of his eye he could see Annabelle, her arms tied and with one of Strutt's oafish sons standing beside her. Belle's safety was his priority. By a supreme effort of will he curbed his anger, fighting it down, clearing his head. When the chance came he must be ready to act.

Belle listened to Hugh's explanation with shock and surprise. Despite her own discomfort and their fearful situation she felt an overwhelming relief for Lucas. If only she could talk to him. He met her eyes briefly and her heart lifted slightly at the faint smile of reassurance he gave her. Darling Lucas, even now he was trying to protect her.

Hugh was bundling the signed papers back into the case. 'Get them into the coach,' he barked.

The landlord checked that the passage was clear and they walked out of the inn, Lucas and Belle with their arms bound tightly to their sides and Belle all the time aware that the men behind them carried a shotgun and one of Lucas's duelling pistols. Her spine was quite rigid with nerves, making every step difficult. A shabby travelling chaise was waiting in the yard, the blinds drawn down. Belle looked around, wildly hoping that someone might be there to help them. She thought she caught the tinkle of bells on the wind. A packhorse train, possibly, crossing the moor, or even perhaps putting up for the night in the fold behind the inn, although she could see nothing in the darkness.

They were bundled unceremoniously into the chaise.

'Hobble them,' ordered Hugh. 'I don't want them escaping on the way.'

'Why not kill 'em out now and be done with it?' muttered Zac, the eldest of the Strutt sons.

'Daft lump.' His father spat on the ground. 'I don't want any mess in me carriage, nor any signs that we was involved in this night's work.

Now do as you're told, then you an' Amos can take 'em to the ridge.'

Zac quickly bound their ankles and stepped back. Hugh looked in, the flare from the carriage lamp throwing black shadows across his face. He ignored Belle and addressed Lucas, his tone genial, as if they had just enjoyed a sociable evening.

'This is where we say goodbye, Cousin. I am going to take the gig back to Stanton and make sure I am seen at the Red Lion tonight, drinking your health.'

The carriage rocked as someone climbed up on to the box. The door was closed and the next moment they were clattering across the cobbles and on to the rough lane. With the blinds drawn down, the interior of the chaise was completely dark. Unable to move her arms, Belle fought hard against her panic.

'Lucas!'

'I am here, love. Give me a moment to get out of these ropes.'

She could hear him grunting and moving beside her. She strained against her own bonds, but the cord only bit into her flesh through the thin sleeves of her walking gown. It was hopeless.

'At last.'

She guessed he had struggled free, for the next moment she was in his arms.

'My poor darling.' He reached around her, feeling for the knot at the back of her bonds. 'Did he hurt you very much?'

'No, not really.' She rested her head against his chest, listening to the reassuring thud of his heart. 'But I have never been so frightened.' She felt the rope grow loose and fall away.

'There.' Lucas began to chafe her arms. 'You will soon feel more like your old self.'

'Yes, thank you.' Tentatively she tried moving, reaching out in the darkness until her fingers encountered Lucas's body and she slid her hands around him. 'I feel much better already.'

His hold tightened and he held her close for a moment, resting his cheek against her hair.

'My brave girl,' he muttered. 'But we are not quite out of the woods yet, my love. Can you untie your ankles, do you think?'

'Yes, I will try.'

Soon they were free, but the coach was rocking too wildly on the stony lane to risk jumping out. When they reached a smoother section of road Lucas pulled aside the blind to peep out.

'We are on the new road.'

'How far will they take us, do you think?'

'They will not risk going through the toll. My guess is that they plan to drive the curricle off the road on the first bend, where the drop is steepest. That is not far now. Be ready to move when I say.'

The chaise slowed and came to a halt. It rocked as their driver alighted and rough voices sounded outside the door as he talked to his brother.

'This is it, Zac. Let's get 'em into the curricle and be done.'

'Nay, Amos, hold on, I bin thinking.'

'There's nowt to think about. We have to drive 'em over th'edge and make it look like an accident. The Captain's payin' us good money to do it.' They heard a savage laugh. 'And he'll have to keep on payin' us, too, if 'e wants us to stay quiet.'

'Ah, but them horses is valuable,' protested Zac. 'I've never driven anything like 'em afore. They'd fetch a pretty penny at market.'

'And get us hanged for it, too,' growled Amos.

'But we could take 'em to market elsewhere, Skipton, mebbe. No one knows us there.' A long silence followed, then Zac said persuasively, 'It'd be a sin to waste such grand cattle. Prime 'uns, they are. Best bits of horseflesh I've seen in many a day. We should sell 'em.'

'Nay, Zac. If it's to look like an accident then the horses would have to be trapped with the carriage. There'd be broken legs at best.'

'But who's to say it needs to be an accident? Duggan's the one they'd suspect, not us.'

'I dunno…'

'Come on, Amos, think on! We can still put the bodies in the curricle and push it over th'edge, but the horses comes back with us. We'll take 'em away afore it gets light in the morning, and no one will be the wiser.'

'But Father said—'

'You leave Father to me. He's not one to turn his nose up at a small fortune and that's what we'd get for these two.'

Another pause. Belle found herself holding her breath until she heard Amos speak again.

'All right, Zac. Let's do it. Get the cattle un-harnessed and tether 'em to the coach wheel while we gets rid o' the curricle.'

The voices grew more distant and Lucas pulled Belle close. 'This is our chance,' he breathed. 'When I say—'

'Lucas!' She gripped his arm, shaking. A thin sliver of light was widening around the door as it began to open.

Lucas pushed her behind him. After the complete darkness of the closed carriage the light of the half-moon seemed very bright and it flooded in as the door swung wide. A man stood in the opening, the wide brim of his round, shallow-crowned hat shadowing his face. She was thinking he did not look big enough to be one of landlord Strutt's sons when Lucas growled softly, 'By heaven, George, you took your time.'

'Lord love you, Major, we was waitin' fer the right moment.' George Stebbing cocked his head as a confused mix of grunts and thuds was heard. 'Sounds as if Rudd and Clegg have made the acquaintance of your captors.'

As the man stepped back Belle saw the left sleeve of his coat swinging empty.

'Your valet?' she asked, unsteadily.

'Aye, it is,' said Lucas. 'You stay with him while I go and see what is happening to my horses.'

Lucas was out of the carriage even as he spoke. George Stebbing put out his hand to help Belle to alight, but his grip tightened as she went to follow Lucas.

'Beggin' your pardon, miss, but you'd be best stayin' here.'

'At least let me *see*...'

She stepped out to look beyond the carriage. The curricle was drawn up directly before it and the two highly strung bays were snorting and shifting nervously as a brawl took place on the road in front of them. Even at a distance Belle could see that the Strutt brothers were much bigger than their opponents and had the advantage, until Lucas reached the first grappling couple, pulled them apart and felled the bigger of the two with a punishing fist to the jaw. The other Strutt was similarly dispatched and Belle heard George Stebbing's grunt of satisfaction.

'Thought I was going to have to give a hand, but it seems the Major has dealt with that very nicely. Just have to decide what we're going to do with 'em.'

'The rope they used to tie us up is in the carriage,' offered Belle.

'Excellent idea, miss.'

Minutes later the two brothers were securely bound and shut in the closed carriage. Annabelle leaned against the door, suddenly weak now the immediate danger had passed.

'Are you all right, miss?' Clegg peered at her anxiously.

'I am well,' she assured him, 'but how did you know where to find us?'

'I told them to follow me,' said Lucas, coming up. 'However, I didn't expect them to leave it this late to intervene!'

George Stebbing pushed up his hat and scratched his head. 'Well now, Major, there was too many men at the Boar's Head and with the rascally landlord holding the shotgun we couldn't be sure of getting you away unharmed. But we saw Strutt's lads getting the carriage ready and heard them saying how their father didn't want you killed on his property. But Rudd and Clegg would have come in if they'd heard anything amiss coming from that private room.'

'You were in the taproom?' said Annabelle, bewildered. 'I thought there were only packmen there.'

'Me and Rudd,' said Clegg, grinning. 'We paid the teamster to borrow three jaggers' coats and his ponies for the night.'

She looked at Lucas. 'Then the bells I heard, when they took us out to the carriage...'

'That was me,' explained George. 'I stayed out in the fold with the ponies—'

'Aye,' chuckled Rudd, 'Clegg and I might pass for jaggermen, but there was a fair chance they would have rumbled George with his one arm. Someone might've remembered he was Mr Blackstone's man.'

'Since you tell me the ale was pretty poor stuff I'm glad I stayed outside,' retorted Stebbing. 'Anyway, it meant I could ring the leader's bells, just a touch, like, so the Major would know we was on hand.'

'And, of course, no one would take any notice of packhorses on that trail,' said Annabelle. 'How clever of you.'

'It was the Major's idea,' explained George.

'Something we picked up in the Peninsula,' added Lucas. 'People don't notice the obvious. But enough, we have not finished yet. George,

Rudd, will you take the carriage? Take our friends to the lock-up in Stanton for the night. And you had best inform Sir John Rishworth, he will want to send the constable to bring the landlord and his other boys in tonight, too. By morning Strutt will know something is wrong and may well make a run for it.'

'And Captain Duggan, sir?' asked George.

'I shall deal with him.' Lucas held out his hand. 'Let me have the Manton, George. Duggan already has its mate.'

'You mean to kill him,' stated Belle.

'I do.'

She caught his sleeve. 'No, Lucas, you cannot do that.'

He took the pistol and placed it in his pocket. 'I must,' he said shortly. 'He is a murderer.'

'And killing him would make you one, too.' She placed herself in front of him. 'Let the others tell Sir John what has occurred and Captain Duggan can stand trial. The law shall punish him, not you.'

'You can say that, after what he has done? Besides, I want those documents!'

She read murder in his eyes, but would not step aside.

'I would have justice, but not your way. You know as well as I that the papers he has are worthless. They were signed under duress, you do not need to fight him to get them back.' He did not move. She could feel the tension in him. Every muscle, every sinew was hard and inflexible. He was like some terrible, avenging deity. She raised her hands and cupped his face, saying softly, 'Please, Lucas, no more vengeance.'

Time stopped while she waited for his response. Every fibre of her being was willing him to give in. Beneath her hands, his jaw was clenched hard and she could feel the muscle working in his cheek. She knew his temper, but he could master it. She had to believe that, or there could be no future for them.

Like a silent sigh the rigidity left him; the implacable look in his eyes was replaced by something softer. He raised his head.

'George, inform Sir John of all that has gone on here. Tell him he will most likely find Duggan at the Red Lion. And retrieve my Manton if you can!' He turned back to Annabelle. 'I shall take Miss Havenham to her father.'

The tiny whisper of hope in Belle's heart burst into full song as she took his hand. She did not speak. She knew he would see the happiness shining in her eyes when he looked at her.

'I am taking you home.' Lucas gave Belle a fleeting smile as he helped her into the curricle. 'To Oakenroyd.'

'But my father—'

'He's waiting for you there, Miss Belle,' said Clegg, scrambling up into the rumble seat. 'Mr Blackstone instructed me to take him and Abel to Oakenroyd before I came on here to join the others.'

Lucas said gruffly, 'I could not bear to think of him living in that cottage another minute, so I invited him to return to his home.'

Belle squeezed his arm. 'Oh, Lucas, thank you.'

'You have no need to thank me. Samuel would never have consented to move if I hadn't persuaded him that we could better look after you there.'

She bridled at that. 'I do not need looking after!'

They were about to move off, but Lucas delayed, controlling his restless team with one hand while with the other he pulled Belle to him and kissed her, hard, regardless of the groom sitting behind them.

'I intend to look after you for the rest of your life, madam, whether you need it or not.'

Already shaken from her ordeal, Belle could not pull away. She remained passively within the circle of his arm, gazing up at him. The moonlight shadowed his face, but she could feel the power of his glance burning into her. His arm tightened.

'Agreed?' he demanded.

'Agreed, Lucas,' she replied meekly.

'Good.' He released her and took up the reins again. 'Now. Let us go and see your father.'

Chapter Eighteen

The half-moon had dropped to the west but it was still light enough for Lucas to drive his team at a cracking pace. Annabelle sat quietly beside him, the cold night air keeping sleep at bay. So many thoughts raced through her mind that she could make no sense of any of it.

When they arrived at Oakenroyd they found the house blazing with light. Lucas helped her down and escorted her to the front door where Gibson was waiting.

'Welcome home, Miss Havenham.' The butler beamed at her as he ushered her into the house. 'You will find Mr Havenham waiting for you in the drawing room. He refused to retire until he had seen you.'

Lucas took her arm and as they crossed the hall the housekeeper came bustling out of the shadows. After the briefest of curtsies to Lucas she launched herself into speech.

'Oh, Miss Havenham, it is so *good* to see you here once more. Your old room is ready for you, and the master's—Mr Havenham, I *should* say— and I have taken wine and cakes into the drawing room, in case you are hungry, but I will fetch you a hot chocolate if you would prefer, or tea…'

'Thank you, Mrs Wicklow, wine will be very good.' Belle smiled at her and as the housekeeper turned away she saw her lift her apron to wipe away a rogue tear.

Lucas put his hand over her fingers where they rested on his sleeve. 'You have been missed,' he said quietly.

'But I do not understand. Have you told them that you are making the house over?'

'Not a word.'

'Then…how do they know?'

He smiled down at her, the glow in his eyes setting her pulse racing. 'Servants always know.' He squeezed her fingers briefly as they entered the drawing room. Samuel rose as the door opened and Belle flew across the room and into his arms, laughing and crying at once.

It took a considerable time to explain everything to Samuel. Belle sat beside him on the sofa while Lucas stood before the fire and told him all that had occurred that evening.

'So it has all ended well,' said Samuel, when he had finished.

'Well, almost, sir,' said Lucas. 'My only concern is the property and the loans I signed over to Duggan. I know he used threats to obtain the signatures, but if he should contest that and Strutt should back him up… Unlikely, perhaps, but everything could become bound up in the courts for years.' He looked up. 'I cannot lie to you, sir. Most of my capital is tied up in the properties. If I lose them I shall have some money left, not a great fortune, perhaps, but sufficient to look after you and your daughter.'

'I am sure we shall come about,' said Samuel gently.

'But you may still lose Oakenroyd,' said Lucas. 'At least in the short term.'

'We can always go back to Croft Cottage,' put in Belle.

Lucas smiled. 'No, it won't come to that, I promise you.'

'I think you are worrying unnecessarily,' said Samuel. 'For my part I think we have a great deal to be thankful for. I am relieved to learn that Jonas was not responsible for the fire at Morwood. As you must be, my boy, although I am sorry you had to discover it in such unpleasant circumstances. But more than that, I cannot express my gratitude to you for bringing Annabelle back safely to me.'

Lucas's face darkened. He rested one arm on the mantelpiece and stared down into the fire. 'You have nothing to be grateful for, sir,' he said curtly. 'On the contrary. If I had not been such a crass fool none of this would have occurred—'

'But sometimes God likes to test us with adversity.' Samuel shook his head at him, smiling. 'I know you will not agree with that, Lucas, but you must allow an old man his beliefs.'

'I will allow you anything, sir, if you can forgive me—' He broke off, his jaw working as he considered his next words. 'But, can you forgive me enough to change your mind and allow me to marry your daughter?' He looked at Samuel, such uncertainty in his eyes that Belle's heart turned over. 'I have learned a great deal tonight, sir. Not only about my father, but also about myself. I know I have no right to ask it, but if you would consent, I believe I could be a good husband to her. I will see to it that she wants for nothing.'

'We know you have money enough,' said Samuel, gently, 'but is that all, Lucas?'

'If you mean do I love her, sir, then, yes. With all my heart.'

Belle caught her breath. She felt her father's

eyes upon her and turned to look at him, hoping he could read the silent appeal in her own. With a smile he patted her hands before responding.

'My dear boy, if ever a knight deserved to win his maid it is you. If Belle loves you, then I will gladly give my consent.'

Belle gave a little sob. 'I do, Papa! You know—'

He held up his hand. 'No, no, I am not the one you have to tell, my love.' He pushed himself to his feet. 'It has been a long day, and if you will excuse me I shall go to bed.' He turned to Belle, who had risen with him, and took her hands. 'My child, you know how dearly I loved his mother. If you love Lucas only half as much, then you should marry him and with my blessing.' He kissed her cheek and made his way slowly out of the room.

Belle stood with her hands clasped, looking at the closed door. She was very much aware that Lucas was watching her. Only the crackle of the fire disturbed the silence.

'So,' he said at last, 'I have your father's permission to address you.' When she did not reply, he continued. 'I believe I even have his blessing to do so. Not that you should let that influence your decision. For it *is* your decision, Belle. Having put my cousin into the hands of the law it may not be possible for me to make Oakenroyd

over to your father for a while, but I shall set up
an annuity for him immediately, enough to keep
you both. You will be independent again. There
is no need for you to marry anyone, unless you
really want to do so.'

Silently Annabelle sank back on to the sofa.
She looked about the room. Everything was as
she remembered it. This had been her home and
might well be again, but it would never be the
same. Adversity had taught her to appreciate the
comfort and luxury of Oakenroyd, but not to take
it for granted.

Lucas dropped on to one knee before her and
reached for her hands.

'I asked you once before to marry me,' he said.
'Then it was for all the wrong reasons and you
turned me down. I am asking you now, my love,
to accept my hand in marriage and this time I
hope I am asking you for all the *right* reasons.
Because I love you, because I want to make you
happy. I want to honour, cherish and protect you
all the days of your life.' He looked down at her
fingers clasped in his own. 'And lastly because
my life will be so damnably empty if you are not
in it.' She waited for him to continue and heard
the note of tension in his voice when he spoke
again. 'So I lay everything I have at your feet,
Belle, and beg you to make your choice. If you
say yes, you will make me the happiest man in

the world, but if…if this is not what you want, then you only have to say and I shall importune you no more.'

'Can you do that? Can you really leave the decision to me, and if I say no you will leave me alone, for ever?'

'You have my word on it.'

Gently she disengaged her hands and got up. She began to walk slowly about the room. 'You see,' she said, 'I think that, deep down, I am even more unforgiving than you, because I have known for many months now that I love you, and when you and my father decided between you that it would be best that we did not see each other again I found myself railing against it quite, quite *violently*.' She came back to stand before him, looking down into his face. 'What your father did, or did not do, was of no interest to me. I could never bring myself to believe that you would hurt me, despite what had happened and I *raged* against your decision not to marry me. I swore I would never forgive you for that.'

'And now?' He was looking up at her, his eyes dark and wary, afraid to hope.

'Now,' she said, her lip trembling, 'now I would think myself the luckiest woman alive if I could be your wife.'

When she saw the joy in his eyes she could no longer hold back her smile, but it was smothered when he jumped up and dragged her to him, kissing her so savagely that for a while she could think of nothing but the sheer pleasure of being in his arms.

When Belle at last came to her senses she was half-sitting, half-lying on the sofa with Lucas's arm around her. He had discarded his neckcloth and the top buttons of his shirt were open, while the pins had fallen from her hair, allowing it to tumble over her shoulders.

'I do not deserve such happiness,' he murmured between kisses. 'How soon will you marry me?'

'As soon as you like.'

'Then we will have the banns called immediately. I am all too aware that I have already compromised you.'

She smiled up at him. 'You did not compromise me,' she said softly, touching his cheek. 'I gave myself willingly. To comfort you.'

Without thinking she slipped her hand into the neck opening of his shirt and traced the hard, muscled contours of his breast. The crisp hair curled around her fingers. He clapped his hand over hers.

'Careful,' he growled. 'Or you will have to comfort me all over again.'

She blushed, but continued to run her hand over his skin, giving him a provocative smile.

With a sound between a groan and a laugh he sat up.

'Shall we continue this upstairs?'

Taking her silence for assent he swept her up into his arms. Smiling, she slipped her hands about his neck, but felt obliged to protest as he carried her out of the room.

'Lucas, the servants!' she hissed, casting an anxious look around her, but the hallway and stairs were deserted. A few dim lamps were burning, giving sufficient light for Lucas to see his way up the stairs.

'Your room or mine?' he whispered, nuzzling her ear and making her wriggle with pleasurable longing in his arms. 'I gave instructions before I went out for my things to be moved to the blue bedchamber, so that your father could have his old room.'

'I have never slept in the blue chamber,' she murmured.

He gave her a wicked grin. 'I was not proposing that we *sleep* there tonight, my love.'

He carried her along the corridor to his bedroom where the fire had been banked up and was blazing merrily. He set her down gently on the bed and she watched, fascinated, as he undressed. Belle's throat dried when she saw his body, golden in the firelight, shadows playing over the corded muscles of his shoulders.

'Come,' he said. 'Let us get you out of your clothes.'

She slid off the bed and pulled off her gown, but any thoughts of hastily shedding the rest of her garments were soon dispelled. Lucas moved behind her and slowly, oh, so slowly, began to unlace her stays. She felt the vibration against her body as he pulled the ribbons free and when she put back her head he fastened his mouth on the smooth slope of her shoulder, nibbling his way along to her neck. She leaned against him and was almost moaning aloud by the time the corset was finally removed. He pulled her to him, his chest hard against her back and only the thin chemise between them. He slipped his hands under that last flimsy defence and cupped her breasts, working his magic on them with the thumb and finger of each hand.

Unable to bear any more she turned, reaching for him, but with a laugh he gathered up her chemise and lifted it over her head. Obligingly she reached up, but instead of pulling it free he imprisoned her arms in its folds while his head came down to wreak more havoc on her breasts, suckling one then the other until her whole body was pulsing with excitement. At last he released her and lifted her on to the bed. He stretched out beside her, raising himself on one elbow and with his free hand he traced a figure of eight around her breasts, then moved down to circle her navel. He began to lay a series of kisses across the soft skin of her belly. Her hips began to move restlessly as desire unfurled deep inside. She reached for him, but he evaded her.

'Patience,' he murmured.

Lucas pulled out a pillow and placed it beneath her hips. He took one stockinged foot in his hands. Belle shivered at the touch of his fingers on her ankle. He untied her garter and began to roll the stocking down, pausing frequently to plant kisses on the bared skin. The silk slid away with a whisper and he ran his hand from calf to the ankle, lifting her foot high to kiss it. He repeated the action with the other stocking, but this time, once he had finished, his mouth trailed back along her leg, licking and kissing her skin until she was tingling with anticipation.

He began to stroke the soft mound at the hinge of her thighs, his fingers smoothing over the dark curls while his thumb dipped towards the opening beneath. The cushion was holding up her hips, presenting her to him. She could not pull away from that teasing thumb as it circled and pressed the delicate skin, exciting her until she thought she would swoon with the pleasure of it. She gasped when his mouth moved over her, replacing the thumb. His tongue flickered in and out, lapping at her very core and rousing in her such delight as she had not known possible.

Belle groaned and moved restlessly beneath the onslaught, opening herself to his touch. She had never known such sensations—her body was throbbing, she wanted to pull away, yet at the same time she wanted him to go further, deeper. As if he had read her thoughts, his fingers began to stroke her again, even as his mouth worked its magic, until she was bucking wildly with the combined pleasuring. Ecstasy convulsed her. She gasped, her hands pulling at his shoulders and at last he released her, but only long enough to slide up her body, covering her mouth with his own while he slipped into her. She could taste herself in his kiss, feel him moving deep inside her and the heady exhilaration of their union sent her soul flying. She cried out, her fingers digging into his skin as he carried her with him to the explosive culmination of pleasure. His arms tightened, he held her close as her world fractured and they fell together into oblivion.

The sun was shining on her. Annabelle slowly opened her eyes. She was in her own room at Oakenroyd, but the curtains had not been drawn around the bed, nor had the curtains been pulled across the window and now the low morning sun was shining directly on to her. She turned away from the light. She had been having such a lovely dream about Lucas.

She was no longer sleepy. It had not been a dream. A feeling of well-being came over her and she shifted restlessly as she remembered what had happened when he had carried her up to the blue bedchamber.

She had fallen into a deep sleep after they had made love so wonderfully and it had been dark when she next woke up. She had felt incredibly safe and comfortable, and as the fog of sleep left her mind she realised why. Lucas was wrapped around her, his naked limbs entwined with hers and his mouth close to her cheek. She shifted around until she could kiss his lips. He stirred.

'I love you.' His softly murmured words lifted her soul.

'I love you, too,' she whispered and kissed him again, pressing her body against his, exulting in his reaction to her closeness. They made love again, slowly, languorously before sinking back into sleep.

It had still been dark when Lucas next roused her with a kiss. Sleepily she opened her eyes. A single candle burned beside the bed, casting a dim glow over everything. She reached out and tried to wind her arms around Lucas's neck, but he held her off.

'Come along, sweetheart, I think you should go back to your own bed before the servants are about.'

'Why?' she complained, nuzzling into him. 'You said yourself they know everything.'

He chuckled. 'They might *know* what we have been up to, but we have to observe the proprieties.' He eased her from the bed and wrapped her in his own dressing gown. Walking her to the door, Lucas pressed the candlestick into her hand. 'Off you go to your own room now, love, and I will see you at breakfast.'

Breakfast! She sat up quickly. Had she missed it? Why had no one woken her? She reached out and rang for Becky, then remembered that she no longer had a maid. The pitcher on the washstand was full of fresh cold water so she quickly washed her face and hands, then opened the linen press. All the clothes she had left behind were there, just as she had left them. She pulled out a fresh gown and was just scrambling into it when there was a scratching at the door.

'Becky!'

'Yes, miss.' The maid came into the room, grinning broadly. 'Mrs Wicklow sent for me at the crack o' dawn, said you would be needing me again, only I was not to wake you this morning. But I am right pleased to be back, I can tell you.

Working as a chambermaid at the Lion was not the same thing at all!'

'And I am glad to have you,' declared Belle, smiling. 'Help me into this dress, will you, Becky? But I do not know how I am to do my hair—oh.' She stopped, staring at the ivory-backed hairbrush and comb on the dressing table.

'Mrs Wicklow says Mr Havenham brought some of your things with him from Croft Cottage,' said Becky, following her glance.

'He was sure that Mr Blackstone would find me, then.' Belle smiled as she picked up the brush. Of course. Papa had as much faith in Lucas as she.

'Oh, yes, miss. What an adventure! Mr Stebbing and Rudd had just got back when I arrived, telling everyone about how that wicked Captain Duggan had tried to do away with you and steal Mr Blackstone's property.'

'Oh, they must have been up all night. Have they gone to bed now? I would like to talk to them.'

'Nay, miss, Cook was feeding them ham and eggs in the kitchen when I came upstairs, the master—Mr Blackstone, that is—saying he would see them once he had finished his breakfast.'

Belle waited to hear no more. Having hastily put up her hair she ran down the stairs to the breakfast parlour, almost skidding to a halt at the door. She must enter with at least the semblance of composure.

Lucas was alone at the table. She hesitated in the doorway, suddenly shy, but his smile was reassuring. He got up to pull out a chair for her, dropping a kiss on her head as she sat down at the table.

'No regrets about last night?' He murmured the words in her ear, his hands resting lightly on her shoulders.

She blushed. 'No, none.'

'Good. Then I propose we visit the parson later today. What do you say?'

'I say, yes, if you please. And...'

'Yes?'

'May I come with you when you see Rudd and Mr Stebbing? I should like to know how they went on.'

He pressed her shoulder. 'Of course. I have no secrets from you now, my love.'

When they had finished breakfast he took her to the study where they found George Stebbing and the groom waiting for them. They almost stood to attention when Lucas walked in. Belle noticed that Rudd was sporting a black eye, but he was looking very pleased with himself.

'All locked up right and tight now, Major,' said

George cheerfully. 'Those two boys of Strutt's was squealing like stuck pigs by the time we got to the lock-up, happy enough to put the blame for everything on Captain Duggan. Sir John sent the constable and a couple of stout fellows to the Boar's Head immediately to pick up Strutt and the two other lads while we went with him to the Red Lion to, er, *hap-ree-hend* the Captain. Quite a kick-up there was, when we turned up. The Captain quite lost his head, admitted in front of everyone that, having failed to kill you when he burned Morwood all those years ago, he was determined to do so now.' George chuckled. 'The Captain didn't want to come quietly. He put up a fight and tried to make a run for it. In all the confusion that case of his came open and all the papers fell into the fire.' The old soldier met Lucas's eye for one pregnant moment. 'We set ourselves to rescue them, of course.'

'Aye,' said Rudd, trying to subdue a grin. 'Burned to cinders, every one of 'em. Sir John asked what they might be, but the Captain wouldn't say, and o' course we had no idea, so then Sir John says that what with the statements from the Strutts and the Captain's confession, made in front of a dozen witnesses, he didn't want to be bothered with any more bits of paper.'

'Very wise of him,' said Lucas gravely. 'We will let the law deal with my cousin now.'

'Aye, sir.' Stebbing smothered a yawn. 'Now, if you would excuse us, Major, me and Rudd will be off. After we'd helped Sir John put the Captain in the lock-up with his cronies we had to go back to the Boar's Head and collect the pack ponies we'd borrowed, so we ain't been to bed yet.'

'Of course,' said Lucas, 'off you go and get some sleep.'

'Aye, sir, that we will, although there's a few things to be done first, like trying to rescue those boots you was wearing yesterday. Fair scratched they are and caked with mud....'

The old sergeant followed Rudd out of the room, still muttering darkly. Lucas waited until they had shut the door, then he turned to Belle and held out his arms. She walked into them as if it was the most natural thing in the world.

'Papa was right,' she said, reaching up to kiss him. 'It has ended very well.'

'It is not over yet,' he warned her. 'Sir John will want to talk to us and there will be a trial. You will have to give evidence.'

'I do not mind that if you are with me, Lucas.'

His arms tightened around her. 'I shall be with you always from now on, my love. Which reminds me, fetch your cloak while I send for my curricle. We will drive into Stanton and find the vicar. There is still time for him to marry us before Christmas.'

* * *

Down in the servants' hall, George Stebbing held one of Lucas's boots between his knees while he brushed it vigorously with his one hand. He looked up in time to see the curricle speeding away from the house, sending up a shower of gravel as it swung sharply around the drive. He chuckled.

'Clever man, the Major. Always said so. But not clever enough to avoid the parson's mousetrap.'

'And why shouldn't he want to marry Miss Belle?' demanded Becky, bridling in defence of her mistress. 'She's a fine lady and more than a match for your Major, Mr Stebbing!'

'Oh, she is that, I grant you,' he said, chuckling. 'He chased her as hard as ever he could— but in the end he was the one as got caught. Ah well, 'tis the way of the world, I suppose!'

* * * * *

&

A sneaky peek at next month...

HISTORICAL

IGNITE YOUR IMAGINATION, STEP INTO THE PAST...

My wish list for next month's titles...

In stores from 6th September 2013:

☐ Mistress at Midnight – Sophia James

☐ The Runaway Countess – Amanda McCabe

☐ In the Commodore's Hands – Mary Nichols

☐ Promised to the Crusader – Anne Herries

☐ Beauty and the Baron – Deborah Hale

☐ The Ballad of Emma O'Toole – Elizabeth Lane

Available at WHSmith, Tesco, Asda, Eason, Amazon and Apple

Just can't wait?

 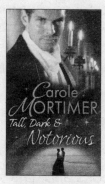 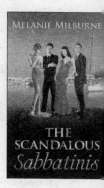

Join the Mills & Boon Book Club

Want to read more **Historical** books?
We're offering you **2 more** absolutely **FREE**!

We'll also treat you to these fabulous extras:

- 🌹 Exclusive offers and much more!

- 🌹 FREE home delivery

- 🌹 FREE books and gifts with our special rewards scheme

Get your free books now!

visit **www.millsandboon.co.uk/bookclub**
or call **Customer Relations on 020 8288 2888**